# Cesspool

## A Novel

By

Phil M. Williams

Printed in the United States of America
First Printing, 2016

Phil W Books
www.PhilWBooks.com

ISBN: 978-1-943894-10-9

Cover design and interior formatting by Tugboat Design

# Contents

Dear Reader,

**If you're interested in receiving my new book releases for free, go to the following link:** http://www.PhilWBooks.com. You're probably thinking, *what's the catch?* There is no catch. I hope you enjoy the book!

Sincerely,
Phil M. Williams

# Chapter 1

## White Slaves Get Sunburnt

James Fisher sat at the dining room table, his laptop open. His coffee steamed within reach of his pasty arms. He grabbed the mug, took a sip, and scanned the headlines on the screen.

Tent Cities in the Heart of Silicon Valley

ECB Supports More QE

Ponzified Pensions in Pennsylvania

National Debt Ballooning Beyond $18 Trillion

Health Insurance Costs Outpacing Wages

Russia's Economy in Decline

Greece's Stock Market Collapsing

Portland-Area Water Rate Skyrocketing as Pipes Burst

He moved the cursor over the Ponzified Pensions in Pennsylvania link and clicked it. He scanned the graphs and quotes from officials, grappling with the unforgiving nature of mathematics. *Coming soon to a state near you.* He heard quick steps down the wooden stairs. The first floor of his home was open, with no dividing wall between the kitchen and the living room. He turned toward the kitchen, where the stainless steel appliances glistened in the morning light. A small round table for two sat against the bay window.

Lori's sneakers squeaked as she rushed into the kitchen, her keys in hand and an Adidas bag slung over her shoulder. Her straight brown hair was pulled back in a long ponytail. Her nylon jacket was unzipped to chest level, showing her ample cleavage held together by two sports bras.

She opened the fridge and removed a bottle with greenish liquid. James stood with a groan and trudged across the hardwood to the kitchen. She shook the bottle, avoiding his gaze. Lori rifled through a drawer, grabbing an energy bar and dropping her keys in the process.

"Damn it," she said as she bent over and snatched her keys from the tile.

James saw the outline of her labia through her yoga pants. *The guys at that stupid-ass gym see her vagina more than I do.*

"Won't you be cold?" James asked.

She rolled her eyes. "The box gets pretty hot."

"Why can't you guys just call it a gym?"

"You wouldn't understand," she said as she unzipped the side pocket of her bag and shoved the energy bar inside.

"Maybe you could wear regular shorts and a T-shirt. That would be comfortable."

She glared at James. "This is what everyone wears now."

"It's just a bit … revealing."

Her pale face flushed red. "What do you want me to do, James? I can't change now—I'm late."

"You just have a lot of … curves." He winced.

She crossed her arms, still holding her green drink concoction. "You think I look fat?"

*Shit.* "No, you look great. You've always looked great. I loved your body forty extra pounds ago."

"I'm late." She brushed past James and slammed the door on her way out.

* * *

James fast-walked down the empty hallway, a loaded backpack over his jacket. Classroom doors were closed, decorated with snowflakes and snowmen. A murmur of preteen chatter spilled into the hall. He stood at his classroom door, fishing his keys from his khakis. He caught a glimpse of himself in the door window. His nose was too large, his eyes too squinty, and his chin too small.

"Mr. Fisher, I'd like a word."

James took a deep breath and turned around.

The principal was short, with narrow shoulders, low body fat, but a big head. It looked as though he had the body of one of his middle-schoolers, with an adult head shoved on top.

James smiled, looking down at his principal. "Good morning, Dr. Richards."

"We need to have a talk—now." The principal marched toward his office, without waiting for a reply.

James skulked after him. Dr. Richards didn't look back or hold the door as he entered the main office. Two middle-aged women worked behind the L-shaped reception desk. One was on the phone; the other glanced at James and went back to her work. He shuffled into the principal's office, shutting the door behind him. Dr. Richards sat at the wooden desk with his fingers interlaced, as if he were praying. James sat across from him in a wooden chair that wasn't built for comfort. *He might be five three, but at least he has a man's chin. My chin's like a girl's. If only I could grow a decent beard.*

"Mr. Fisher, are you paying attention?"

"Yes, every word," James replied. *He'll repeat it.*

"What I asked was, 'Do you remember what we talked about last month?'"

"Shoot, I'm sorry about being late today. I had a family emergency."

The principal sat quiet, his eyes on James.

*He's trying to get me to talk. Not going to happen, Dr. Dicks.*

"It's not just today," Dr. Richards said.

James raised his eyebrows. "As far as I know, I've been on time since our last conversation."

"We had a complaint that you haven't been monitoring the hall at the start of school."

"That's surprising."

"Now I know you have your planning time first period, but you cannot show up late just because you don't have class."

James nodded along with his principal. "Absolutely. I agree 100 percent. That's why this is so surprising, because I've been here on time. Did you check my scan card?"

The principal tightened his jaw. "It appears you haven't been scanning in."

"That's odd. I definitely scan. Doors won't open if you don't."

"I assume you come in through the main entrance."

"No, the back by the gym."

The principal narrowed his eyes. "And why would you do that? Your classroom is on the other side of school."

James smiled. "I like to stretch my legs early in the morning and walk a bit."

"We've had some problems with that door." The principal exhaled. "It will be fixed. It has been moved to the top of my list. Do you understand me?"

"Loud and clear, boss." James saluted his principal as he exited.

He entered the nurse's office across the hall. The placard on the open door said, School Nurse Yolanda Mendez. There were two rooms, one with a desk and an exam table, and the other with cots. A heavyset Latino woman in peach-colored scrubs sat at the desk. She had short wavy hair with brown highlights. James knocked on the open door.

"Knock, knock," James said.

She turned with a toothy grin that stretched her wide nose and round cheeks. "Good morning, Mr. Fisher. Dare I ask what you're doing in the principal's office?"

"Apparently Dr. Dicks had a complaint about me being late."

She shook her head. "Probably that little tart across the hall from you. You better watch yourself."

James shrugged with a grin. "She's just mad that the kids like me better."

"Don't you have work to do?"

James put his backpack on the floor and sat on the examination table, the paper covering crinkling under him. "I don't really function until nine. It's insane that we start so early. The kids are zombies in the morning anyway."

She laughed. "Well, *I* have work to do."

"I guess that's my cue." James stood up, the paper cover hanging off the table.

"And look what you've done to my table."

He straightened the paper. "Sorry. I'll see you at lunch." He started for the exit.

"James," she said.

He turned around. "Yeah?"

"I know you stay late, but you need to be here on time. You can't keep sneaking in the back. Dr. Dicks is just looking for a reason."

James smiled again and blew the nurse a kiss.

\* \* \*

"The Emancipation Proclamation—what did it do?" James scanned his classroom. The faces were blank. A dark-skinned boy in front was turned around in his seat, whispering. "Vernon, pay attention. This *will* be on the quiz tomorrow."

Vernon turned around with a half-smile. He had a thin mustache and acne bumps on his cheeks and forehead. He was built more like a linebacker than an eighth grader.

"Can we just get through this?" James asked. "We only have a few more."

"On the real, Mr. Fish, this is borin' as hell," Vernon said.

"Sometimes we have to follow the curriculum."

"Come on, Mr. Fish," Maurice said from the second row. "Tell it to us for real, like you do." Maurice was dark-skinned, thin, with high cheekbones and a bright smile.

James smirked. "I'll tell you the real story of the Civil War, but you guys have to promise me two things. Number one, we have to learn the real story *and* the government propaganda version. Number two, what happens in Room 124 stays in Room 124."

"Y'all better not be snitchin'," Vernon said, glaring at his classmates.

"Don't worry, Mr. Fish. We got your back," Maurice said.

"Okay, let's play a game," James said.

The class sat up straight and leaned forward.

"Everyone take out a blank sheet of paper and a pencil."

The kids argued, begged, and borrowed, but eventually everyone had a piece of paper and a writing utensil.

James continued, "I want you to imagine yourself in 1860, living in the South."

Vernon turned to Maurice. "You'd be picking that cotton, nigga."

The class laughed.

Maurice smirked. "You'd be gettin' your black ass whipped."

The class hooted and hollered.

"Cut it out, guys," James said with a frown. The boys and the rest of the class composed themselves. "For this game—"

The classroom door swung open, and a short young blonde stomped in. Her face was red.

"Mr. Fisher, we are taking a test," she said. "Your class is *much* too loud."

A spattering of oohs came from the class. Someone said, "Bitch be crazy."

"Quiet down, guys," James said to the class. He turned to the teacher. "I'm sorry, Mrs. Scribner."

The teacher turned on her high heels and slammed the door behind her.

"Damn," Vernon said. "Why she always trippin'?"

"Where were we?" James asked.

"You were tellin' us about the game. Then *she* interrupted *us*," Maurice said.

James grinned. "Right, … for this game, you will be wealthy plantation owners."

"Could I have white slaves?" Vernon asked.

"There weren't no white slaves," Maurice said.

"Yes, there were," Janelle said from the back. Her hair was black and braided, her skin a shiny chestnut brown.

"Janelle's right," James said. "There were white slaves." He rubbed his chin for a moment. "Raise your hand if you would like your slaves to be white."

Half the class raised their hands.

"I'll give each of you one hundred slaves. So write down one hundred white slaves—or one hundred black slaves, if you prefer." The kids scribbled on their papers; James wrote on the whiteboard. "Now write 1 million dollars next to the one hundred white slaves and write 1.5 million dollars next to the black slaves."

"Hold up, Mr. Fish," Vernon said. "Why are the white slaves less?"

"White slaves weren't as productive. They cost less and were worth less because, in general, they did less work, and they were more likely to get sick and die."

Vernon frowned. "Damn. I shoulda went with the brothers."

"I bet them white slaves were burnin' up in the heat too," Maurice said.

"No sunblock neither," Janelle added.

"I'll also give each of you three hundred acres of land," James said. "So add three hundred acres of land and write 3.5 million dollars next to the land. And you'll all get a barn and housing for your slaves, and a great big plantation for yourself and your family. So write housing and barn with 1.5 million next to that."

"Damn," Vernon said, "even with these busted-ass white slaves, I got six million dollars."

"Not exactly," James said. "You have six million dollars invested in land, slaves, and buildings. Now that's in today's dollars adjusted for inflation. At the bottom write income $1,000,000 per year and expenses $600,000." The kids scribbled on their plantation balance sheets. James wrote on the whiteboard.

100 Slaves (Black) $1,500,000

300 Acres of Land $3,500,000

Housing and Barn $1,500,000

Income per Year $1,000,000

Expenses per Year $600,000

Profit $400,000

"A $400,000 profit," a girl said, as James wrote it on the whiteboard.

"We're doing pretty well, right?" James scanned his audience.

"We're gettin' paid," Vernon said.

"In those days," James said, "if you were from the South, you bought a lot of your manufactured goods from Europe, because it was cheaper than buying from the North. The government stopped that by levying a tax on European goods to make them more expensive. So, just like that"—James snapped his fingers—"you have to pay more for almost everything. Change your expenses from $600,000 to $700,000. What's your profit after the tax?"

"$300,000," Maurice said. "We're still okay."

James continued, "In response to the tax the US government levied on Europe, the Europeans stopped buying US cotton. Now change your income to $800,000."

"We still have $100,000 left," Janelle said.

"We've lost 75 percent of our profits, and the North is talking about abolishing slavery, the same slaves who you paid $1,500,000 for. As Southern plantation owners, how do you guys feel about that?"

"Slavery's wrong," a girl said.

"You're absolutely right," James replied. "Upton Sinclair said, 'It is difficult to get a man to understand something when his salary depends upon his not understanding it.' What do you guys think Mr. Sinclair meant by that?"

Vernon had a crooked grin. "We're not gonna think slavery's wrong if we're gettin' paid."

James nodded. "I agree, Vernon. And we see that every day in our society, with people rationalizing what they do because of the paycheck."

"So that's why we had the Civil War?" Janelle asked.

"That was a big part of it," James said, "but there was a spark from Europe that started us on the path to war. The European bankers wanted a war to divide the United States. If they had a war and two broke countries that were in debt, the bankers stood to make a lot more money than with an intact United States that was self-sufficient and debt free." James glanced at the clock. "We're almost out of time."

The class groaned.

"We'll finish this tomorrow. I have a homework assignment for you."

The class grumbled.

"Come on, Mr. Fish," a boy said.

"Relax, it'll be interesting," James said, walking over to his desk. He picked up a stack of papers. "I have a quote for you guys. I want you to take it home, read it, and think about it." He handed a small stack of papers to each person in the front row to pass back.

"And what else do we have to do?" Janelle asked.

"Nothing, just think about it. We'll discuss it tomorrow. And I expect everyone to have an opinion to share."

The quote read:

> I am not, nor ever have been, in favor of bringing about in any way, the social and political equality of the white and black

races; that I am not, nor ever have been, in favor of making voters or jurors of negroes, nor of qualifying them to hold office, nor to intermarry with white people; and I will say, in addition to this, that there is a physical difference between the white and black races which I believe will forever forbid the two races living together on terms of social and political equality. And, in as much as they cannot so live, while they do remain together there must be the position of superior and inferior, and I, as much as any other man, am in favor of having the superior position assigned to the white race.

—Abraham Lincoln

# Chapter 2

## WOD

James covered a plate of chicken and mashed potatoes with Saran Wrap, then set it in the refrigerator. He rolled up the sleeves of his button-down shirt and went to work on the dishes. The front door pushed open as James started the dishwasher. Lori tramped into the foyer, her laptop slung over her shoulder. She marched past James without a glance. He followed her beyond the foyer and the living room to her office. She was setting up her laptop on the desk. She wore a gray skirt suit, her hair tied up in a brown bun.

"I made chicken," James said, standing in the doorway.

"Ron and I ordered in," she replied, her eyes focused on her computer.

"I made real mashed potatoes. I think they turned out pretty good … almost as good as yours."

She glared. Her face was full and round and symmetrical. "You know I can't eat that."

He pursed his lips. "I'll eat the potatoes. You can have the chicken and peas."

She nodded, her mouth a flat line. "Thanks. That was nice of you to make dinner. You should have called though."

"I didn't want to bother you. Last time I called you seemed annoyed."

"I told you that I'd be working crazy hours."

He exhaled. "I just miss you."

"Don't start with me. It's been a long week."

"I can't miss you?"

She rubbed her temples. "I need this promotion, especially now. I still can't believe I listened to you. You have no background in finance whatsoever."

James crossed his arms. "It's not my fault everything's rigged."

"Then whose fault is it? Our savings has been decimated."

"I may have been wrong about the timing, but I'm not wrong."

"I believe that *you* believe that." She shook her head. "I actually calculated how much more money we would have if we had kept things the way *I* had it."

"We just have to be—"

"Three times, James. We would have three times more."

"That's the paper price. They can manipulate that, but they can't manipulate the supply. Silver's scarce. Supply'll dry up at these prices. We just have to be patient."

She bit the inside of her cheek. "You and your asinine conspiracy theories."

"The analysis is correct. We both agreed. Nothing's changed except for the paper price."

"I don't want to talk about this."

"Lori—"

"Can you just go somewhere else?"

* * *

"I thought we could have a nice brunch, like we used to," James said, sitting up in bed.

Lori pulled her sports bra over her teardrop-shaped breasts. "I need to get my workout in. I don't have time for a leisurely breakfast."

James wiped the sleep from his eyes. "I just want things to be good between us. I miss how we used to be. I feel like we've drifted apart."

She pulled a second sports bra on to hold her chest firm. "It won't always be like it was in the beginning." She capped her ensemble with a tight T-shirt.

"Why?" He pulled off the covers and stood in boxer briefs. His body was pale and thin. "Is it because we have different interests?"

She exhaled. "That doesn't help."

"Then maybe I should come with you."

She frowned. "I don't think you'd like it."

"But you used to beg me to go, when you first started there."

"And you said it sounded retarded." She grabbed her nylon jacket.

"You shouldn't say *retarded*. It's *mentally challenged* or *handicapable*."

"You don't want to go."

"I do. Let me get dressed." He grinned. "You have another pair of those yoga pants?"

\* \* \*

The gym—or box, as they would say—was a warehouse with forty-foot-tall ceilings and exposed metal beams. Ropes and rings hung from the beams. The floor was rubber. A banner the size of a scoreboard hung from the far wall that read CrossFit, Fairfield, VA. Above the banner was a huge digital clock set on 0:00.

Lori dropped her bag among a sea of bags near the entrance. She removed her jacket and T-shirt as if she were dying to. Despite two sports bras, her nipples were visible. Muscled men and women stretched and socialized in a large group. Some men were shirtless, and the women were in sports bras and tiny spandex shorts or yoga pants. James was comparatively overdressed in his gray sweats. *Are we going to work out or have an orgy?* Lori marched toward the crowd, her midriff exposed, and her shape on full display. James followed like a child, staring at the steel cages and weights, set up along the far wall like personal torture chambers. Lori beamed as her tribe greeted her return.

"Hey, Lori," a built young man said.

"Lori, what's up, girl?" asked a fortysomething woman with a round ass.

"Lookin' good, young lady," a middle-aged man with a tank top said.

A bearded man, his muscled arms crossed, stared at James. Tattoos ran from his wrists to his T-shirt sleeves and probably beyond. He looked part soldier, part lumberjack, part biker, and part NFL linebacker.

The bearded man lifted his chin toward James. "And who's this guy?"

Lori turned around and looked at James as if she had forgotten he was there. Her face was flushed. "Oh, ... this is James."

The man moved toward James with his head up and his back straight.

*This guy has great posture.*

"I'm Matt, the head trainer here," he said, holding out his hand and squeezing James's tighter than necessary. "Why are you here, James? Do you have any fitness goals?"

James massaged his hand. "I'm just here to support my wife."

Matt grinned and turned to Lori and the crowd. "This is the *husband*? He's different than I expected." He turned back to James.

Lori smiled, but her face was tight and still flushed. "He's different all right."

"What did you expect?" James asked Matt.

"I pictured Lori with someone built."

"Sorry to disappoint."

Matt smacked James on the shoulder. "There's no disappointment here. Only people trying to be the best they can be. Let's get you squared away. You're about to experience your first WOD."

A large man with a face full of stubble exited the bathroom in shorts and a tight T-shirt. James recognized him as Lori's boss.

"I never thought I'd see you here," the man said as he strutted over.

"Hey, Ron," James said.

Ron was in his early forties, ruggedly handsome, with short dark hair and a solid physique.

Ron turned to Lori. "You think he's ready for this?"

Lori rolled her eyes. "I hope so."

"A hundred bucks says Lori beats James in the WOD today," Ron said with a grin. He looked at James. "What do you say, James?"

"It's not smart to bet with people used to playing in a rigged casino," James replied.

Ron chuckled. "I heard about your theories on the stock market. It's funny how those theories always come from people who *lose* money."

Lori frowned.

Matt intervened. "We're gonna start soon."

James stripped down to his baggy shorts and T-shirt. His limbs were skinny, tattoo-free, and bright white. Matt showed James how to do each of the exercises on the workout of the day—or WOD.

Matt opened the garage door enough for everyone to walk under. James had goose bumps from the cold air. A line of tape was on the floor just inside the door. Everyone spaced themselves just behind the line. The buzzer sounded, and everyone ran to the parking lot. James waited for a moment then followed. He jogged, keeping pace with the women. He stretched his legs and passed a few people, Lori included. He touched a mailbox a few hundred yards away, turned around, and ran back toward the warehouse. Inside, he grabbed the kettlebell from his station and swung it under his legs and above his head as he had been instructed. His legs were bent, and he thrust his hips as he moved the weight like a pendulum. He was breathing hard; his shoulders and legs burned. After twelve repetitions, he stopped to rest.

"Let's go, James. Don't stop," Matt said.

James picked up the kettlebell and finished the prescribed twenty-one repetitions. Then he moved to the pull-up cage. He placed a strong band under his foot to assist him. Even with the support, he had to rest frequently.

Ron smiled at James as he ran for the door. "You're falling behind."

After pull-ups James moved to a wooden box. He stumbled and slipped off the box the first time he tried to jump on top of it.

"Bend those knees," Matt said.

James jumped on the box. His legs felt like Jell-O. Each time he rested, Matt scolded him. Halfway through his box jumps, he realized that the women were already running to the mailbox for the second time and many of the men were halfway to round three.

On the fourth round, he felt dizzy and nauseous after the mailbox run. Everyone was already finished. The crowd circled him, offering encouragement as he swung the kettlebell and struggled through the pull-ups. He tasted hot vomit in his throat as he jumped on the box. He swallowed it back. The crowd was close, intimate. He only had seven more. The room was spinning. The sweaty people around him were spinning. His face was surely green. He jumped again. Standing on top of the box, he projectile vomited into the crowd. The puke was yellowish-gray and chunky, like foamy scrambled eggs. The crowd dispersed. Ron and a fit young woman in a sports bra were covered in James's vomit.

"Motherfucker," Ron said as he flicked puke off his sweaty T-shirt.

The woman hurried to the bathroom. Lori walked away. James slipped off the box and collapsed to the floor. He heaved and more foamy-egg vomit spilled out, followed by greenish-yellow bile. James lay on the rubber floor, sweating, the room still spinning.

"It's lactic acid," Matt said, laughing. "He'll be all right."

# Chapter 3

## Guest

James sat alone at a round table covered in white linen. The placard next to him read Lori Wells-Fisher in fancy cursive. His placard read Guest. He ate yellow cake with white icing and silver sprinkles. He finished his cake, reached into his suit jacket pocket, and pulled out his phone. He scrolled through the headlines on his favorite alternative news site.

Retailers Wish for Last-Minute Shoppers as Christmas Nears

Your Professor, Your Waiter

Abysmal Conditions for Makers of Apple Products

IEA Cuts Forecast for 2015 Oil Demand

NY Governor Bans Fracking

Tsunami Survivors Rebuild

He shoved his phone back in his jacket pocket. He stood and surveyed the ballroom. The ceiling had sheer white fabric hung across the room like elegant clouds. In between the clouds, white lights shone like stars. The expansive room was raucous with men in suits and tuxedos and women in formal dresses, all standing and talking and drinking. Lori was across the room, wearing a clingy black cocktail dress and spiky heels, holding a glass of wine. She held the attention of two men in tuxedos. James trudged across the ballroom. He sidled up to Lori and tapped her on her lower back. She turned with a scowl.

"It's getting late," James said.

"I haven't seen *you* all night," Ron said.

"Hey, Ron," James replied, his eyes on Lori.

"I'm not ready to leave," Lori said. "You can go. I'll catch a ride with Ron."

"It's still early," said the man next to Ron.

"James," Ron said, "this is my friend and managing partner, Walt Davidson."

James turned toward Ron and his balding, bookish friend. "Hi, Walt. I'm James Fisher, Lori's husband."

Walt's beady eyes lit up as they shook hands. "You're the one with all the interesting theories."

Ron dipped his head and covered his laugh with his fist.

Lori groaned.

"I guess so," James said, blank-faced.

"He thinks the stock market'll blow up in our faces," Ron said.

"I've seen some insiders with dire forecasts," Walt said. "The S&P down as much as 20 percent in 2015."

Ron chuckled. "He's not talking about a bear market. He's talking about a total collapse."

"Like 1929? The seventies?" Walt asked.

"Much worse." Ron lifted his chin to James. "Tell him, Jimbo."

"Why don't you go home," Lori said to James.

James ignored his wife. "It's a mathematical certainty. And it won't just be the stock market. It'll be our entire way of life."

Lori shook her head. "Here we go." She frowned at Ron. "See what you did."

Ron smiled back at Lori like a mischievous child.

"We've always had doomsday predictions," Walt said, "and yet here we are."

"The problem is that our system must grow exponentially," James said, "but we live in a world with limits in terms of raw materials and energy and food and water and a million other things we need in modern society."

"Are you familiar with a book from the early seventies called *Limits to Growth*?"

"Great book," James said.

Lori gulped the last of her wine. "We're going for refills," she said, holding up her empty glass. Ron and Lori moved toward the bar.

"I agree with you that our system must grow," Walt said. "A debt-based money system has to grow or the debts can't be paid."

"We saw what happened in 2008," James said. "GDP growth was down but still positive, and it was like the end of the world."

"What I don't agree with is that we can't overcome the limits you talk about with respect to energy and raw materials. We're becoming more efficient every day, and technology is growing, keeping up with our growth rate."

James nodded. "I agree that we're finding ways to be more efficient, but technology is not an energy source. All this technology requires more energy, not less."

"Solar and wind technologies have had vast improvements over the past few decades," Walt said.

"We get less than 5 percent of our energy from renewable sources, and most of it is in the form of hydroelectric and biomass. Solar and wind are just a drop in the bucket. And how much oil and coal do we burn to dig up the metals required to make a solar panel or a wind turbine?"

"In Brazil they get a lot their fuel from sugar cane."

"There are some bright spots. Human beings are certainly ingenious. I'm not disputing that." James pursed his lips. "I'm just saying that our economic system requires growth, and that growth has been destructive in terms of using up natural resources and polluting the environment in a way that's unsustainable. And every day it gets worse. Every day we have more people, with more energy used, more stuff, more of everything. Anything that's unsustainable will eventually end."

Walt smiled. "And yet the stock market is near all-time highs, and commodities are in a bear market."

"That's true," James said with a crooked grin, "but I would imagine it's easier to manipulate computer digits than the real world."

Walt cackled. "You know what, James? You might be on to something there. Prior to 2008, we used a proprietary trading system that worked very well for us, but, after 2008, it's been ineffective. Thankfully we were smart enough to follow the herd back into equities, and we're using high-frequency trading algorithms now."

"And what's changed since 2008? Do we have more or less derivatives? Are the banks bigger or smaller? All we've done is postpone the inevitable, making the outcome more destructive."

"What's the solution?" Walt held out his hands. "Go live in the woods with a truckload of canned goods?"

"There isn't one. We have a predicament, not a problem. Problems have solutions. Predicaments have outcomes. You joke about living in the woods with a truckload of canned goods, but it isn't the worst idea. I definitely wouldn't want to be here, where everything's trucked in. Seriously, where's the nearest farm?"

Walt smirked. "Ultimately you may be right, my friend, but not in my lifetime."

James deadpanned, "I wouldn't be so sure about that."

Walt glanced over James's shoulder. "Do you and Lori have any big plans for the holidays?"

"I assume we'll go see her parents and her sister, but we haven't had a chance to talk about it. How about you?"

"We have two boys, but they outgrew the Christmas magic long ago. Now it's all about the electronics."

James nodded.

Walt looked around the room. "I should probably find my wife."

"It's been a pleasure talking to you," James said, holding out his hand. "I should do the same."

They shook hands and parted ways. James trekked to the bar but found no sign of Lori or Ron. James did a lap around the ballroom but still nothing. He had to pee, so he exited the ballroom and walked down a marble-floored hall to the bathroom. He placed his hand on the brass handle, and the door burst open. He stepped back, the door almost hitting him in the face. Two young men in suits departed, laughing. James entered the marble-tiled bathroom. One wall had a bank of mirrors and sinks. Opposite the sinks were eight stalls. Against the far wall were a slew of urinals, with two thirtysomething men peeing side by side. He heard groans from the handicapped stall as he walked to the urinal at the end, as far away from the pee buddies as possible.

One man said, "Aah," as his flow started.

The other said, "Fuckin' beer runs right through me."

James unzipped his fly and pulled out his penis from the hole in his boxer shorts. He stood, the pressure building in his bladder, but not a drop released. The men walked away, one after the other, pulling up their pants and zippers in one grand motion. They left without visiting the sink, and James then began to pee.

Afterward he zipped up and moved to the sink. The urinal flushed automatically. He washed his hands, grabbed a towel from the stack, and wiped them dry. He gazed into the mirror. His nose dominated his face. James forced a smile. His teeth were straight and white. Like a predator, his eyes locked on movement in the mirror. He saw spiky heels and shiny men's dress shoes intertwined under the handicapped stall door. James frowned. *Get a room.*

James marched past the stall toward the exit. He heard a giggle that stopped him in his tracks. He turned around and knocked on the stall door. She squeaked in surprise.

"Occupied," Ron said.

"Let me talk to my wife," James said.

He heard hushed whispering, the rustling of fabrics, and a zipper zipping. The stall opened just enough for Lori to fit through. She appeared with her head down, and her lipstick smudged.

"How long?" James asked.

She didn't reply.

"How long!"

She jumped at the volume and looked at James through red eyes. "A year—I was going to tell you. I'm sorry."

"And all this time … I'm a fucking idiot."

She bit the inside of her cheek. "We grew apart."

James rubbed his eyes with his thumb and index finger. "And Ron? Seriously? He's a superficial douche bag."

The stall door yanked open. "Watch it," Ron said.

James clenched his fists, his face red. "Or what? What are you going to do? Fuck my wife? Oh, you already did that."

"James, stop," Lori said.

"Aren't you married?" James asked Ron.

"They're going to get a divorce," Lori said.

James nodded. "That's great. That's fucking great. You guys have it *all* figured out." He pointed at Lori. "You're a lying, … fucking … bitch."

James didn't see the fist that connected with his glass jaw. He was sprawled out on the marble floor, Ron standing over him.

"Get up, you fucking coward," Ron said.

"Stop it, Ron," Lori said, grabbing her man and pulling him away from James.

James stood, rubbing his jaw. He looked at the couple, their arms interlocked in solidarity. He marched out of the bathroom to the parking lot and yanked open the door to his Honda Accord. He drove fast and erratic, almost hoping for an accident. The tires screeched as he pulled into the parking space in front of their town house. He slammed the front door and plopped down on the sofa in the dark living room. He kicked off his shoes and lay on his side, his legs pulled to his chest. Tears slid down his face, until he fell asleep.

* * *

James was jolted awake by banging on the front door. He rubbed his eyes. The house was dark. He moved his aching jaw back and forth as he stood. He was still in his rumpled suit and jacket. More banging came at the door. He glanced at the clock on the DVD player. It read 2:44 a.m. He staggered to the front door and peered through the peephole at two uniformed police officers. They held their hats in their hands. James's stomach turned as he opened the door.

"Yes?" James said.

"Are you James Fisher?" the stocky officer asked.

"Yes."

"I'm Officer Koch, and this is Officer Johnston," he said, motioning to his thin partner. "Could we come in?"

James let the officers in. He turned on the overhead light in the dining room. They sat at the square table. As soon as they sat, Officer Koch delivered his message, like ripping off a Band-Aid.

"I'm very sorry sir, but your wife died in a car accident at approximately 12:15 a.m."

# Chapter 4

## Dr. Dicks

James sat at the end of the front pew, squeezed in among Lori's family as an afterthought. He gazed at the stained-glass windows and the ornate ceiling. *They extol the virtues of humbleness, at the same time spending a fortune on extravagant churches and lawyers for child molesters. What a bunch of bullshit.*

James glanced around at Lori's friends and family, many of them unfamiliar to him. The men wore dark tailored suits, the women in black designer dresses. He saw Yolanda a few rows back. She flashed a sympathetic smile. He put his hand up in acknowledgment and turned back around. He heard Lori's sister, Rebecca, whispering to her husband. In the cavernous church, voices carried farther than the gossipers realized.

"They were going to get a divorce," Rebecca said. "She wasn't happy."

"It's not the time," her husband whispered.

"At least she and Ron are together now."

James remembered the steely stare he had received when he called her Becky and not Rebecca.

"My parents met him you know," Rebecca continued.

"Who?"

"Ron. Who else?"

"*Shhhh.* People can hear you," he whispered.

"I'm not being loud. I'm just saying, they liked him ... a lot."

"Rebecca, stop."

"That's all I was going to say."

A white-haired priest began the funeral service with a prayer. The old man was the only person in the church that didn't get on his knees to pray. James was lost in his own world as the priest spoke in clichés and platitudes about a life taken too soon. Lori's father, Mr. Jack Wells, was invited to the lectern to speak. *I wonder if he let Ron call him Jack.*

James felt hot as the bald man told stories portraying Lori as daddy's little girl. James loosened his collar, but it didn't help. He felt sweat rings developing under his arms. He was having trouble breathing. James slipped out of the pew and raced along the edge of the church toward the exit. He heard whispering in his wake. He stumbled outside and sucked in the cold air, his hands on his knees. He staggered down the concrete steps and headed for the parking lot. The lot was full of shiny luxury cars. He fumbled for his keys as he approached his Honda. He heard heavy steps behind him as he opened the car door.

"James," Yolanda said.

James turned around as Yolanda huffed toward him, an overcoat covering her black dress.

"Are you okay?" she asked, catching her breath.

James exhaled. "I can't be in there anymore."

"You want to get some lunch and talk?"

James shook his head. "Thanks, but I'm okay."

She frowned. "You don't look okay."

"Have you ever heard of the term *hypergamy*?"

"No."

"It basically means marrying up or trading up. When I married Lori, she was fifty pounds overweight."

Yolanda scowled.

"I didn't have a problem with it. I loved her the way she was. Her being overweight, me being skinny and mildly ugly—"

"James."

"No, it's true. Neither of us felt we could get someone better. Then she lost the weight, and she looked great to other men too. Did you know she was overweight her entire life, until she lost the weight last year?"

"I didn't know that."

"She never knew what it was like to be desired by real men, alpha men who could attract lots of women. It made her feel special. Ron was everything I'm not. He was wealthy, good-looking, someone who could make her friends jealous. As bad as it hurts, in a way, I don't blame her."

"I *do* blame her."

"Her parents knew." James took a deep breath and exhaled, condensation spilling out of his mouth. "They actually liked him." He pursed his lips, his eyes filling with moisture. "When my dad died, and my mother went that next year, I thought of them as my surrogate parents." He swallowed. "It was one-sided. I was never good enough."

"I'm sorry, James."

"I'm pretty sure they didn't think I would be here today. They didn't even reserve a seat for me. I was her fucking husband." He looked at the asphalt. "I miss her."

Yolanda wrapped her arms around James. He held on as the dam broke, and the tears flowed.

\* \* \*

James's cell phone vibrated on the dining room table. His hair was disheveled, and his sweats needed a wash. He ignored the phone, as he scanned the headlines on his laptop.

I See Bubbles

Protect Your Portfolio

EU Eyes Personal Savings to Plug Financing Gap

James clicked on the link to "The Algorithm That Can Predict a Revolution" article. His cell phone vibrated again. He rubbed the stubble on his chin as he read. Afterward he hit the Back button, returning to the headlines. He clicked on the I See Bubbles link. His phone vibrated. He exhaled and glanced at the screen. He had seven text messages and four missed calls. They were all from Yolanda. He read through the texts. The last one said she was coming over. James selected her number and tapped the green phone icon. Yolanda picked up on the first ring.

"James," she said.

"I'm at the store," he said, "so I won't be at home."

"I just thought you might want to come over and have dinner with us tonight."

"Thanks, … but I don't feel up to it. Besides, I shouldn't be near anyone on Valentine's Day. I'm a walking cautionary tale. It would be like inviting Kissinger to a peace rally or a vegan to a barbecue or Dr. Dicks to an NBA tryout or Freddy Krueger to a sleepover or—"

"Stop," she said, giggling. "I'm worried about you."

"I'm fine."

"Really?"

"Yes," James said.

"You need to get out of the house."

"I have been. I'm at the store, remember?"

"What store?"

"The one that sells stuff." James chuckled.

"Uh-huh."

"Seriously I'm fine. I'll see you on Monday."

"Are you sure you don't need more time? I could talk to Dicks for you."

"I'm sure he would love to extend my *unpaid* leave of absence. He doesn't have to see my ugly mug, and he can save money with a sub."

"Didn't you get paid bereavement leave?"

"Five days."

"Oh. Are you okay … financially?"

"I'm fine. We had life insurance, and some savings."

"The kids miss you. They've been bugging me about when you're coming back. I didn't tell them about Monday, in case you changed your mind. They'll be excited to see you."

\* \* \*

James stood near the door and greeted his students as they entered the classroom.

"Good morning, Janelle," he said.

Her eyes were wide, her mouth open. "Mr. Fish," she said, giving him a hug.

James held out his arms, so he didn't touch the girl. The top of her head was braided in a perfect swirl pattern.

She released her grip, stepped back, and said, "We missed you."

Maurice smiled at James through bright white teeth and high cheekbones. "Hey, Vernon, Mr. Fish is back," he yelled down the hall as he sidled up to his teacher. "I'm glad you're back. The subs we had …" Maurice shook his head. "I can see why they only get a hundred dollars a day."

"We had eleven different subs," Janelle said.

Maurice laughed as Vernon strutted into the classroom with a crooked smile.

"Thank God," Vernon said. "Mr. Fish, it was borin' as hell in here."

James swallowed the lump in his throat. "Thanks, guys. It's good to be back."

The rest of the class spilled into the room and greeted their teacher long after the bell. The mood was jovial and rambunctious.

"Mr. Fisher," Mrs. Scribner said from the doorway. She stood with her toe tapping and her arms crossed over her chest.

James glanced at the tiny blonde. She looked like a teacher strip-o-gram.

"It's great that you're back and everything," she said, "but my kids are really distracted by the noise."

James marched over and shut the door in her face. The class laughed and commented on the diss. The kids finally settled into their seats. James stood in front of his class in khakis and a button-down shirt. "So what did you guys learn while I was away?" James asked.

"Nuthin," Maurice said.

"He's right," Janelle said. "They were teachin' stuff we already learned. Dr. Dicks said there was no way we were as far as we were."

"You guys are a lot smarter than they give you credit for," James said. "Did you learn about the Reconstruction?"

"Yes," several kids said in unison.

"Since we're so far ahead on government propaganda, why don't we concentrate on learning things that will help everyone become a more successful adult?" James scanned the classroom. The kids sat up straight, with their eyes locked on him. "What do you guys think is the purpose of school? Why do you have to go to school for thirteen years?"

"To learn," a Bolivian kid said.

James nodded.

Vernon frowned. "To learn what they want us to learn."

"Who's *they*, Vernon?" James asked.

Vernon shrugged. "People in power. Who else?"

"Can you be more specific?"

"The government," Vernon said.

"And bankers," Maurice added.

"And the fascists," Janelle said.

"Janelle, can you explain to everyone what a fascist is?" James asked.

She stood, taking the spotlight. "Fascism is when you put together private companies with the government."

James chuckled. "So what do all these people want you to learn? And for what motive?"

"Stuff that makes 'em look good," a heavyset girl said.

"To keep us from knowin' the truth," Maurice said.

"And why wouldn't they want us to know the truth?" James asked.

"So we don't get mad. So we're easier to control," Maurice replied.

"There's this comedian that I really like," James said. "His name was George Carlin."

"Never heard of him," Vernon said.

"He died in 2008, so he's probably a bit before your time. In one of his shows he explained what you guys are talking about. I'm paraphrasing here, but he said something like, 'They want obedient workers. People who are just smart enough to run the machines and do the paperwork. And just dumb enough to passively accept a lower and lower standard of living. What they don't want is a population of well-informed, well-educated people, capable of critical thinking. That doesn't help them. That's against their interests.'" James paused and looked around at the diversity in the classroom. Boy and girls, black and white, and everything in between. He thought about how they all had one thing in common. *The deck is already stacked against them.* He continued, "That's what I want for you guys. I want you to learn to think for yourselves. So, for the rest of the year, that's what we'll concentrate on."

\* \* \*

Dr. Dicks sat behind his desk, noticeably higher than James across from him. *Does he have a booster seat back there?* The gold placard on his desk read Dr. Paul Richards. Early summer sunlight pierced through the window. Dust motes were suspended in the rays. The principal leaned forward, his elbows on the desk.

"This is a real problem, Mr. Fisher," the principal said.

Dr. Dicks was hairy—his forearms, his neck, even the collar of his polo had hair bursting forth. He was like a cross between a caveman, a dwarf, a marine, and a golfer.

"I don't see what the problem is," James said. "My students learned the state-mandated curriculum."

"But they also learned quite a bit of controversial and inappropriate material."

James exhaled. "Are you telling me that it's controversial and inappropriate to teach kids to think for themselves?"

"We've had several complaints from teachers. Many of your students have been argumentative and disrespectful in their other classes. They've challenged teachers and administrators. I had to deal with Janelle yesterday. She called me a statist and said my argument was wrong because I was appealing to authority. I was just assigning her detention for being insubordinate. We've had a teacher corroborate that this disobedience has been encouraged by your class."

James shook his head with a frown. "These kids are learning. They're gaining confidence. They're thinking for themselves. And someone who is a critical thinker will not stand for half-truths and manipulations. These teachers who are upset are bullies. They're not used to kids questioning them. But that's what we should be encouraging."

The principal sat silent, his jaw tight.

James stared. *Here it comes.*

"I will not tolerate such deviation from the curriculum. I'm giving you an unsatisfactory evaluation for the school year. Next year you will have to meet with the instructional coach, and you will be subject to unannounced visits from me and the coach to see how you're progressing. If you do not adhere to the standard, I will be forced to initiate termination proceedings."

James cackled. "*Initiate termination proceedings*? Are you going to fire me or launch me into space?"

The principal's face was set in stone. "I assure you this is no laughing matter."

"Does it feel good to have power over others?"

"Mr. Fisher, you are not helping your cause."

"Seriously I'd like to know. Do you enjoy making people do what you want them to?"

The principal clenched his fists. "I suggest you leave before you say something you'll regret."

James leaned back in his chair. "The kids hate you. Shit, the staff hates you. Ole Dr. Dicks. What an asshole."

Dr. Dicks slammed his fists on the desk. "You're fired, Mr. Fisher. You're what's wrong with education. You think you know everything, but you offer no discipline."

James smirked. "I doubt you can fire me for that. The union would have your head. I'm just telling you what people say."

The large vein in the principal's neck looked like it would burst. "I'll find a way to get rid of you. You can be certain of that." He stood. "Now get out of my office." He pointed at the door.

James exhaled. "I'll save you the trouble. I quit."

# Chapter 5

## Protect and Serve

James pulled a cart loaded with trees across the gravel lot to his F-150 pickup truck. He dropped the tailgate and heaved the potted fruit trees into the rusted truck bed.

"Hey, mister. You need a hand with those trees?" said a young man with a T-shirt logo that read Growing Dreams.

"I think I have it, thank you," James replied.

James laid down the trees, so they wouldn't get windburn on the drive home. He shut the tailgate and drove away. When his cell phone rang, he glanced at the number and tapped the green icon.

"Hey, Yolanda," James said.

"I was just calling to see how you were settling in up there," Yolanda said.

"It's different, … but I like it. Everything's slower, more natural."

James drove through town, past three- and four-story brick and stone buildings plus a fountain that shot water ten feet in the air.

"How's the cabin?" Yolanda asked.

"Rustic. I shower outside and use an outhouse, but I like the simplicity of it all. Maybe Thoreau was on to something."

Yolanda laughed. "Sounds like my childhood, but I'll keep my indoor plumbing. The novelty might wear off in the winter."

"I do have electricity."

James drove past a police cruiser poised to exit a Sheetz gas station. The officer scowled.

"Can I call you later?" James asked.

The cop followed James, tight to his bumper.

"I have a cop on my ass," James said.

"I'll call you later," Yolanda replied.

James placed his phone in the cup holder and checked his speedometer. He glanced in the rearview mirror, with a sinking feeling in his stomach. The cruiser was still tight to his bumper. He drove through town, the business district giving way to farms and wilderness. After a few minutes the police officer turned on his flashing lights. James pulled over. The police officer gunned the V8 of his Crown Victoria, zooming past. James parked on the shoulder, his heart pounding. After a moment he continued home.

Gravel crunched under the tires of his old Ford. James fiddled with the radio stations, scanning the channels. *Country, classic rock, Christian music, and Christian talk radio.* He frowned and turned off the radio as he motored down the narrow country road, with a dense oak, hickory, and maple forest on either side. Driveways leading to cabins and trailers were scattered about a quarter mile apart.

As the bright sun heated the cab, he rolled down the window. Birds sang; squirrels scurried over dead leaves on the forest floor. He heard a high-pitched holler as he passed a single-wide trailer home. James stopped his truck and spied. The home was partially concealed by a stand of young trees. There was a red Ford Ranger parked in the driveway. An older man dragged a young woman by the crook of her arm. He took her to the backyard, out of view. James sat in his truck, listening. Nothing.

He continued down the gravel road for two miles. He pulled into his driveway and parked in front of the one-story cabin with its front porch that ran the length of the house. The roof was cedar shake, with a black hose that snaked back and forth and ended at the far corner of the porch roof. It hung over a wooden enclosed shower. The front yard was cleared, a mix of sparse grass, dandelions, and clover.

James donned his straw hat, pulled on his leather gloves, and moved to the rear of the truck. He dropped the tailgate, flexed his reddish-tan arms, and picked up a potted fruit tree. He placed the trees in the front yard to take advantage of the only sun he had. A square-shaped garden was placed near the driveway. He kept the trees far enough away from the garden so their mature size wouldn't shade the vegetables. James used a tape measure to space the eight fruit trees according to the tags.

He stepped on the shovel to press the spade into the hard ground, working it, making the hole twice as wide as the tree pot. James pulled the tree from the pot and massaged the roots to help break the root binding. He sprayed some water in the hole before he set the tree inside and backfilled the soil, tamping it down as he went to avoid air pockets. Once the tree was planted, he added more water and applied wood mulch.

With the afternoon sun still high in the sky, he spread mulch around the last fruit tree. He pulled the hose toward the spigot, passing the garden. The lettuce and spinach leaves were scorched by the early summer heat wave. The plants were going to seed, trying to ensure their genetics lived on. The tomatoes and peppers were wilting, and the eggplant leaves looked like someone had taken a tiny shotgun to them. The ground was dry and cracking underneath the plants. A hunk of quartz, the size of a shoe box, sat in the center of the garden. James frowned at his plants and watered the garden, before rolling up the hose.

He trekked around back. The backyard was mostly wooded but cleared near the house and around the outhouse—a small wooden structure, twice the size of a Porta-John. Inside, a bag of lime with a scooper was on the wooden floor. Two holes with toilet seats were side-by-side. One was open; one was closed. He peed in the open hole, then hiked to the back door of the cabin and entered, wiping his feet on an oversize doormat.

The cabin was a single room containing a bunk bed, dresser, and a wardrobe along the front wall. A ratty recliner sat in front of the stone fireplace with a wood-burning insert. A love seat and wooden cubbyholes for storage were along the back wall. Opposite the fireplace was a small kitchen, with a square kitchen table for two. He washed his hands in the kitchen sink and filled a glass with water. He sat down at the kitchen table with a groan, opened his laptop, and inserted the Verizon AirCard into the USB port. After waiting for the computer to load, he scanned the headlines.

> Budget Cuts Blamed for Jump in Chicago Murder Rate
>
> California Traffic Tickets Leading to Debtor Prisons
>
> Italian Banks Made Bad Loans of 192 Billion Euros in April
>
> NJ Supreme Court Rules State Doesn't Have to Pay $1.59 Billion on Pensions
>
> Greek Failure Could Mean End of Eurozone
>
> ECB's Balance Sheet Balloons to 2.43 Trillion Euros
>
> Greek Pension System Failure

\* \* \*

Low on the horizon, the sun was a fiery orange orb. James walked along the concrete sidewalk in khakis and a short-sleeved polo shirt, passing the Community College of Central Pennsylvania sign. Inside his classroom, he setup his laptop as students trickled in. Most were in their late teens, early twenties, white.

"Hey, Mr. Fisher."

"Welcome, Jessica. Good evening," James said.

Jessica had ratty blond hair, an attractive round face, and a medium build. She wore a T-shirt and cut-off jungle fatigues. She looked like a movie star playing a tomboy.

"Kurt, Heather," James said to the couple sneaking into his classroom, "where were you guys last class?"

Kurt frowned. "It's summer," he said, sitting at a desk, barely making eye contact.

Kurt was pudgy with tan skin, a backward-facing baseball cap atop his head, and a beard trimmed in a thin line.

"And this is summer school," James said. "You have to at least show up and give me some effort. What about you, Heather?"

She shrugged. "I wasn't feelin' good."

Heather sat in the desk next to Kurt. She wore neon yellow sneakers with painted-on tight jeans and heavy makeup around her eyes. She had long wavy brown hair, a pretty face, and a thin build.

"You're still responsible for the work we did," James said. "It's on the syllabus. I expect you two to catch up."

"Yeah, we'll get to it," Kurt said with a frown.

The classroom filled with students. James checked his watch and shut the door. "I guess that's about everyone," he said. "You should all have your Civil Rights presentations. Remember guys, this is Current Events, so you must use current issues for your presentations. And we need to know both sides of the issues, not just the one *you* believe in. Your positions have to be about logic and reason, not culture, bias, and emotion. Who would like to present first? Any volunteers?"

The sole hand that went up was Leon's. He was tall with dark skin, his hair cut short. He was the only student who wore slacks and a tie.

"Come on up, Leon," James said, motioning.

Leon took long strides to the front of the classroom. He stood at the wooden podium, arranged his papers, and straightened his tie.

He cleared his throat. "My issue is police shootings in the United States."

"Figures," Kurt said under his breath.

Leon began, "Our police are supposed to protect and serve us. They are supposed to be the people we go to in a crisis. They are supposed to save lives, not take them. Unfortunately, that is not what is happening. From an article in *The Guardian* just last week, they cited the following statistics. 'In the first twenty-four days of 2015, police in the United

States fatally shot more people than police in England have over the past twenty-four *years*. Police in the States have shot and killed more people in every single week of this year than are killed by German police in an entire year. Also US police killed more people in Stockton, California, in the first five months of 2015 than police in Iceland have killed in the past seventy-one years.'"

Leon turned over his paper. "The other side would argue that the shootings were justified, that officers' lives were in danger. I would also like to cite a Bureau of Labor Statistics report on the most dangerous jobs in America. The topmost dangerous job in America is logging, followed by fishing, then pilots and flight engineers, followed by roofers. Police officers do not even crack the top ten. In fact, a report put out at the beginning of 2014 by the National Law Enforcement Officers Memorial Fund shows that 2013 had the lowest law enforcement fatalities in sixty years, and the fewest officers killed by firearms since 1887.

"I would also argue that police officers disproportionately attack poor minorities, black people in particular. The Black Lives Matter movement—"

"All lives matter," Kurt said with a smirk.

"Let him finish," James said.

Leon continued, "Black Lives Matter began as a social media hashtag after George Zimmerman was acquitted in the shooting death of Trayvon Martin. The group became nationally recognized with its protests of the police killings of Michael Brown and Eric Garner.

"Peter Moskos, an assistant professor at the John Jay College of Criminal Justice, compiled a report that, after adjusting for population, stated blacks are 3.5 times more likely to be killed by police than whites. However, if you factor in homicide rates, whites are actually 1.7 times more likely to be killed by police. On the other hand, ProPublica.org cited a statistic that found that black males between the ages of fifteen and nineteen were twenty-one times more likely to be killed by police than whites in the same age cohort. Also *The*

*Washington Post* reported that *unarmed* black men were seven times more likely to be killed by police than an unarmed white man."

Leon glanced at James, then to his paper. "My conclusion is that young black males *are* being disproportionately abused by police, but also that the civil rights of all races are being abused by police in the name of safety and the law. This should not be an issue of white against black or vice versa. It is an issue of government abuse of power. None of us are safer when we have an interaction with the police. Thank you." Leon looked up from his paper.

"Very good, Leon," James said. "Thought-provoking and I liked that you used statistics to back up your thesis." James turned to the class. "We can now open up the class for questions and comments. Remember, be respectful, and bear in mind, part of your grade is based on class participation, and how well you can defend your thesis."

Kurt raised his hand.

"Go ahead, Kurt," James said.

Kurt said, "Just because cops in America are tough on crime don't mean they're doin' anything wrong, and just because cops are gettin' killed less don't mean it's not a dangerous and stressful job. They're just gettin' better, safer trainin.'"

Leon frowned. "Everything you just said was opinion. Do you have any facts to back up your argument?"

"My dad's been a cop for thirty years. He said they have to be so careful now so they don't get sued. He said more guilty people get off now."

"Everybody's got a camera now," Heather added.

"I actually agree with you," Leon said. "I agree that cops are probably less abusive than in the past simply because people have cameras. However, your anecdotal evidence does not prove anything. It still does not invalidate my thesis that rights are and have been trampled on."

Kurt glared. "You talk about racism, but your Black Lives Matter movement is divisive and racist. Should be All Lives Matter."

Leon nodded. "The group isn't called *Only* Black Lives Matter. During the Civil Rights Movement of the sixties, black men hung signs on themselves that read *I am a man.*" Leon flipped through his papers and pulled out a black-and-white image of men marching with that very sign hanging from their necks. He showed it to the class. "Do you think these men were saying only black men are men and white men are something else? They were simply stating the fact that they are men and should be treated as such. Black Lives Matter is simply saying that black lives are just as important as any other race."

"I don't see why they need to even say that," Kurt said.

"Because they're being killed and arrested at a far higher rate than other races."

"Because black men are committin' all the crimes. That's why they're gettin' killed and arrested."

Leon shook his head. "There are problems in the black community, no doubt. Black people do have the highest crime rate by race. I'm not denying that, but how much of the black crime rate is influenced by targeting and racial profiling, and how many white people get away with things because they're white? For example, statistics show that white people do more drugs than black people, yet black people are three times as likely to get arrested for drug possession. And then what happens? They go to prison, where they're likely to be subjected to rape and assault. Then, when they get out, they can't get a job. Nobody cares about them. Meanwhile, the white guy has a good job and a family. Who's more likely to commit a violent crime now? Some of this is circumstance, and another big part is racial profiling."

Kurt shook his head. "You people always say that."

Jessica rolled her blue eyes.

Leon said, "*You people* need to stop arresting us more than everyone else."

"Let's try to keep the opinions to a minimum," James said. "Logic and reason, guys."

"I'll say one more thing about racial profiling," Leon said, scanning the audience of white faces. "Everybody who's been pulled over by the police in the last month, raise your hand." One white hand went up. "How many times?"

"Once," a white male from the back said.

"And for what?" Leon asked.

"I was going forty-five in a twenty-five-mile-per-hour zone."

"And you still got your license?"

"The cop gave me fourteen over, so I wouldn't get any points."

Leon pursed his lips. "Anyone wanna guess how many times I've been pulled over in the past month?"

The room was silent.

"Three times," Leon said. "And I didn't do anything. They searched my car and didn't find anything. How many of you could say the same thing if your car was searched?"

"Maybe your car was suspicious," Kurt said. "If you put tint on your windows, cops think you might be hidin' somethin'."

"I don't have no damn *tint* on my windows." Leon glowered at Kurt, "I wasn't gonna say anything, but this is more to my point of racial profiling. Kurt's brother was the one who pulled me over and searched my car."

"You better watch your mouth, boy."

"Stop it," Jessica said to Kurt.

Heather glared at Jessica.

"Who you calling a boy?" Leon said.

Kurt grinned.

"You can go home now," James said

"For what?" Kurt asked.

"You know what."

"Whatever." Kurt grabbed his backpack. "Let's go," he said to Heather.

Heather stood with her book and notebook in hand.

"If you leave," James said to Heather, "you'll get a zero for class participation today."

"This is bullshit," Heather said.

Kurt slammed the door behind them as they left.

\* \* \*

Dot's Diner was clad in shiny metal, the sign lit in orange fluorescence. James parked a few spaces away from two police cars. Inside, the floor was black-and-white checkered tile. A dozen stools were evenly spaced along the glistening counter. Booths were set up along the walls. Two police officers, one old and one young, sat at a secluded corner booth. A grizzled-looking middle-aged man sat out of earshot. Two young men, with shirts that read Northfield Gas, sat at one end of the counter. James sat at a stool on the other end. Jessica filled their coffee and glanced at James. She smiled at the men and made her way to her teacher.

"Hey, Mr. Fisher," Jessica said. "What can I get for you?" She wore black jeans and a white polo shirt with Dot's Diner embroidered on the upper left corner.

"I didn't know you worked here," James said.

"Three nights a week, after class. I've been trying to get a few lunch shifts, but those are hard to come by. Ladies have been working those shifts for thirty years or more. If you come at lunch, you'll see a bunch of sixty-year-old waitresses."

"I thought you did a very nice job on your presentation tonight. It was well-researched, and you're an excellent speaker. Are you planning to transfer to a four-year school?"

She shrugged. "I'd like to go to Penn State, but money's an issue. I figure I'll knock out my associates at the community college and then see. In the meantime, I save every dime."

James nodded. "Good for you."

"So what'll it be?" she asked.

"I know it's late, but I could go for some scrambled eggs and bacon. Oh, and some coffee too."

* * *

As James finished his eggs, Jessica topped off his coffee.

"Do you know Leon outside of class?" James asked.

"We went to high school together," she said, "but he keeps to himself. I think his mom's a doctor or a nurse or something." She frowned. "I heard his dad's in prison for murder, but that might not be true. People gossip so much around here."

The police officers stood from the booth and strolled to the door as if they didn't have a care in the world.

"He's a smart kid," James said.

Jessica nodded, her eyes on the officers. The younger one was wiry, with tan skin and thin dark hair. His nose was pointed, almost beaklike. The older one was broader, with a mustache, and dark obviously dyed hair that was receding. His neck skin was loose and hanging.

The older cop tapped his large gold ring on the counter. "You be good, girl," the cop said.

"I will," she replied through a tight smile.

"See you next week," the younger officer said.

After the men left, she said to James, "That's Kurt's father and brother. You know, the one Leon was talking about."

James nodded.

"They come here every Monday night—same time, same place. They even sit in the same booth."

"Is Kurt's dad the police chief?"

"Yes."

"I thought I saw his picture on the township website."

"You should probably be careful."

"Why?" James asked.

Jessica bit the corner of her lower lip. "I think Kurt's used to doing whatever he wants. You just might not want to piss him off."

James chuckled. "So I'm supposed to have a different standard for

PHIL M. WILLIAMS

this kid because his family has a little power?"

"How long have you been living here?"

"About three months."

"And I'm guessing you came from a big city?"

"A suburb of DC."

"People talk about how quaint and safe it is in a small town, and I agree it can be. But the problem with small towns is that people don't like outsiders, and they don't like people who are different from them."

James nodded.

"The other thing you have to understand is the police have a lot of power. It's not like the ritzy suburbs where people have money and lawyers. Around here, everyone's poor, so the police can do whatever they want. I believe what Leon said about being harassed."

"So they just go around and harass anyone they don't like?"

"Maybe." She shrugged. "I don't know." She glanced around to make sure everyone was out of earshot. "There is one thing I do know," she said in a hushed voice. "Last year Kurt and the Callahan brothers got caught up in this meth bust. They were all holding enough drugs to show that they were selling. Anyway the Callahan brothers are in prison for I don't know how long, and Kurt, well, you saw him in class. I'm pretty sure nothing happened to him. I'm just saying, they have rules for us and rules for them."

\* \* \*

Kurt stood at the podium, facing the class, his backward-facing base-ball cap pulled down to his eyebrows. "You don't see people filmin' police officers doin' all the good stuff they do. The police are the differ-ence between havin' a peaceful place and thugs runnin' things. If we didn't have police, people would be crazy. Without law enforcement, people would just do whatever they want. It's easy to sit back and look at a video and criticize, but it's a hard job, and those people bitchin' couldn't do any better." Kurt looked up from his paper.

44

"Thanks, Kurt," James said. "As always, we'll open up the class for questions and comments. Remember, be respectful, and, bear in mind, part of your grade is based on class participation and how well you can defend your thesis."

Leon's hand shot up.

"Go ahead, Leon," James said.

"First of all," Leon said, "your whole presentation was opinion. You didn't have one fact."

Kurt narrowed his eyes. "What about the murder rate in Baltimore going up because police are afraid to do their job?"

"Who do you think controls the crime statistics?"

Kurt laughed. "So you're sayin' the cops lied about the statistics to make it look like there were more murders? Now look who's sayin' shit without proof."

"The police lie. That's what they do."

"I'll agree with you there. The police lie, but they do it to arrest thugs."

Leon shook his head. "They don't care about arresting criminals. They care about maintaining power and control. You're biased because of your family."

"Let's not get personal. Stick to provable facts, guys," James said.

Kurt had a shit-eating grin. "So I'm biased because my dad and brother are police officers?"

"That's what I said."

"That's enough, you two," James said.

Kurt stroked his pencil-thin beard. "If that's true, then you must be biased because your dad's a rapist and a murderer."

Leon shot out of his seat.

"That's enough, Kurt," James said. "Leon, please sit down."

Kurt cackled. "See? Already tryin' to murder me. It's in his blood."

Leon sat down. "The police are corrupt and incompetent," Leon said. "That's why my dad's in prison."

"If my dad was a murderin' rapist piece of shit, I'd prob'ly wanna blame the police too."

"You need to leave," James said to Kurt.

Kurt held his palms up. "It's okay for him to insult my family with lies, but I can't tell the truth about his? This is some reverse-racist bullshit."

"Good-bye, Kurt."

# Chapter 6

## The Girl Next Door

James leaned on his truck, watching the gallons and dollars soar skyward on the digital pump. When his phone rang, he reached into his pocket and fished out his cell. He glanced at the number and tapped the green icon.

"Shouldn't you be working?" James said. "I'm telling Dr. Dicks."

"I'm on my lunch break," Yolanda replied. "What are you doing?"

"Filling up my truck. I'm surprised I haven't spontaneously combusted. I'm staring at a sticker of a cell phone with a big red *X* over it."

"I can call you later."

"Hell no. I love to live life on the edge."

Yolanda giggled.

"How are you doing?" James asked.

"I'm good. Busy. How's the fall semester?"

"It's going well. I'm teaching Modern American History and Ancient Greece at night. I have some nice kids. A lot of my summer school students from Current Events signed up with me again."

"What about that problem student you were telling me about?"

"Kurt?"

"Yes."

"Thankfully no. That's one kid I was happy to see go. Every once in

47

a while you get a kid who you just know is evil. It's scary. I was afraid to give him the grade he deserved."

"What did you give him?"

"A C-."

"What did he deserve?"

"A C-, but I really don't know what I would have done if he would've failed. I may have passed him to avoid any blowback. That kid gives me the creeps. Unfortunately, I still see him Monday, Wednesday, and Fridays."

James removed the gas nozzle, placed it on the pump, and screwed on his gas cap.

"I thought you said he wasn't in your class."

"He's not. I think he's taking English Lit. He makes a point of staring at me as he walks by my class on the way to the parking lot."

"Can I call you later? A patient just walked into my office."

James drove from the gas station toward his cabin. He turned down the gravel road, admiring the scenery. Oaks, maples, and hickory trees displayed their fall color. Movement to his left diverted his attention from the October glory. James stopped his truck and rolled down his window. *Again? If this is what goes on outside, I can only imagine what goes on inside.*

He squinted through the trees that partially concealed their single-wide trailer. The young woman, her hand on her cheek, backed away from the porch and the middle-aged man. He had a salt-and-pepper beard with no mustache, like the Amish, but James was pretty sure the man wasn't Amish. He said something inaudible and pointed to the ground in front of him. The small woman stepped toward the man, with her head down. As soon as she was within his reach, he grabbed her and forced her inside.

James exited his truck and crept toward the trailer. The same red Ford Ranger was parked in the driveway. He stopped and hid behind a large oak, one hundred feet away from the house. He listened.... Nothing. He returned to his truck.

James pulled into his driveway and carried two grocery bags to the front door. Two stacks of cardboard boxes sat on the front porch, with UPS shipping labels attached. He put away the groceries and carried the boxes inside one at a time. He placed them near the back door and pulled the oversize doormat from the floor, revealing a two-by-two square hatch. James grabbed the rope and pulled the hatch open. He carried the boxes down steep steps to the basement, where pallets were stacked with similar-looking boxes and fifty-gallon buckets.

He set them down and pulled a string on the solitary bulb. The ceiling was low, six feet. The walls were stone rubble, the floor dirt. One small window was near the top of the wall that faced the backyard. It was boarded up and covered from the outside with earth. He added the new boxes where he had space. Afterward he pulled the string on the light, shut the hatch, and covered it with the doormat.

He made lunch and turned on his laptop. He ate as he read.

Technology Is Slipping out of Control

Appalachia Walking Away from Coal

Soft Drink Makers in Decline

Taxpayers' Alliance: Cut Pensions

The Week in Energy: US Production Data a Farce

After a leisurely lunch, James walked out the front door and inspected his fruit trees. The trees looked smaller. *Are they losing their leaves?* He looked closer.

"God damn it," he said, inspecting the jagged ends of the branches.

A couple trees had bark scraped off their trunks. He exhaled. *That can't be good.* He pulled the hose from the reel and watered the trees. Then he pulled the hose to the garden near the driveway. The plants were wilted, yellowish, and stunted. Half of the tomatoes had dark spots on the bottom of the fruit. He took the diseased tomatoes to the backyard and tossed them in the woods. He heard a twig snap and instinctively looked in that direction. He saw a flash of white in the woods. James crept toward the forest edge. Once inside the wood line, leaves crunched under his feet, negating any surprise.

"Is anyone there?" James called out.

The young woman he saw in the domestic dispute stepped from behind a large hickory tree. She wore a soiled white sweater, no bra, baggy jeans, and a scarf.

"Hi. I'm James," he said as he walked toward her.

"Hi," she said, frozen to the forest floor with her head down.

James closed the gap, getting a closer look at the woman, only to realize that, if she was a woman, it was just barely. She looked young, sixteen or seventeen maybe. She was short, five feet tall, thin, and smelled like cigarettes.

"How are you doing?" James asked within arm's length.

"I'm fine," she said to the ground.

"I think I saw you earlier, a couple miles from here. Was that you in front of the trailer with the older man? Is that your father?"

She shook her head, her stringy brown hair stiff and dirty.

"That wasn't you?"

She looked up through puffy eyes. "That's not my dad."

Despite her disheveled appearance, she had pretty blue eyes, full pink lips, and an attractive symmetrical face.

"Can I help you with something?"

She was unresponsive.

"How did you get here?"

She turned around and pointed. "Trail back there."

"The older man, is he a friend or a relative?"

She turned back to James, her eyes glued to the forest floor. "He takes care of me."

"If you don't mind me asking, how old are you?"

"I'll be nineteen on Christmas."

James chuckled. "So you've been getting ripped off for eighteen years."

She looked up at him with wide eyes.

"With presents," James said. "People with Christmas birthdays always get ripped off with presents. People say they'll give you separate presents for your birthday, but it all gets lost in the Christmas madness."

The corners of her mouth turned up for a split second. "That's true."

"So, are you still in school?"

"I just help Mr. Harold. Whatever he needs."

"I teach at the community college. History. I moved here from Virginia this past spring."

"I seen you when you moved in."

James raised his eyebrows. "You did?"

She blushed. "I go on the trail a lot. We don't get too many new people around here."

"I've noticed."

"How come you ain't had nobody help you move in?"

James smiled. "You can always tell how many friends you have by how many people are willing to help you move."

She giggled.

"When I saw you, I was throwing out diseased tomatoes. I'm about ready to give up on gardening. I have a serious black thumb." James took a couple steps and picked up one of the bad tomatoes. He held it out to the girl. "See? This is what they look like."

She took the tomato from his hand. "It has blossom rot. You're prob'ly waterin' too much. Too much water washes all the good stuff out. My grammy used to say rain's enough. She said, if you give plants too much, they'll be weak, just like people."

"That's good advice. Your grandmother sounds like a smart lady."

She nodded.

"Could you take a look at my garden and orchard? I could really use some pointers from an expert."

Her mouth turned up for a split second. "I ain't no expert."

James chuckled. "You are in comparison to me."

James led her to the front yard.

"This is the orchard," James said. "Something's eating my fruit trees. The bark is torn off the trunks. The ends of the branches are chewed up."

"Deer," she said. "They love fruit trees. You have to fence 'em."

James nodded. "That makes sense. It all happened in one night."

"A herd prob'ly came through."

"The garden is over here," James said as he walked toward the driveway.

The girl followed a few paces behind. They stood looking at the garden with wilting yellowy plants and bare cracked earth.

"So this is it. Pretty sad, huh?" James said, motioning to his garden plot.

"I like your rock," she said, pointing at the pinkish-white quartz in the middle of the garden.

"It's the only thing I can't kill."

She laughed. "You definitely need some mulch."

"What kind of mulch should I use?"

"Don't matter. I would just take leaves from the woods. That'll keep the soil from dryin' out."

James nodded. "I'm so dumb. I mean, I mulched my trees. Why wouldn't I think to mulch the garden? Where did you learn to garden?"

"My grammy taught me to garden and cook when I was little."

"Do you see her much?"

"She died." The girl frowned.

"I'm sorry."

She was blank-faced.

"What about your parents?" James asked.

"I should prob'ly get back," she said.

"I just realized you never told me your name."

"I'm Brittany."

"It was nice to meet you, Brittany. Feel free to visit anytime. And thank you for all the expert advice."

She flashed a small grin and marched back to the trail.

* * *

James sat on a stool at the end of the shiny countertop, finishing his coffee. Jessica attended to a trucker a few stools down from him. The police officers, Kurt's father and brother, stood from their corner booth. James glanced over. *Every Monday night. Same time, same place.*

The old man tapped on the counter with his large gold ring as he passed Jessica. "Be good, girl," he said before exiting the diner.

*Does anything change in this town?*

James finished his coffee, thanked Jessica, and left a generous tip. He started his truck and headed home. Shortly after leaving the diner, a car pulled behind him, headlights illuminating his rearview mirror. His stomach turned at the sight of the police car tailing him. He watched his speed and observed every traffic signal. The police officer tailgated him but did not turn on his flashing lights or his siren. They drove for ten minutes like this. James was nervous as he turned down the secluded gravel road that led to his cabin. They continued down the dark road for a few minutes. Finally, the officer turned on his blue and red lights.

James stopped his truck and cut the engine. The blue and red lights circled, and a bright white spotlight pierced the cab of his truck. He leaned over and fumbled through the glove box for his insurance and registration. The officer tapped James's window with a lit flashlight.

"Roll down your window," the officer said.

James obliged, setting his documentation on the seat next to him. The officer shone his flashlight in the cab, snooping with his eyes. James recognized him as the younger cop from the diner. His gold name tag read D. Strickland. Despite his bird beak, thinning hair, and faded acne scars, he was relatively handsome.

"License, registration, and proof of insurance," Officer Strickland said.

James handed him his documentation. The officer took the papers and walked back to his cruiser without a word. Ten minutes later, the officer returned and handed James his documents.

"Do you know why I pulled you over?" the officer asked.

"No," James replied.

"Where you headed?"

"You should know that. You spent ten minutes looking at my address."

Officer Strickland smacked the truck door with his flashlight. James jolted upright in his seat. The officer grinned. "You better watch your mouth, boy. I said, 'Where you headed?'"

"Home."

"Now was that so hard? People always gotta be so damn hard-headed. And why are you drivin' on my roads at ten on a Monday night?"

James gritted his teeth. "I have class until 8:30. I did some paper-work, then I went to Dot's Diner for dinner. Now I'm on my way home."

"I know you're new around here, so I'll fill you in on a couple things. First off, people here treat police officers with respect. We don't have that us-against-them crap you see on the news. This ain't Ferguson. This is a small town, and everyone knows everyone. So, if you break the law, we'll know about it. Do you understand me?"

"Yes, sir."

"All right then. Be safe now." Officer Strickland tapped on the door with his flashlight as he walked away.

* * *

James dumped leaves into the wheelbarrow with his pitchfork. The soil under the leaves was dark and crumbly. He spotted Brittany hiking the woody trail just beyond his property line.

"Brittany," James called out.

She gave a wave and headed toward James.

"Hey, Brittany," James said with a smile as she approached. "I'm following your expert advice from yesterday." He forked another load of leaves into the wheelbarrow.

She blushed. "You listened to me?"

James shoved the fork in the wheelbarrow and turned to Brittany. She wore baggy jeans, a hooded sweatshirt, and a scarf that covered her neck.

"Of course I did," he said. "It was good advice. You know, when I pulled out these leaves, the soil underneath was black and loose, not gray and compacted like my garden."

"My grammy used to say, 'Nature's the best teacher.'" Brittany tucked her brown hair behind her ears.

"Sounds like she was a great lady."

She nodded, her head down.

"Are you growing anything at your house?" James asked.

She looked up. "Mr. Harold don't like fruits and vegetables. He says he's a meat-and-potatoes man."

James frowned. "So you don't eat any fruits or vegetables?"

"I get 'em from the woods sometimes."

"Really?" James asked with raised eyebrows.

She nodded. "I could show you."

As they walked around his property, she pointed out the oxalis he had growing in his front yard.

"It tastes lemony," she said.

James agreed as he munched on the cloverlike plant.

"Don't eat too much of it. It's a little poisonous."

James grinned. "A *little* poisonous?"

She giggled and pointed out another plant. "This is goosefoot," she said. "It's kinda like spinach."

James munched on a dark green leaf. "It does taste like spinach."

"I seen you got a shagbark hickory too." She led James into the woods separating their houses. She patted the enormous hickory trunk. The bark was loose and shaggy. Golf-ball-size green nuts littered the forest floor. Most still had the green shell covering, but some were cracking open, exposing the rock-hard light-brown shell inside. She picked up a nut. "You can eat these too. They can be tough to open. I use some stones, but my grammy used a nutcracker. They taste like pecans."

James picked up a nut, the green covering already off.

"That one's no good," she said.

"What's wrong with it?"

"It got that little hole. Means it got worms inside."

James tossed the nut. "What about fruit?"

"In the summer, I get lots of berries." She grinned, her eyes twinkling. "For fall I know a spot that got persimmons and pawpaws. Nobody knows 'bout it neither."

"I never had a persimmon. And what the heck is a pawpaw?"

She laughed. "You never heard of a pawpaw? It tastes kinda like banana custard, but you gotta try it for yourself, because nothin's like it. Only a few pawpaws left for the season. I could take you sometime."

"Sounds like fun."

"We could go tomorrow or Friday. Mr. Harold's a volunteer firefighter. He's at the firehouse those days."

James pursed his lips. "Does Harold not want you outside?"

She shrugged. "When he's nappin', I can go outside. He says I make too much noise."

"I work nights, so my days are free. Why don't we do it tomorrow?"

She smiled. "I'll come here. It's on the way to the pawpaws. I gotta get goin'. He might be up soon." She hurried toward the trail.

"What time?" James called out.

She turned around. "When he goes to the firehouse."

\* \* \*

James followed Brittany through the forest. She moved gracefully, avoiding rocks and branches along the rustic trail. Her baggy jeans were rolled up several times at her feet, the belt cinched tight around her tiny waist. James stumbled along, his breathing elevated. She turned around and smiled. Her facial features were small and buttonlike.

"You need a break, Mr. James?"

He nodded.

They sat on a fallen tree trunk. She adjusted her scarf, covering up her neck. James pulled two water bottles from his backpack. He handed one to Brittany.

"I packed one for you," he said in response to her wide eyes.

She took the water bottle and sipped. James guzzled his.

"I brought some trail mix too," he said, pulling out two Ziploc bags filled with a variety of nuts and M&M chocolate candies.

She gorged herself on trail mix with a slight grin, her legs kicking back and forth against the tree. She glanced at James's left hand as he pulled nuts from his Ziploc bag.

"Are you married?" she asked.

James's mouth was a flat line.

"You got that wedding ring," she said.

"I was." James took a deep breath, holding up his left hand. "I guess I shouldn't be wearing this anymore."

"Did she die?" she asked, as if it was a common question.

James nodded. "She did … car accident."

Brittany looked at James for a moment. "I'm real sorry."

"Thanks, Brittany. I appreciate that."

"It's okay if you still wanna wear the ring."

James looked at her with a small smile.

"When my gram died, … it was the saddest time for me," she said.

"Is that when you came here?"

She shook her head and stared at the trail mix. "I was only ten when she died. I had to go back home."

"How was living at home?"

She shrugged and pushed herself off the log. "You wanna get movin'? We're almost there."

James followed Brittany off the trail. They hiked downhill, grabbing trees to stabilize their descent. At the bottom of the slope, the ground was spongy, the land flat. Small tropical-looking trees grew in a grove under the forest canopy. Oblong fruits the size of a child's hand hung in sporadic clusters. Brittany turned around, beaming.

"We're here," she said.

James set his backpack on the ground and pulled out a couple plastic bags. He handed one to Brittany. "I thought we could take some back with us. I read online that you can freeze them."

Brittany's mouth turned down. "I can't."

"We can keep everything in my freezer. You can come by and eat them whenever you want."

She nodded and tucked her straight hair behind her ears, exposing a bruise on her cheek.

James winced. "What happened to your cheek?"

"I don't know." She shrugged. "Must've hit it on somethin'. Doesn't hurt." She rushed into the pawpaw grove and called back to James. "I'm gonna find the best one for you."

She returned with a kidney-shaped greenish-yellow fruit. "Try this one. It's soft. You just cut it in half."

James took the fruit, inspecting the dark bruising on the skin. He removed the knife from his scabbard and sliced the fruit long ways. Inside looked like vanilla custard, with four evenly spaced large black seeds.

"That *is* a good one," she said.

"Can you hold these?" James asked, handing the halves to Brittany. "I have spoons." He removed his backpack and pulled two plastic spoons from the side pocket.

They dug their spoons into the pudding.

James savored the flavor before swallowing. "Wow. It's like mango, banana, and little bit of citrus mixed together. But that's not even exactly right."

Brittany beamed. "I told you it was like nothin' you ever had." Her face turned serious. "You can't tell anyone about this, okay?"

His eyes were wide. "About what?"

"About this place. If people find out, we'll never get none."

"Your secret's safe with me." He smiled at Brittany. "Thank you for trusting me."

"This is fun," she said. "I could show you the persimmons tomorrow."

"We could wait until Friday, if it's easier for you."

"The persimmons aren't too far. I could get away. Harold always naps after I give him his lunch."

"Are you sure it's okay? I don't want to get you into trouble."

"It'd be easy. They're right off the trail, about halfway between us."

"We could meet on the trail, so you don't have to walk as far," James said. "What time do you think?"

"Lunchtime," she replied.

James grinned. "I was thinking more of an exact time."

"He eats at twelve, so I guess 12:30."

"I'll leave at that time too. We'll meet in the middle."

# Chapter 7

## Pie in the Sky

James hooked wire fencing on green T-posts, encircling each fruit tree just beyond the drip line. *Ugly but hopefully effective.* He gazed up at the clouds, dark and heavy. He fished his phone from his pocket and checked the time. *Already 12:27 p.m. I should get moving. Hopefully the rain holds off.*

He hiked along the rocky path, wondering when he would run into Brittany. *She's quick. She'll probably beat me to the halfway point.* He glanced up at the clouds and picked up his pace.

A few trailers and cabins were visible from the trail. He counted each house, trying to remember how many were between his cabin and the single-wide trailer. *I have to be over halfway there at this point. Maybe she got a late start. Maybe she thought it was going to rain.* He thought about turning around. *But what if I turned around and she was coming down the trail? She'd walk all the way to my house and get soaked in the process.* He continued, quickening his pace, a sense of urgency coursing through him.

*I have to be close to the trailer. Maybe I already passed it. You can't see all the houses from the trail.* He looked up at the clouds. They were closing in on the last remaining bits of blue. *Five more minutes and I'm turning around. What are you doing anyway? I don't know. She needs a friend. … Maybe I do too.*

Between the hardwoods, he saw the back corner of the vinyl-sided trailer. *I think that's it. What now? You can hurry your ass home, so you don't get soaked. She probably figured you were smart enough not to go outside when a storm's coming.* He heard glass shatter. His stomach turned. *Shit.* He heard a thud, followed by a high-pitched yelp. He broke into a sprint, crashing through the brush and briars. He ran around the trailer to the front door. A man was yelling.

"Get your fuckin' dumb ass over here."

James banged on the door. The house went quiet, except for the Lamisil commercial on the television. There were hushed voices and soft steps. The blinds parted for a moment. James banged on the door again. Harold yanked it open. He stood, his arms crossed, guarding the threshold. The middle-aged man was thin and short, with a full head of hair and a salt-and-pepper beard to match. His skin was pale, with blotchy red chafing under his eyes and over his eyebrows.

"What the hell you want?" he asked. His teeth were yellow, one missing from the bottom row. He smelled like cigarettes.

"I can hear what you're doing," James replied, his jaw set tight.

"You best get the fuck off my property before I get my shotgun."

"Brittany," James called out. "Are you okay?"

Harold's eyes were wide. "You been talkin' to my girl?" He stepped out of the doorway and poked James in the chest with a bony finger.

James backed up. "Don't touch me."

Brittany appeared at the doorway behind Harold. Her lip was split, her eye black. Bruising was evident on her neck. She looked like a little girl in loose pajamas.

"Go on home before you get yaself hurt," Harold said.

James pushed past the scrawny man toward Brittany. "Are you okay?" James asked.

She nodded, her head down.

Harold stepped in front and pushed her inside. She hit the wall behind her and fell in a heap. She pulled her legs to her chest, tucking her chin, and covering her head with her arms. Harold tried to slam the front door, but James stuck his foot inside, forced his way in, and stood between Harold and Brittany.

"You're not going touch her anymore," James said.

Harold punched James in the jaw with a weak right cross. James was stunned by the blow but uninjured. He shoved the little man, and Harold stumbled backward, falling on the soiled carpet. He scurried to his feet, and James pushed him back down.

He pointed at Harold. "Don't fucking move."

Harold gritted his teeth, but he stayed on the floor.

James turned to Brittany, holding out his hand. "Let's go."

She grabbed his hand, and they left the trailer.

Harold yelled from the front door. "You ain't gettin' your stuff, you little whore. You best be watchin' your back."

Brittany hiked with James along the trail in her dirty slippers. She glanced back, her brow furrowed. James pulled her forward. Once they were a safe distance from the trailer, James stopped and inspected her face.

"Are you okay?" he asked. One eye was black and swollen, partially shut. Her lower lip was split, blood trickled to her chin. Her neck was covered in bluish-black bruises.

"I have to go back," she said. "It's gonna be really bad if I don't."

"Do you want to go back?"

She shook her hanging head. "But I have to. I don't have anywhere to go."

"We'll figure it out. Let's get to my cabin, so we can get you cleaned up, and I can make some calls." He glanced up at the sky. "It's about to pour."

They entered his cabin. He sat her down at the kitchen table, cleaned her lip, and gave her some ice for her eye.

"I'm calling the police," he said, pulling his cell phone from his pocket.

She put down the ice, recoiling, her eyes wide. "No, please don't." She shook her head. "It won't do no good."

"What he did to you is assault. All you have to do is tell the police what's happening, and they can make it stop."

"They won't. He's—"

"I'm sorry. I can't sit by and do nothing anymore." James dialed 9-1-1.

Brittany sat in silence, icing her eye. James paced, looking out the windows, waiting for the police. He glanced at the clock on his phone. *Jesus Christ, it's been twenty minutes. Where the hell are they?* James took the melted ice, and Brittany laid down on the love seat. He gave her a flannel comforter. She covered up and closed her eyes. An hour later, a single police car crept up the driveway. Officer Dale Strickland stepped out of the cruiser. James met him on the porch before he had a chance to knock. He wore dark shades and moved as if he was out for an autumn stroll.

He lifted his chin to James. "Are you James Fisher?"

"Yes. We met before."

"And you witnessed an assault?" He didn't acknowledge that they had met.

"Yes."

James told the officer what he had seen and heard.

"And the complainant is here, in your custody?" Officer Strickland asked.

"Yes, but I wouldn't consider her in my custody. She's here of her own free will."

The officer smirked. James opened the door. "Brittany, we're coming in."

She sat up on the love seat. Officer Strickland marched through the door and turned to James. "I'd like to interview her *alone*," he said.

James waited outside as Officer Strickland talked to Brittany. James peered through the window. Her head was down as the officer spoke. After five minutes of what appeared to be a one-sided conversation, the officer departed the cabin.

"Are you going to arrest him?" James asked Officer Strickland.

One side of his mouth turned up in a crooked grin. A few raindrops pelted his shirt. "You gotta have a complainin' victim. And you didn't actually see him hit her, did you?"

James scowled. "I saw him push her pretty hard."

"It ain't enough."

The rain began in earnest. The officer jogged to his cruiser. Thunder cracked in the distance. James entered the cabin, the downpour pounding the roof. Brittany sat on the love seat, her knees pulled to her chest, her head down. She was more shell-shocked now than before she spoke to the officer.

"Are you okay?" James asked.

She was silent.

"Brittany, are you all right?"

She lifted her head. Her eyes were red and puffy. "Why'd you have to do that? I told you it wasn't goin' do no good."

"What did he say?" James grabbed a wooden chair, positioned it in front of the love seat, and sat down.

She clenched her fists. "He told me to keep my mouth shut. What'd you think he was gonna say?"

"I thought he would arrest Harold."

She laughed, a few tears spilling from her eyes. "You think he's gonna arrest his uncle?"

"What?"

"Harold's always braggin' that I can't never call the cops 'cause his brother's the police chief and his nephew's a cop too." She shook her head. "He was right."

James exhaled. "I'm sorry. I didn't know they were related."

"I tried to tell you," she said.

"You're right. I should have listened to you." He looked her in the eyes. "You tell me what you want to do. I can take you anywhere you want to go. Do you have any family who you'd like to stay with?"

She burst into tears. "I can't go back there. Please don't make me." She threw her arms around him, pressing her braless pajama top against him. "I'll do anything you want."

He pulled back, uncoupling himself from her. She put her head down and sobbed. He lifted her chin.

"Hey," he said, "I'm not going to make you do anything you don't want to. Do you have any friends you could stay with?"

She shook her head. "Can I stay with you? Just for a little while. I won't be no trouble. I'll cook and clean—"

"Okay."

Her sobbing subsided.

"Brittany, listen to me. This is important. You don't have to do anything for me. I'm your friend, and I'll help you out, because I want to. No strings. Do you understand?"

She nodded her head. "Thank you." She looked down at her soiled pajamas. "I don't have any clothes."

"It's fine. We can get you what you need."

"I'll pay you back. Every penny, plus interest if you want."

James shook his head. "We'll call it payment for your gardening and foraging consultations."

She smiled, her nose and eyes red.

"This has to be temporary, okay?" he said. "Until you can get a job and get your own place."

"I ain't never had a job."

James took a deep breath. "We'll figure it out. In the meantime, I should cancel my class tonight, and run by Walmart to get you some clothes and toiletries."

Her eyes were wide. "Can I go with you?"

\* \* \*

James slept in the bottom bunk.

He heard "No, don't. No, please stop."

His eyes popped open to a dark face in the window, the features indistinguishable. His heart pounded as he scrambled back, sitting up. He rubbed his eyes. The window was dark. *I'm losing it.*

Again he heard "No, don't. Stop."

He rolled out of the bunk and turned on the floor lamp. Brittany tossed and turned in the top bunk.

"I said no," she said. "Please don't."

James edged closer. "Brittany, wake up. You're having a bad dream."

"Please don't."

He grabbed her arm.

She pulled away from his touch, curling in the fetal position. "No! No!"

"Brittany, wake up!"

Her eyes popped open. Her face was taut.

"It's me, James. You were having a bad dream."

She relaxed at the sight of him. "Oh, … I'm sorry. Did I wake you up?"

"I think I was having a bad dream too. Do you want some tea?"

"Okay."

James put water in the teakettle and turned on the electric stove top. He sat down at the kitchen table, across from Brittany. She wore brand new flannel pajamas.

"We could prob'ly find some mushrooms tomorrow." She stared out the window into the darkness. "After the rain."

"You okay?" he asked.

She tucked her brown hair behind her ears. "I don't usually remember 'em."

"The nightmares?"

She nodded. "I just wake up stressed. The ones I remember make me glad that I don't."

"Do you want to talk about it?"

She shook her head. "Do you wanna talk about yours?"

"I don't remember them either."

"Can I ask you something?"

James chuckled.

She frowned. "What's so funny?"

66

"I used to say that to my wife before I asked her something important, and she would get mad at me and tell me to just ask the question. She said that she didn't like it when I prefaced things."

"Sorry."

"No, don't be. She was wrong. It's polite to ask."

Brittany took a deep breath. "How come you're here all by yourself? Don't you have friends and family who wanna see you? People like Harold, live up here all by themselves 'cause nobody likes 'em."

He bit the inside of his cheek. "Lori was my wife's name."

Brittany nodded, her blue eyes on him.

"I wasn't the best husband, and she went elsewhere. The day she died, I found out she was having an affair with her boss."

Brittany put her hand over her mouth.

"I called her a lying, f-ing bitch. That was the last thing I said to her. They had been drinking. Her boss wrecked his car, killing her and him in the process. They ran into a telephone pole." James rubbed the stubble on his chin. "Anyway, we had friends, but our friends were really her friends, and, when she died, I realized they weren't my friends at all."

"What about your mom and dad? Brothers or sisters?"

"They're gone, and I'm an only child."

"I'm sorry." She sucked in her plump lower lip and pushed it out.

The teakettle whistled. James stood up and turned off the stove. "Is chamomile okay?" James held up a small box of herbal tea. "It doesn't have caffeine."

"I never had that kind. I only ever had Lipton."

"You're in for a treat then."

James placed the tea bags in two teacups and poured the hot water. He set the cups on the table with a plastic bear full of honey.

"We should let them steep for a couple minutes."

"Were they nice, your parents?"

James sighed. "Very nice. My mom would have loved you. She was into nature like you. My dad was stuffier, like me."

She giggled. "You're not *too* stuffy."

"My turn. What do *you* want to do? You're young, talented. You could do anything."

She tapped her lips with her index finger. "Anything?"

"Sure. Why not?"

"I wanna have a family of my own." She paused. "And a job that helps people."

"Have you thought about college?"

Her mouth turned down. "Don't you have to finish high school?"

He winced. "When did you drop out?"

"Halfway through my junior year. I had to leave. That's when I came here, and Harold found me." She looked down. "I wasn't that good at school anyway."

"Look at me, Brittany."

She looked up.

"What you want—a family and a job helping people—that's not a pie-in-the-sky dream. That's very possible. We just need to get you moving in the right direction."

"How do we do that?"

"You've been through a lot. You need help that I can't give you."

Her eyes watered. "Are you gonna make me leave?"

"No, I'm not. I just want you to talk to a nice lady who works at the counseling center on campus. She can help you."

She wiped her eyes with the side of her index finger. "I'm fine. I just get nightmares sometimes."

James had a lump in his throat. "I just ... I'm just so sorry for what you had to go through. I can't even begin to imagine how hard things have been for you."

Tears spilled down her cheeks. She shrugged, wiping her face with her sleeve. "It's over now."

"That's the problem, Brittany. Some things can make you really sad for your whole life if you don't get some help. If I made you an appointment, would you go?"

# Chapter 8

## Help Wanted

James spoke into his cell phone. "I know it's really short notice, but can you fit her in tonight?"

"Bring her in at five."

"Thank you so much, Diane. I really appreciate it." James hung up and shoved his phone in his pocket. "You're all set for tonight."

Brittany sat at the kitchen table, blank-faced. She had a black-and-blue shiner, her neck was bruised, and she had a scab on her lower lip.

"You okay?"

"Do I have to answer all her questions?"

"No. She'll mostly want you to talk about how you're feeling."

Brittany frowned.

"I know it sounds weird, but it'll help, and she's really nice."

She nodded. "Okay."

James packed his backpack with trail mix, water, and a few plastic bags.

She surveyed the one-room cabin. "Don't you get bored without TV?"

"The opium of the masses," James replied.

"Huh?"

"It's like a drug that makes people complacent and docile and stupid."

69

"Harold watches TV all day."

"Maybe that's why he's so stupid."

Her mouth turned down. "He thinks I'm the one who's stupid."

James set down his backpack and looked at Brittany. "I've been teaching for eighteen years. I've seen thousands of kids. I can tell you, without a doubt, that you're not stupid."

She smiled for a moment. "So, what do you like to do, if you don't like TV?"

"I like to read. Your imagination can be more interesting than the best movie. Haven't you ever heard people say, 'The book is better than the movie'?"

She shook her head.

"A lot of the most popular movies were books first. And the books are *always* better than the movie. Do you like to read?"

"I used to read the Goosebumps books when I was little."

James attached his knife and scabbard to his belt. "We'll stop by the library on the way to your appointment. I'm sure we'll find something that interests you." He slung his backpack over his fleece. "You ready?"

They stepped outside. The air was crisp, the sun playing peekaboo with the clouds. They walked past the outhouse.

"I have to go the bathroom real quick," she said.

James stood waiting. He gazed into the woods. He heard a rustling of leaves, and he saw movement in the distance. He strained his eyes, trying to determine if it was human or otherwise. Brittany appeared from the outhouse.

"I just need to wash my hands," she said as she walked back to the cabin.

"Could you grab my keys and lock the door on your way out?" James asked. "They're sitting on the kitchen table."

She turned around, her brow furrowed. "Is everything okay?"

He nodded. "We need to get in the habit of keeping the doors locked."

James hiked through the woods, following Brittany along a

well-established trail. She walked ahead, unburdened by a pack, testing out her new footwear.

She waited for James. "It's just ahead at the fork," she said.

They stopped on a small bluff, in front of a wooden post emblazoned with a yellow mark. To their right, a country road was visible from the bluff. A few farmhouses lined the road. The trail beyond the post snaked down the hill toward a gravel parking area large enough for three cars. Across from the parking area was a dilapidated self-storage center, with rows of garages, and boats and trailers parked along the chain-link fence. To their left was an unkempt trail.

"This way," she said, as she traipsed down the overgrown trail.

The forest canopy was thick, the ground leaf-covered. She slowed at a cluster of dead and dying oak trees. One was horizontal across what was left of the trail. She searched the base and the trunks of the trees, circling them like she was playing ring around the rosie.

"Found one," she said.

James followed her voice around the trunk of a standing oak. She stood smiling at the enormous cluster of vibrant yellow-orange mushrooms growing from the tree.

"Wow," he said.

"Chicken of the woods." She put her hands on her hips. "Pretty, huh?"

"Beautiful." James inspected the human-head-size mushroom cluster. "How do you know it's not poisonous?"

"I been eatin' from here for two years. Plus I know what the good ones look like and the bad ones that look like the good ones. My grammy used to say, 'They taste like crabmeat, not chicken.' But I never had no crab."

James removed the fixed blade from the scabbard attached to his belt. He sliced the mushroom from the tree trunk and placed it in a plastic bag. He put it in his backpack, and they hiked home.

James checked his watch as they returned to the cabin. "We should get moving if we're going by the library before your appointment."

\* \* \*

Brittany browsed the middle-school section of the public library, with a stack of books under her arm. She wore jeans that fit her, a sweatshirt, and a scarf that covered her neck. Her hair was brushed and tucked behind her ears. She was on her tippy toes trying to reach a book on the upper shelf. James walked over and grabbed the book for her.

"Thanks," she said, stepping back. Her shiner was under heavy concealer.

"Why don't I take those to the librarian?" he said. "She's holding our books."

Brittany handed James her stack of books.

He smiled. He was clean-shaven, his hair purposely disheveled. "It looks like you found a few things."

"I wanna do that reading workshop you were tellin' me about. A book a week makes you smart, right?"

James nodded. "The research shows that kids who read a book a week outperform their peers."

"That's what I wanna do."

\* \* \*

James sat in the waiting room of the counseling department. He graded research papers on the political system of ancient Greece. Every few minutes he glanced at the windowless door. The placard read Diane Fitzgerald, PhD. The door opened, and a thin woman with wispy white hair came out with Brittany. He gathered his papers and stood.

Diane smiled at Brittany. "Same time on Monday?"

Brittany nodded.

Diane waved at James over Brittany's shoulder. James waved, and Diane retreated into her office. Brittany turned around as James approached. She wiped her nose with a tissue.

"You okay?"

She nodded.

"Do you want me to run you back to the cabin? If we hurry, I can make it back in time for class."

"I don't wanna be left alone, if that's okay." She looked down for a moment.

"You can come with me to class every night if you want."

They walked to his classroom in silence.

"Aren't you gonna ask me what we talked about?" Brittany said.

"That's between you and Diane."

She smiled at James.

"I do have one question," James said.

Brittany looked up at him with red-rimmed eyes.

"Did you like her?"

"She's really nice."

During class, she sat in the back reading *Wonder* by R. J. Palacio. Leon, Jessica, and a handful of others debated whether or not taxation was moral. After class, James and Brittany went to Dot's Diner for dinner.

They entered the shiny metal-clad diner. A Help Wanted sign hung in the window. They sat at the end of the metal counter, reading plastic-covered menus. Jessica sauntered over with a crooked smile. Her blond hair was pulled back in a ponytail, exposing her round, attractive face.

"Hey, Mr. Fisher. What can I get you two?"

"Jessica, this is my friend Brittany," he said motioning to the petite eighteen-year-old sitting next to him.

Jessica smiled. "It's nice to meet you."

"You too," Brittany said, barely audible.

"You were in class tonight, right?"

Brittany nodded.

"You look really familiar," Jessica said, her eyes narrowed. "Did you go to Schuylkill High?"

"No," she said, her head bowed. "I'm not from around here."

"You just have one of those nice faces then." Jessica grinned. "So what can I get you?"

She shrugged, looking up at Jessica. "How much is a peanut butter and jelly sandwich?"

"What about your crab cakes?" James asked, his finger pointing to the dish on the menu. "Are they any good?"

"Depends on the day," Jessica said. "They're usually pretty good on Wednesday because the seafood shipments come on Tuesday."

"Brittany's never had crab," James said.

"You haven't?" Jessica asked.

"Should I try 'em?" Brittany asked James.

"That's up to you."

"If you don't like them," Jessica said, "I'll buy you a peanut butter and jelly sandwich."

Brittany smiled. "Okay, I'll try 'em."

"What about you, Mr. Fisher?" Jessica asked.

"I'll have breakfast again," James replied.

Jessica put her index finger to her temple. "Scrambled eggs, bacon, coffee, and ... wheat toast."

"You're good."

Jessica took their order to the kitchen and waited on her other customers.

"She's nice," Brittany said.

"And smart too," James replied.

"They have a Help Wanted sign. You think *I* could get a job here?"

"Do you have any identification cards at Harold's? Like a social security card or a birth certificate?"

"No."

"Do you know your social security number?"

She shook her head. "What do I need that for?"

"If you want a job or financial aid for college or a driver's license, you'll need your social security number."

She frowned; her head sagged. "I don't have that stuff."

"It's all right. We can go get it."

She raised her head and looked at James. "From where?"

* * *

They drove past trailer homes, modular homes, a house with a blue tarp for a roof, and farmhouses with dilapidated barns. The cloud-filtered sunlight made everything seem dull and gray. They saw yards filled with cars and car parts, aboveground pools with cold green water, bicycles and sports equipment, and large dogs attached to chains. Brittany pointed out the tidy yard on their right. James stopped the truck across the street from a rusted double-wide trailer.

"I can't do it," she said, her face pale.

"I'll be right there with you," James said.

She shook her head; her body trembled. "I can't."

"You can. I know you can. Nothing'll happen to you. I promise."

"It's just …" She looked at James, her eyes wet. "I'm scared."

"I know. We don't have to do anything you don't want to."

She pursed her lips. "What did you say about courage before?"

"The truly courageous aren't without fear. They're afraid, but they go anyway."

"I wanna be like that."

He looked at her, his eyes unblinking. "You are."

She opened the truck door and hopped out.

They trudged up the gravel driveway, past a beat-up Oldsmobile Cutlass from the mid-90s and a Plymouth Duster from the 70s. The Plymouth had a sparkling orange paint job and shiny chrome rims. The rear wheels were much larger than the front wheels. They climbed five wooden steps to the front door. James glanced at Brittany and knocked.

A short middle-aged man with a potbelly opened the door. His eyes locked on Brittany, scanning up and down. He had scraggly dark facial hair and a bright red T-shirt with a Dodge Ram logo. His sweatpants had stains on the knees. "Damn, girl. Never thought we'd see you again."

Brittany looked down.

His eyes darted to James, glaring. "Who are you?"

"I'm James, a friend of Brittany's."

"A friend, huh?" He chuckled. "I know how that goes." He turned his attention back to Brittany. "How old are you now girl?"

She didn't respond.

The man counted on his fingers. "You must be eighteen at least." He grinned. "Legal now."

"We just came to get her birth certificate and her social security card. Or just her birth certificate, if that's all you have."

The man frowned. "Her what now?"

"Brittany needs her birth certificate and her social security card."

"Hold up." He turned around and called out, "Hey, Terri, come out here."

"What?" a female called from the house.

"Get your ass out here," he said louder. "Brit's here."

The female replied, each word getting louder as she approached. "What the hell you talkin' 'bout her—" The petite woman's mouth hung open as she caught a glimpse of Brittany. The woman's hair was perm-curly and dull brown. She wore painted-on tight jeans and a fitted turtleneck. Her face was decorated like a shopping mall glamour shot.

She pursed her lips and said to Brittany, "You ain't got nuthin' to say?"

Brittany looked at her mom. "I just want my birth certificate."

"Ain't nuthin' changed," the man said, still staring at Brittany. "Always wantin' somethin'. Never givin' nuthin.'"

The woman looked at her man, staring, then narrowed her eyes at Brittany.

"Brittany needs her birth certificate and social security card," James said.

The woman scrunched her face. "Who the hell are you?" she said.

The short man smirked. "Her friend."

She glared at James's left hand. "Your wife know you're runnin' around with this little homewrecker?" she asked.

James said, "I'll ask you one more time to please produce her birth certificate and social security card."

The man snickered. "Or what?"

"We're just now gettin' over all them problems we had," the woman said. "Lil' hussy comin' on to my man. Ain't no man gonna say no."

Brittany stared at the ground. The man looked away.

James pulled his keys from his pocket and turned to Brittany. "Could you please go to the truck and wait for me?"

Brittany took the keys without a word, her head down.

Once she was safely out of earshot, James said, "Do you know what the statute of limitations is for statutory rape?"

"The statute of what?" the woman said.

"I ain't never raped nobody," the man said with his hands up. "That little whore came on to me."

"Doesn't matter," James said. "She was too young to consent. She can bring charges on you until she's fifty."

The man's eyes were wide.

"You some kinda lawyer?" the woman asked.

"Yes, I am," James said. "Brittany doesn't want to dwell on the past. She wants to move on with her life, but she can't do that without her birth certificate and social security card. And, if she can't move forward, the only place to go is backward. What's it going to be?"

The woman exhaled. "Lemme see what we got."

Brittany's mother and her boyfriend left James on the stoop as they hunted for the paperwork. He heard them arguing.

"I don't know *where* it is," she said.

"You better find that shit," the man replied.

"It ain't my fault you got shit all everywhere. Can't find nuthin' in this house."

James waited on the stoop for half an hour as the couple rummaged through their house. They finally appeared at the door with a thick rumpled folder. James opened it and found Brittany's medical records, birth certificate, social security card, and even a couple school report cards. He shut the folder.

"Brittany's a good person," James said. "I don't know how, given you two—"

"You best watch your mouth," the man said.

"We ain't did nuthin' to her," her mother said.

"Shut up, both of you," James said. "You will listen to me now, or we *will* press charges."

The man crossed his arms. The woman clenched her jaw.

James continued, "She'll go on with her life. She'll make something of herself. *That* I can guarantee. And you two will have to live with what you did to her."

The door slammed as James turned and walked toward his truck. He climbed into the cab and handed the folder to Brittany. "I believe this is yours," he said.

She sniffled and looked at James with red eyes. "You got it?"

"It's all there. We should separate out the really important stuff and get you a lock box."

She scooted across the long bench seat and hugged James sideways. "Thank you," she said as she let go.

"I'm really proud of you."

She frowned. "I didn't do nothin'."

"Facing them took a lot of courage. And I don't think we would have gotten this folder if they didn't see you face-to-face."

She blushed. "Can we go home now?"

He cranked the engine. "Let's never come back here again."

"Never again."

They drove to the end of the block and turned on the main road, leaving her old neighborhood in the rearview.

# Chapter 9

## Detect, Barricade, and Evade

Raindrops pelted the cabin. The sun couldn't penetrate the dark cloud cover.

"Do you have cabin fever yet?" James asked, sitting at the kitchen table in front of his laptop. He was dressed in khakis and a button-down shirt.

Brittany lifted her nose from her book—*Schooled* by Gordon Korman. She was curled up on the love seat in sweats. "Huh?" she asked.

"Do you have cabin fever yet?"

"I'm not sick."

James chuckled. "*Cabin fever* is when you're stuck inside, and you really want some fresh air and sunshine."

"Oh, ... I don't know. I like the rain. It's cozy here. Plus I'm totally hooked on this one." She held up the yellow dust-jacketed book.

"What do you think about taking the GED test?"

"I don't think I would pass."

"I'm on this website that has test prep software. Are you interested?" She sat up straight. "Yes."

"I'll download the software to my computer, until we can get you one of your own."

She raised her eyebrows. "One what?"

"A computer. You can use mine in the meantime."

"You would do that for me?" She placed her hand on her chest.

"Why wouldn't I?"

"It's a lot of money."

"Maybe, if you just sit around and play World of Warcraft. It's an investment if you use it to earn a high school diploma, go to college, and get that great job helping people."

James downloaded the software, shut off his laptop, and stowed it in the computer bag. He packed some trail mix in Ziploc bags.

"It seems like the ratio of M&M's to nuts is dwindling," James said.

Brittany looked up from her book and deadpanned, "Must be an M&M shortage."

"Shortage, huh? Probably not a shortage in your stomach."

She giggled.

"We should get moving. I need to be on time for office hours, and you need to be on time for Diane."

"Do you think Diane would care if I went in sweats?"

"I have girls that come to class in pajamas." He smirked. "You've seen it. Real live pajamas with little bunnies on them. I doubt your sweats will raise an eyebrow."

\* \* \*

Brittany sat in the back of class, her eyes glued to James's laptop, working on her GED prep. She was unaware when James dismissed the class. The students filed out.

"Jessica, could I talk to you for a minute?" James asked, standing behind his desk.

"What's up?" Jessica said, walking over, her book and notebook in hand.

"Brittany wanted to get a job at the diner. Do you think they would hire her?"

Jessica glanced at Brittany. She was still glued to the laptop. Jessica spoke in a whisper. "I think I've seen her before. Like before you introduced us."

James raised his eyebrows.

"When I first starting working there, two years ago," Jessica said. "I think she used to pick food out of the diner's Dumpster. The night manager, Rod, told her to stop, but she kept coming back. He called the police on her. They took her away, and I didn't see her again until you brought her in."

"She's had it rough—"

"It's not that. If it were up to me, I would definitely hire her. She seems real sweet. It's just that Rod's an asshole. He might remember her."

James frowned.

"On the other hand, he might not. He's kind of a dumb ass."

"We'll keep looking."

Jessica turned and looked at Brittany, then back to James. "You know, she looked pretty rough then. But I can see she's cute. I bet, with some girly clothes, a haircut, and some makeup, Rod wouldn't even recognize her."

"You want to give her a makeover?"

She smiled and stepped back from the desk, motioning to her jeans and fleece. "This is about as girly as I get, but my younger sister is all into that stuff. She helped me for *my* interview."

"You think she'd do it?"

"She loves that crap."

"This is really nice of you. I'll ask Brittany about it first. Also please don't say anything about the Dumpster-diving. I don't want her to be embarrassed."

"I understand, Mr. Fisher. I won't mention it." She whispered, "Can I ask you why you're doing this? I mean, I know you're not a creeper."

"The guy she was living with was … not so nice. I'm just trying to help her out, until she gets on her feet."

\* \* \*

James paced back and forth in the dim light of the cabin. He pulled his cell phone from the side pocket of his sweatpants and glanced at the time. *It's 11:34. She should have been home a half hour ago. What if Harold got a hold of her?* He moved next to the window. He pressed his face near the glass. He saw darkness and the outline of trees. He flipped the switch for the porch light up and down, up and down. The porch stayed dark. He heard leaves rustling in the wind. He continued pacing. *Relax. She's an adult ... technically. She's probably just having fun.*

He heard the faint sound of an engine and the crackle of gravel beneath car tires. He saw headlights moving toward him. The car turned into his driveway, the headlights sweeping across his front yard, illuminating a dark figure for a split second. His stomach leapt. He ran to the kitchen and fished the flashlight from the bottom drawer. James flicked on the flashlight as he sprinted outside. He moved the beam of light back and forth across the front yard. ... Nothing. He ran past the car to the backyard, shining his flashlight toward the woods and the trail. Nothing but trees, leaves, and brush. *Jesus, I really am losing it.*

"What's wrong?" Brittany called out.

James turned around and walked toward the Honda Civic in the driveway. Brittany was illuminated by the headlights. She stood in tall boots, a skirt just above her knees, and a blousy top. Her hair was styled and cut to shoulder-length.

"What's wrong?" Brittany asked again.

"I thought I saw something. It was nothing."

Jessica marched over and put her arm around Brittany. "What do you think, Mr. Fisher?"

James nodded with a smile. "Very pretty."

"Pretty?" Jessica replied with a scowl. "She's freakin' hot."

James chuckled.

A striking well-dressed young blonde exited the passenger door. Jessica introduced James to her sister.

Afterward James said, "Jessica, I'll see you in class. It was nice to meet you, Denise." He started back to the cabin.

The girls said their good-byes, making plans to hang out again. The little Honda reversed down the driveway. Brittany strutted into the cabin, her hands full of shopping bags, and her face smooth and even with the understated makeup. James moved past her and locked the door.

She looked at him with raised eyebrows. "Is everything okay?"

James stepped away from the door and forced a smile. "Everything's fine. How did it go?"

Her words spilled out in rapid-fire excitement. "Jessica and Denise are really nice. Denise taught me how to do my makeup so I look classy, and she taught me what to look for with clothes, and she took me to her hair stylist." She set the bags next to the dresser and spun around. "So what do you think?"

"You look fantastic," he replied.

"Guess what else?"

He shrugged.

"You know how I'm 'posed to interview on Monday?"

"Yeah."

"Well, when we were at the mall, Rod called Jessica, asking her to work on Sunday. I guess they had someone quit or somethin'. Anyway, he asked Jessica if she had my number because he wanted to move up the interview. Jessica said I was with her. We just came from the diner." She smiled.

"What happened?"

"I got the job." She jumped up and down, clapping her hands together. She threw her arms around him, hugging him tight. "Thank you, thank you, thank you," she said in quick succession.

He pulled away with a grin. "Congratulations. We should celebrate tomorrow. Why don't we go to dinner? Anywhere you want to go."

She bit her lower lip. "We could celebrate tonight." She sashayed into his personal space, her hips rocking back and forth. She gazed up at him, the heels on her boots putting her lips within striking distance. She pressed her lips to his, and reached down and rubbed her hand over his crotch.

James recoiled, his breath heavy. "I'm sorry," he said. "We can't."

She moved back into James's personal space, her teeth raking her lower lip. "Why not?"

James put his outstretched hands on her shoulders, keeping her at arm's-length. "I'm too old for you."

She scowled, her eyes watering. "You don't think I'm pretty?"

"Of course I do, but this is not good for you. Especially …"

She crossed her arms over her chest and stomped to the love seat. She sat down and unzipped her boots. She pulled the boots off her feet and dumped them on the wood floor. "What are you doin' with me then?" she said. "Why are you buyin' me stuff and helpin' me? What are *you* gettin' outta this? Are you some kinda freak?"

James sat in the recliner and swiveled toward her. "Would you believe that it makes me happy to help you?"

"Then why won't you let me pay you back?"

"Your dream job, that job helping people, do you want to do it because of the money, because of the payback?"

She was quiet for a moment. "Knowin' that I did somethin' good for someone is the payback."

"If you can do it, why can't I?"

"I'm just used to men …" Her eyes filled with tears.

"A lot of nice guys are out there. You'll find one who's right for you."

"How?" She sniffled.

"You have to work on *you* first. Understand?"

"I think so." She wiped her eyes with the side of her index finger, smudging her mascara. "I'm sorry. I'm just not used to this."

* * *

James stared at the tiny wires dangling behind the porch light. *Was it always cut? Did the porch light ever work?* He exhaled and entered the cabin. Sunlight pierced the windows. James made coffee and sat at the kitchen table in sweats, his laptop in front of him. Brittany sat across from him, eating cereal.

"What time are you working today? James asked.

"Four to twelve," she replied.

"We need to get you a driver's license."

"Jessica said she'd drop me off."

James shook his head. "It's out of her way. I'll be there to pick you up. Have you ever driven a car before?"

"No," she replied.

James rubbed the stubble on his chin. "I'm not sure you'll reach the pedals on my truck."

She set down her spoon. "You're really not gonna let me drive, are you?"

"Sure. Why not?"

"Because I'll break somethin' or *someone.*"

James smiled. "We'll go somewhere out of the way to practice."

She stood and washed her bowl in the sink. James scanned the headlines on his favorite alternative news site.

Tensions Rise over Refugee Crisis

ACLU Accuses Biloxi, Mississippi, of Running Debtors' Prison

The Disappearing Pension

Half of American Workers Make Less than $30,000 a Year

The Nightmare Created by Quantitative Easing

Brittany read over his shoulder. "Why do you read all this depressin' stuff?"

"I like to be aware, to know what's coming."

She sat back down across from him. "What's comin'?"

He shut his laptop. "Nobody knows for sure. We can only talk in probabilities."

"What does that mean?"

"When you're talking about future events that are affected by millions of different factors, you can only estimate the likelihood of occurrence. You never know for sure."

She frowned. "That still don't make sense."

"For example, what is the likelihood that I will die in a car accident on my way to class tonight?"

She glared at James. "I don't even wanna think about somethin' like that."

"Bear with me. It's a thought exercise. I'm a pretty good driver, if I do say so myself. There's very little traffic on the way to work, and the weather's good. All these factors lead me to believe that it's very unlikely that I'll die in a car accident tonight. But what if I was drunk, and there was a huge rainstorm, and the traffic was heavy?"

"It would be more likely."

"Exactly. So, when I keep up with the news, I'm calculating the likelihood of various events."

She furrowed her brow. "You didn't answer my question."

"What question?"

"What do you think's comin'?"

"There's a lot to be concerned about, but the big problem, as I see it, is that we have an economy that has to grow or it falls apart, but we live in a world with limited resources. So here we have an economy that requires more of everything every year, but we live in a world that is becoming more and more polluted with less and less high-quality resources to go around."

"So people end up with less."

"Pretty much."

She shrugged. "Seems to me that's already happenin'."

He nodded. "You're right."

"Is that why you came here?"

He sighed. "Partly maybe. Nothing was really holding me to northern Virginia. It was so expensive and crowded. Definitely not the place to be if you're trying to live a more self-reliant lifestyle."

"Is that what you're tryin' to do here? Live a self-reliant lifestyle?"

"I've been trying. I'm terrible at it. The best thing I've done is meet you."

She smiled.

He continued, "You know things in nature like the back of your hand. It's all unfamiliar territory for me."

"Don't worry. I'll keep you alive."

He laughed. "That's what I'm counting on."

"We should prob'ly get more wood and food for the winter. Gram used to have a root cellar filled to the brim with stuff from the growin' season. I'm surprised this cabin don't have one."

"It does."

James removed the oversize doormat and showed Brittany the hatch. He opened it, led her into the cellar, and turned on the single bulb. She gazed at the boxes and fifty-gallon buckets on pallets.

"Food?" she asked.

"The boxes have freeze-dried meals," he said. "The buckets have dried stuff, like rice and beans. It's all vacuum-sealed. Should last twenty to thirty years."

She nodded. "Are you gonna eat this stuff?"

"I hope not. It's for emergencies."

"Like a blizzard or a war or somethin'?"

"Anything that might stop the trucks from rolling. Our grocery stores operate on just-in-time inventory. If the trucks don't run, we only have three days until the food runs out."

James shut the hatch and covered it with the mat. "I'm going to check the mail," he said.

He walked to the end of the driveway and grabbed a small stack of letters from the mailbox. He flipped through the letters as he strolled back to the cabin. *Shit.* He stopped in his tracks, looking at a return address—North Schuylkill Township Police. He hurried to the front porch and sat on the wooden bench. He opened the envelope, quickly scanning the typed page.

10-22-2015

It was recently brought to the attention of the police department that the property you own or occupy is in violation of the North Schuylkill Township Ordinance, Chapter 10, Section 101, which covers the area of grass, weeds, and other vegetation. The ordinance addresses this area in part by indicating that grass, weeds, and other vegetation may not exceed six inches in height.

It is the responsibility of the owner or occupant of the property to trim, cut, or remove all grass, weeds, or other vegetation and maintain the property in that fashion. You will have seven days from the date listed above to complete the work, or the township may be obligated to take further action as outlined in the ordinance; this would include ongoing fines and possibly other appropriate action to bring the property into compliance, such as the township will cut the grass, and a lien will be placed against the property. This warning will be effective for three years from the date of this notice. No further warnings will be issued in regard to this ordinance, and future violations will result in a citation being filed.

I look forward to you complying with this request to avoid any future hardship. Should you have any questions, feel free to contact me at the above number.

Sincerely,
Chief Wade Strickland

James exhaled, shaking his head as he pulled his cell phone from his pocket. He glanced at the date: *10-26, three fucking days*. He heard a scream from the outhouse. James dropped the mail and ran around the cabin. Brittany came from the outhouse, a hand over her mouth.

"What's wrong?" he said as he approached.

She had tears in her eyes. She pointed to the outhouse. "He was in there."

James stepped to the wooden structure and opened the door like it was booby-trapped. A pair of ratty light-blue cotton panties were displayed on top of the right-hand toilet seat. *Whore* was scrawled across the cotton in black marker. The letters were jagged—all capitals, as if the epithet was screamed. James grabbed a mitt of toilet paper and carefully picked up the underwear. Crusty white stains were inside and out. He winced, shaking his head. He dropped the underwear, threw the toilet paper in the hole, and slammed the door as he exited the outhouse.

Brittany stood, frowning, with her arms over her chest. "He was in there," she said.

"I know," he replied, pulling out his cell phone.

James dialed 9-1-1.

"This is 9-1-1. What is your emergency?" a female said.

"Harold Strickland trespassed on my property, went into my outhouse, and left a semen-stained pair of underwear. He also wrote a threat on the underwear."

"Is anyone in immediate danger?"

"I don't think so."

"An officer will be dispatched."

"One more thing. Harold Strickland is related to an officer and the police chief here in North Schuylkill Township. So please do not dispatch a Strickland here. It's an obvious conflict of interest."

"Yes, sir."

James and Brittany waited on the front porch of the cabin.

"This is so fucked," James said as Officer Dale Strickland pulled his cruiser into the driveway. He turned to Brittany. "You should wait inside."

James met Officer Strickland on the driveway.

"Mr. Fisher, what can I do for you?"

"Your uncle Harold left semen-stained women's underwear in my outhouse."

He nodded with a smirk. "No septic here?"

"No."

He grinned for a split second. "Let's take a look at them panties."

James clenched his jaw and led the officer to the outhouse. The officer entered alone. After a minute he exited and asked James for a plastic bag. James retrieved a bag from the kitchen, and the officer placed the underwear in the bag.

"Did you touch 'em?" Officer Strickland asked.

"I picked them up with toilet paper," James replied.

The officer nodded. "Did anyone see Harold on the property?"

"All you have to do is test the DNA that's all over it."

Officer Strickland glared, the sun reflecting off his shades. "And how do you know he put 'em there? Nobody saw him. There's no law against bustin' a load in some panties."

James crossed his arms. "This is bullshit."

The officer moved closer, making James take a step back. "I don't think you understand how close to the edge you really are."

James shook his head, his mouth shut tight.

"Since I'm here makin' a house call," the officer said, "we should talk about those code violations you got."

"If weeds over six inches are illegal," James said, "then you should stop by every house in township."

Officer Strickland motioned toward the four-foot-tall plants against the cabin. "You don't got a weed whacker?"

"That's goosefoot. It's not a weed. I eat the seeds and the leaves."

Officer Strickland scowled. "I don't give a shit what it is. If it's not cut next time I come around, I *will* write you a citation." He lifted his chin toward the outhouse and turned back to James. "And that outhouse … that's against code. You're gonna have to put in a septic system."

James exhaled. "A bunch of houses around here have outhouses."

"It's legal for part time residents."

"When I bought the place, nobody said anything about having to put in a septic."

"Just 'cause you're ignorant of the law don't mean you don't have to follow it."

"How much time do I have to do this?"

"You'll get a letter." He brushed past James toward the driveway.

James entered the cabin. Brittany sat on the love seat with her knees pulled to her chest. She was blank-faced. He swiveled the recliner toward her and sat down.

"I'm sorry," he said.

She was unresponsive.

"I won't let anyone hurt you. I promise."

* * *

Brittany opened the door and climbed into the Ford pickup. She wore a jacket over her white polo shirt and black pants. James flipped on his headlights as he pulled out of the diner parking lot. He asked her about her first day of work.

Her face was expressionless. "I made eighty-eight dollars just from tips. I've never actually touched that much money."

"That's great," James said, looking at her for a moment, then putting his focus back on the road. "You don't seem happy about it."

"I just keep thinkin' about what happened today."

James nodded, his eyes on the dark, empty road in front of him. "I know. Me too. And I think we need a security plan. I did tons of research today. I have a few ideas. The first thing I thought about was a gun."

She looked at James. "Do you know how to shoot?"

"Do you?"

"No."

"Me neither. But I'm sure I could take classes at a range or something, but I don't think a gun's the answer." He glanced at her.

Her mouth was turned down. "Why not?"

"First of all, in this township over the past decade, once you adjust for the small population, you're five times as likely to be killed by cops here than the rest of the country. And guess what the justification for killing was in over 70 percent of the deaths?"

"They said the person had a gun."

He glanced at Brittany. "Bingo. So, if I bought a gun and used it in home defense against Harold, what do you think would happen?"

"Somethin' bad."

"Right. I'd be arrested or shot."

She frowned. "You're tellin' me that we just do nothin', hope for the best?"

"Not at all. I do have my Buck knife if he breaks in, but I'd rather avoid any confrontation altogether. To do that, I'm proposing we 'detect, barricade, and evade.' First, we have to know someone's coming. Then we have to stop anyone from getting in or at least slow them down. And, in the unlikely event they do get in, we need an escape plan already in place that involves more than dashing out the back door."

# Chapter 10

## Payback

James widened the narrow trench across his driveway just enough to fit the magnetic sensor that looked like a pipe bomb. He dropped the coated wire in the trench and ran it across the driveway, through some brambles, and behind a tree. A black plastic box the size of a lunch pail was attached to the tree trunk. Brush and brambles camouflaged it. Thorns grabbed his sweatshirt as he connected the wire to the box. He kicked the earth back into the narrow trench, covering the wire. He grabbed the rake leaning against his truck and moved the gravel over the sensor.

He threw the rake in the truck bed and hiked up the driveway toward the cabin. Three trucks were parked haphazardly in front. A half-dozen men worked around the cabin. A fit young man cut window film. Another predrilled holes in the wood around the windows. The front door was off its hinges, leaning against the cabin. A pudgy man secured metal brackets into the door frame.

James moved to the backyard where a skid steer dumped small trees, brush, and the remnants of the outhouse into a stake-body truck. Browning Septic in faded vinyl lettering had been stuck to the doors of the truck. A tracked excavator sat idle off to the side. An older man stood against the cabin, supervising. His hair was snow white, his face grizzled. A paunch hung over his belt. James walked to him.

"You think we're okay on space for the drain field?" James asked.

Sam Browning nodded. "I think we'll be okay. Lucky your perc's good."

"What about the other thing? Think your guys can do it?"

He chuckled. "I've had some interesting jobs, but this one …" He shook his head. "This one takes the cake. We can definitely do it. That two-foot culvert pipe ain't cheap though. Three hundred bucks per twenty-foot section. You'll need four. We're already here with the digger makin' a mess, so you'll save on setup and labor. How's three grand sound?"

"Will it push you guys back, as far as the schedule?"

"It won't make no difference. The excavatin' guys will be the first done anyway. It's the plumbers that'll be busy."

"All right, let's do it."

"I'll order the pipe today."

"I appreciate you fitting me in so close to Thanksgiving."

"I'm just sorry you was forced into all this. These township people don't know their ass from a hole in the ground. I see it all the time. They use the codes to put pressure on people they don't like."

"What about the people they do like?"

Sam chuckled. "I'll tell you one thing. If your last name's Strickland, you can do whatever the hell you want. Harold up the road from you got a failin' cesspool that's against code." He spat on the ground. "Last year the son of a bitch was tryin' to get me to drain it. Hell, I even dug up the manhole cover and marked it for him for free. I showed him that the sewage was about three inches from the inlet pipe. Stank to high heaven. I told him he needed to replace it with a septic. He was fired up when I told him what the cost would be. Accused me of tryin' to rip him off. Got some shady contractor to pump it for him. No way in hell I'd pump his shit. As bad as his cesspool is, it's bound to cause a sinkhole."

"What's the difference between a cesspool and a septic system?"

"Septic systems are watertight. Cesspools are pits with perforated walls. Nasty things. More likely to fail."

"What happens when they fail?"

"The tank gets clogged and fills up quick. Then the plumbin' backs up. Tank overflows."

"I would hate to be downslope of that."

Sam's face was taut, his jaw set tight. "You don't *ever* wanna be downslope of Strickland shit."

James thanked Sam for the advice and walked to the front porch, avoiding the guys working on the windows and door frame. Two black boxes sat on one of the benches. He opened them and selected matching numbers on the dials. Jessica's Honda Civic crept up the driveway. She stopped short of the chaos. James hiked down to meet them. Brittany stepped out of the passenger seat in black pants and a jacket over her polo.

"Hey, Mr. Fisher," Jessica said from the driver's seat of the compact car. "How's the project coming?"

"You were right about Sam. He really knows his stuff," James said.

"I knew he'd take care of you. Mr. Browning's my favorite customer."

James pulled a twenty-dollar bill from the front pocket of his canvas pants. "Please take this. You're a lifesaver. I couldn't go anywhere today."

She shook her head. "It's really not necessary."

James placed the bill in her hand. "For gas. It's out of your way."

Jessica backed out of the driveway; Brittany waved.

"How was the lunch crowd?" James asked.

She grinned. "I made ninety bucks in like four hours."

"I can see why those old biddies hang on to that lunch shift. Who will replace the lady who died?"

"It won't be me or Jessica. This was just a one-time thing because of the funeral." She looked around at the chaos of contractors. "I was hopin' to take a nap, but I doubt that's gonna happen."

"Yeah, sorry. The security guys will be done today. I wanted to get that done as soon as possible. After today, it'll just be the septic and plumbing guys. But they'll be here for two weeks. Come on. I'll give you a tour."

He led Brittany to the end of the driveway.

"Sam's guys ran a trencher across the driveway here." James pointed to the gravel. "All the way to that tree, where those raspberries are. Hidden in there is a box with batteries that power the magnetic sensor under the driveway. So if a car pulls into the driveway in the middle of the night, we'll know it."

"Detection," Brittany mumbled to herself.

He led Brittany near the front porch, keeping their distance from the workers. A stocky man held up black steel burglar bars over the window as another man installed the lag bolts.

"The windows are being coated with a special thick plastic that, even if you break the glass, it'll still hold together. I saw videos on the stuff. It takes a long time to break through it. Then we have the bars on the windows too. That guy there"—James pointed to the pudgy man measuring and then attaching metal brackets to the door frame—"he's beefing up the door frame. Most home invasions come right through the front door. It's actually really easy to kick in a door, but it isn't the door that breaks. It's the hinges or the frame. Those metal brackets solve that problem."

"Barricade." She nodded, her blue eyes wide.

"I also have a couple motion sensors to install. I'm trying to figure out a way to mount them so they're hard to see, but they'll detect anyone near the front or back door. My only concern is the sensor tripping every time an animal walks by in the middle of the night. I'm thinking that, if I can set it up so it only trips for tall things, it might work okay."

"I didn't realize you were gonna do so much. All this seems really expensive. I can give you my money to help out." She bit her lower lip. "I mean, this is my fault you're doin' all this. If you never helped me—"

"This is Harold's fault, not yours. Besides this security stuff's not that expensive. The septic and the plumbing put a dent in my savings.

That has nothing to do with you either. I should have bought a place with indoor plumbing anyway. It was stupid of me to think I could live up here in the woods like a mountainman."

* * *

James paced. Brittany sat at the kitchen table, working on his laptop. Flurries fell on the frozen ground. Wood burned in the fireplace insert. A tiny artificial Christmas tree sat on top of the storage cubbies. A small bathroom and shower now occupied the corner. She looked up from the laptop. James checked the time on his phone.

"You look stressed," she said.

"I am." He scowled. "I'm tired of waiting. I want to get this over with."

"I just try to concentrate on something else."

He nodded and shoved his phone in the front pocket of his jeans.

She said, "Maybe they're not coming because of the snow."

"It's flurries. They just want me to sweat."

A police SUV turned onto the driveway. The black box in the kitchen that looked like an answering machine chimed and said, "Alert zone one. Alert zone one."

James walked over to the machine and turned it off. He saw Officer Dale Strickland and Chief Wade Strickland marching toward the porch in puffy police jackets. James opened the door before they had a chance to knock. He hated how the police banged on the door when a polite knock would suffice. James greeted them and invited them in. They stepped inside without wiping their boots on the Welcome mat. The chief had an expansive glistening forehead, accentuated by his receding hairline. Above his lip was the obligatory copstache. His son was a better-looking version of the old man with an oversize beaklike nose. Both men stole looks at Brittany. She had tunnel vision, avoiding the stress by submerging herself in GED prep.

"You always have those bars?" Officer Strickland asked.

"I just put them in," James replied.

"Is there a fire code against burglar bars?" the officer asked his father.

The chief nodded. "Yep, you have to be able to get out in the event of a fire."

"That's why there's a quick release on them," James said. "They're up to code. I can assure you of that."

"Let's see that latrine then," the chief said.

James showed the officers the small bathroom that featured a toilet, a sink, and a shower stall.

"It's tight in there," the chief said.

"We don't have a lot of space," James said.

"That's not such a bad thing," the chief replied, his eyes darting to Brittany and back to James.

"Do you want to see the drain field?"

"Not necessary. I trust that Sam did what he was supposed to do."

"I have the permit that says he did, if you want a copy."

The chief brushed his mustache with his thumb and index finger. "Won't be necessary."

"Is that it?" James asked.

"I'll be checking on you come spring," Officer Strickland said. "Make sure you're keepin' those weeds under control."

James bit the inside of his cheek. "I've already complied. This has cost me a lot of money. I would like you guys to leave me alone now."

The chief stepped closer to James. Wade spoke casual, relaxed, at a low volume. "I decide if we're gonna leave you alone. You got me?"

James was silent.

The officers marched to the front door. Officer Dale Strickland flashed a crooked grin on his way out.

The chief stopped at the threshold, the door open, a cold draft blowing in. He said, "Be good now."

\* \* \*

James sat at his desk, reading on his laptop, the classroom empty.

Canadian Budget Deficit Growing

Illinois Budget: It Is Really, Really Bad

Oil Firms Burdened by Debt

China Increases Gold Reserves

Rail Cargo Declines

China's Slowdown Hurts California Exports

Brittany walked through the door, her eyes red and puffy. James diverted his attention from the computer.

"Are you okay?"

She nodded as she sat in the student desk across from him. "We talked about you today."

James raised his eyebrows. "You don't have to tell me. What you talk about with Diane is between you and her."

"I know, but she said I should." She tucked her hair behind her ears.

"Should what?"

"Talk to you about things."

"Okay." He shut his laptop.

"She asked me today if you and I have a physical relationship." She pursed her plump lips.

"What did you tell her?" He leaned forward, his elbows on the desk.

"I told her what you told me about it not bein' a good idea. She said you were right. That it's not a good idea. She also said that we can't live together forever. You might wanna have a girlfriend or get married, and, if I'm here, it might be … a problem. And I want those things too."

"And how do you feel about that?"

"That's what she says. How do you feel about this? How do you feel about that?"

"How *do* you feel about it?"

She took a deep breath. "I don't like it, but I know it's true. I feel like I'm holdin' you back, but I don't wanna feel like I'm holdin' you back. Am I? Do you wanna have a girlfriend and get married again?"

He was blank-faced. "Someday, maybe, but I'm not ready for that now. It's only been a year since … the accident." He shook his head. "Sometimes I think about how Lori and I were, the first few years of marriage. I guess everyone says the beginning is good, but it was *really* good. Then it wasn't. I would give anything for a second chance to make it right."

She sat, her face cute and buttonlike, her blue eyes popping. She said, "My life would be … I don't even wanna think about where I would be without you. Maybe you don't get second chances. Maybe you can only give them."

* * *

"How long is winter break?" she asked.

James stood at the sink, washing the dishes that Brittany bused.

"It's a month," James said, "but I'm teaching a two-week intensive history class, so I'll only get the next two weeks off. I have to be back at work on the fourth."

"The diner only gives us Christmas and New Year's."

"We'll have to do something extra nice for Christmas and your birthday. I think we should devote half the day to Christmas and the other half to your birthday. Is there something special that you want to do?"

She shrugged. "I don't know. It's up to you."

He smirked. "It's not up to me. It's *your* birthday. Think about it."

"Okay." She began drying and putting away the stack of clean dishes on the counter.

"What about New Year's? Do you want to go out to dinner or make something nice here?"

She winced. "I'm goin' out with Jessica and Denise on New Year's."

"Of course," James said with a forced smile. "I forget that you're almost nineteen."

"They have a place rented in Philly for the night. There's some huge party down by the water at this ice skatin' rink. They already bought the tickets. I was going to mention it earlier, but I …"

"It's okay. I'm glad that you're making friends." James dried his hands on a towel. "You *should* be spending time with kids your age. It's pretty expensive on New Year's. Do you need any money?"

She shook her head. "I already paid them for the ticket, and they're not chargin' me for the room, but I have to sleep on the cot—which I really don't mind anyway. I'd sleep on a cot every night if it saved me a hundred bucks."

"I'm going to put on my sweats and brush my teeth." He pulled his shirttail out of his khakis.

"Me too," she replied.

"Do you want the bathroom first?"

"No, you go ahead."

James brushed his teeth. He spat and rinsed. He put both hands on the sink and stared in the mirror. He gazed at his face from different angles, his nose always too large and his chin always too small. With his head tilted down, he had the makings of a double chin. He exhaled. *Now I'm skinny fat.*

He unbuttoned his shirt and replaced it with a sweatshirt. He heard "Alert zone two. Alert zone two." *I need to fix that thing.* He sat on the toilet seat cover and removed his dress shoes. Brittany screamed. James burst from the bathroom in stocking feet. She stood in sweatpants, with her arms wrapped around her bare chest.

"He was in the front window," she said, her eyes wide.

James unlocked the dead bolt and sprinted outside. In the moonlight, he saw a dark form galloping toward the trail. He sprinted after it, his socks immediately soaked from the half inch of snow on the ground. Despite his awkward gait, he gained ground. James tackled the person dressed in black coveralls and a knit hat, just before the trail. There was an audible *yelp* on impact. James turned over the person. Harold's eyes were wide. He tried to cover his face with his arms. James pummeled the diminutive man, some punches blocked by his forearms but many connected with his face. His nose and lips ran red.

"James," Brittany said, grabbing his shoulder.

James stopped, condensation spilling from his mouth. He pushed off Harold as he stood, saying, "Get up."

Harold staggered to his feet. James grabbed him by the collar of his coveralls and pulled him close. Harold wheezed, and blood dripped from his mouth and nose.

James said, "If I ever see you on my property again, I will *fucking* kill you. Do you understand me?"

Harold nodded.

"Speak!"

"Yeah, I got it."

James pointed the man toward the trail, shoved him, and said, "Get the fuck out of here." Harold stumbled in the right direction.

# Chapter 11

## Reckoning

James sat at the kitchen table, reading on his laptop. Brittany stirred in the top bunk.

"Good morning, sleepyhead," James said over his computer screen.

She climbed down from the top bunk in her flannel pajamas. A fire burned in the fireplace insert. She rubbed her eyes, stretched her arms over her head, and sat down across from James.

"You want some breakfast?" James asked. "You must be starving. You slept through dinner last night."

"I had trouble sleepin' at the hotel. When we got back, I was exhausted."

"You have fun?" James asked.

She blushed.

"That good, huh?" James stood from the table. "How about eggs?"

"Scrambled?"

"Coming right up." James cracked eggs into a bowl. "So how was it?" he said over his shoulder.

She grinned. "It was so much fun. I think I met more people in one night than in my whole life. Jessica and Denise were like the center of everyone."

James turned around. He held the bowl, scrambling the eggs with a fork. "What did you guys do?"

"We went ice skatin', dancin'. We hung out."

James removed a frying pan from the cabinet and set it on the stove top. "With who?"

"Huh?"

James added oil to the pan, turned on the stovetop, and glanced over his shoulder. "Who did you hang out with?"

Brittany's face turned scarlet. "We met these guys from Temple."

James grinned as he poured the eggs into the pan. "College guys, huh?"

Brittany smirked. "We were just hangin' out."

James sat down across from Brittany, his grin receding. "I think it's good that you're spending time with people your age. It's important. Just be careful."

Brittany bit the inside of her cheek. "I know."

"Did you like any of these guys?"

She shrugged, but her face betrayed her.

"Are you going to see him again?" James asked.

"Prob'ly not." She smiled. "He was really nice though ... and *cute*."

James smiled. "I'm glad."

\* \* \*

Brittany piled produce onto the small counter next to the self-checkout area. James typed SKU numbers into the screen and placed a bundle of bananas on the scale. The machine told James to place the bananas in his bag.

"That it?" James asked Brittany.

"Yep."

James pressed the Pay for My Order button. He slipped a one-hundred-dollar bill into the machine. A ten and a couple ones appeared at the bottom, along with a few coins.

Bundled in heavy jackets and knit hats, James pushed the cart into the salt-stained parking lot while Brittany walked alongside. The gray sky made everything look dingy. Dirty snow was piled up in the back of the lot.

"It's freezing," James said.

"I'm not cold."

James looked at her long puffy Patagonia coat.

"The best birthday present I ever got," she said.

James grinned, stopping the cart next to his truck. "You mind riding with the groceries?"

Brittany handed bags to James, and he placed them on the middle of the seat and in the passenger wheel well. Brittany climbed into the truck, carefully situating her feet among the groceries. James walked around the back of the truck. A flash of red caught his eye—a red Ford Ranger a couple rows over. A shadowy figure sat in the driver's seat. The engine fired up, and the high beams flicked on and off, on and off. The truck peeled out of the lot.

James climbed into his truck with a scowl. He cranked the engine and gripped the steering wheel strong enough for his knuckles to go white.

"What's wrong?" she asked.

James shook his head as he backed out of the space. "Nothing."

"I know you, James. There's something you're not tellin' me. If you keep things from me, I end up thinkin' scarier things in my mind."

James pulled from the parking lot. He exhaled and glanced at Brittany. "I think I saw Harold."

Her eyes were wide. "When? Where?"

"Right before we pulled out, after we loaded the groceries. He was a few rows over." James looked at Brittany. "Are you okay?" He focused back on the road.

"I'm worried," she said. "Diane said I should be honest about my feelin's, and I'm really worried."

James shook his head. "I won't let him hurt you. He's just a sick little old man."

"I'm worried about you. What if he told the chief what you did to him?"

"He won't. Besides, it's been weeks. I would have heard by now if he had pressed charges."

She crossed her arms with a frown.

James glanced at Brittany. "Do you really think he wants to tell his brother that he was beat up by a skinny city boy? He'll take that to the grave."

* * *

"What would you like to drink?" the tall waitress asked.

"Iced tea, please," Brittany replied.

"And for you, sir?"

"I'll have water," James said, "but I may want wine with dinner."

James and Brittany sat at a corner table of a dimly lit restaurant. James wore a dark suit; Brittany, a black dress. If it wasn't a day for lovers, and if they didn't look so different, they might have passed for father and daughter.

"How does it feel to be a high school graduate?" James asked.

Brittany looked up from the heart-shaped menu. "It's only a GED."

"Don't do that. Don't minimize your accomplishments. You've come a long way in a short time. It's only been four months since you started on the GED prep."

She nodded with a crooked grin. "You sound like Diane."

The waitress returned with water and iced tea. James ordered fish with white wine—Brittany, the New York strip. After the waitress departed, James raised his water glass.

"I would like to propose a toast *to you*," he said. "Congratulations on your high school diploma and your driver's license. I'm very proud of you."

Brittany sat in her seat blushing and smiling.

James said, "This is where you pick up your drink, and we clink glasses together."

*Clink.*

After dinner, James helped Brittany with her coat. He left cash on the table, and they strolled through the restaurant toward the front door. An elderly couple glared at them.

"It's sick," the old man said under his breath.

James stopped. "Excuse me?"

The man glowered at James. "Don't you think you're a little old for her? I got a granddaughter about her age."

The heavyset white-haired woman next to him sat with her arms crossed, a plate of untouched food in front of her. "You've ruined my Valentine's Day dinner," she said.

Brittany stared at the floor.

"Get your minds out of the gutter. I'm her guardian. And I would appreciate it if you wouldn't speak of her that way. You should be ashamed of yourselves."

As James and Brittany departed the restaurant, he said to her, "You can't argue with ignorance. But I still try."

"I know." She forced a smile.

In the parking lot, a bitter wind cut through their clothes. Brittany hurried for the truck. James stopped and glanced at the highway, a flash of red catching his eye. He was weary from feeling like they were being watched. *Was it a pickup? Was it a car?*

"You comin'?" Brittany said, shivering by the passenger door.

James retrieved his keys from the front pocket of his slacks.

"Do you want to drive?" he asked.

"Not in heels."

James cranked the engine and turned up the heat. They drove through town. The town square had a fountain that was dry in the winter. Raised beds made with brick and concrete contained neatly trimmed hollies and junipers. Near the square, on the strip, a handful of three- and four-story brick and stone buildings housed banks, accountants, and relationship salespeople, otherwise known as financial advisors. Traffic was sparse as James and Brittany passed the historic district. When they moved beyond the buildings built with the grift of finance, the architecture became less extravagant, mostly two-story converted row homes with brick and vinyl siding. Many had old rusty metal roofs that needed replacement. A carousel of failed businesses rotated through the row homes. The mainstays were the dry cleaners, two bars, and a sandwich shop.

Outside of town, the road was dark and deserted. James glanced at Brittany. She gazed out the window. *Almost home. I'm ready for sweats. And that cake.* He motored around a bend, and his stomach leapt. Brittany turned to him, her eyes wide.

"It's okay," he said.

James watched in his rearview mirror as he passed the cross street, where the police car was parked. The cruiser pulled out. He could hear the V-8 gaining ground behind him. The car tailed him—close. James scowled. *Here we go.* He turned onto the gravel road that led to his cabin. The cruiser followed. Brittany turned around, gripping the headrest. James stopped the truck as soon as the officer activated his flashing blue and red lights.

James put the emergency brake on, cut his headlights, and took a deep breath. The truck idled, warm air pumping from the vents. James grabbed his documentation from the glove box and his license from his wallet.

The officer was backlit by the spotlight on the cruiser. He shone a flashlight the size of a baton. He marched to the driver's side door in a puffy jacket and black gloves.

James rolled down his window halfway. He was relieved to read M. Emory on the officer's nametag. Officer Emory was clean-shaven, with dark hair and light eyes.

"Turn off the truck," he said, shining his flashlight into the cab.

"It's cold," James replied.

"Turn off the truck."

James cut the engine.

The officer's pants were pulled up high to prevent his gut from lapping over his belt.

Officer Emory said, "License, registration, and proof of insurance."

James handed him his documents. The officer took the papers and shone his flashlight in Brittany's face. "This your daughter?"

"She's a friend," James replied.

The officer leaned forward, almost sticking his chubby face in the truck. "How old are you, miss?"

Brittany was pressed up against the driver's side door, her arms folded over her chest. "I'm nineteen," she said, barely audible.

"You'll have to speak up," the officer said.

"Nineteen." Her head was down.

The officer scowled at James. "Do you know why I pulled you over?"

"Because Chief Strickland told you to."

The officer looked away, breaking character. After a moment, his glare returned. "You were driving erratically. Have you been drinking?"

"I had one glass of wine at dinner."

Officer Emory nodded and returned to his car with James's papers.

James turned to Brittany. "You okay?"

"No," she replied, her face taut, "This is really bad."

"It'll be fine. I haven't done anything. He's just messing with me."

Ten minutes later the chubby officer returned to the truck.

"I'm gonna have to ask you to step out of the vehicle," he said to James.

James frowned and stepped from the truck to the gravel road.

"Turn around, spread your legs, and put your hands on the truck," the officer said.

James spread his legs and leaned forward, his hands touching the cold metal.

"Do you have any weapons or needles or anything that might cut or poke me?" the officer said.

"No."

He frisked James and then told him to turn around. He led him to the middle of the road. "Stand and hold your arms out to your side," the officer said. "Now touch your nose with each hand."

James stood with his arms out and touched his nose without losing his balance. He did it over and over again, gaining speed. "That good enough?" James said.

"Stand on one leg and count to ten."

James complied.

"Now the other leg."

James complied.

"Now stand straight, close your eyes, and tilt you head back for thirty seconds."

James closed his eyes and tilted his head back. After what felt like a minute James said, "Are you keeping time?"

"No, you are," the officer said.

James opened his eyes and tilted his head forward. "It's been like a minute."

"Recite the alphabet backward."

"*Z, Y, X, V, W* ... shit. I'd have to write it forward first. This is ridiculous. I'm clearly not drunk."

The officer attached a tube to a small plastic device. He pointed the straw at James's face. "This is a breathalyzer. Take a deep breath and blow into this straw until I tell you to stop. Do not stop blowing until I tell you to, and do not touch the machine. Keep your hands by your side."

James took a deep breath and blew into the straw.

"Stop," the officer said after ten seconds, extracting the device from James's mouth. He looked at the readout and placed the machine in his pocket. "Turn around and place your hands behind your back. You're under arrest for driving under the influence. You have the right to remain silent and to refuse to answer questions. Do you understand?"

"Yes," James replied.

The officer placed handcuffs on James's wrists, tightening the metal enough to feel immediate discomfort. Brittany watched from the back window of the truck.

The officer said, "Anything you do or say may be used against you in a court of law. Do you understand?"

"Yes."

"You have the right to consult an attorney before speaking to the police and to have an attorney present during questioning now or in the future. Do you understand?"

"Yes."

"If you cannot afford an attorney, one will be appointed for you before any questioning if you wish. Do you understand?"

"Yes."

"If you decide to answer questions now without an attorney present, you will still have the right to stop answering at any time until you talk to an attorney. Do you understand?"

"Yes."

The officer led James to the cruiser. He put his gloved hand on James's head as he guided him into the seat.

"I'm assuming she can take my truck home," James said.

"Does she have a license?" the officer said.

"Yes."

"If she does, then she can. If she doesn't, we'll see that she gets home."

The officer slammed the door. James scooted to the middle of the backseat, his hands bound behind his back. He watched as Officer Emory approached the passenger door of his truck. The officer tapped on the glass with his flashlight. He spoke with Brittany. She handed him her license. He shone his flashlight on it and handed it back to her. Brittany stepped out of the vehicle and stood, shivering on the frozen ground, while the officer searched the truck.

After the search, Brittany hopped back into the truck, scooted across the bench seat, and started the vehicle. The officer marched back to the cruiser and climbed inside with a groan. He turned the car around on the tiny gravel road with a six-point turn. Brittany moved slowly down the road toward the cabin, the red taillights fading.

James sat in the backseat, silent, as the officer drove off, eventually pulling into the police station. Four cruisers sat in the parking lot. He parked and walked James into the one-story brick building. The officer bypassed the public waiting area and scanned into the employee entrance. Inside, it looked like a typical office, with desks, and printers, and computers. Three officers milled about—one in slacks and a rumpled shirt and tie; the others in uniform. James was searched again, and his wallet, watch, cell phone, and belt were taken. Officer Emory undid his handcuffs and reattached them with James's hands in front. Emory forced James's fingers onto an electronic screen to capture his fingerprints. Emory swabbed his cheek for DNA. James was photographed, guided into a windowless room, and forced to sit at a metal desk. Video cameras were hung in the upper corners of the room. Officer Emory departed, shutting the door behind him.

A plainclothes officer entered the room, shuffling papers in a manila folder. He was medium height and stocky with pale skin and blond curls cut tight to his head. He sat down across from James, the folder in front of him.

"I'm Detective Warren." He opened the folder, shaking his head. "Point-zero-eight-two. That's some seriously bad luck, James. *And* we have a confession of drinking alcohol prior to driving."

"There's no way I was over the legal limit on one glass of wine."

The detective winced. "I've seen it happen. I bet it was a big glass. Here's the thing, James. I really don't want this to get out of control. Judge Schaeffer is a real hard ass when it comes to DUI cases. He had a nephew killed by a drunk driver. He gives the maximum penalty over and over again. Do you know what the maximum penalty is for a DUI?"

James was silent.

"Six months in prison, James." He nodded with a frown. "I really don't want to see that happen. It's not like you had an accident or hurt anyone. I mean, you were almost home for Christ sakes."

James nodded.

"Here's the thing, James. As a police officer, I like to put away bad guys. You're not a bad guy, but you broke the law, and the laws are pretty stiff. I think just about everyone in this country has driven drunk at one point in their life. If you make this process easy for us, we can make it easy for you."

James nodded.

The detective slid a blank piece of paper and a pen across the table. "If you write down exactly what you drank at dinner, before driving home, I can guarantee you will not serve any jail time. You might have a small fine of like three hundred dollars and maybe a month or two of probation. You won't even lose your license. All you have to do is write that you had four glasses of wine at dinner before driving."

James frowned.

The detective continued without missing a beat. "And I know you said that you only had one glass, and I believe you, but that glass was a doozy. If you write that you only had one glass, with your breathalyzer test score, it'll seem like you're lying, and, if it seems like you're lying, I can't do a deal for you."

James was silent.

"This is the best option, James," the detective said with a straight face.

James narrowed his eyes at the detective. "I don't think so."

"If it would make you feel more comfortable, we could say it differently. We could say something like you admit to consuming enough alcohol to raise your blood alcohol to the level that we recorded. You're not admitting to anything we don't already know."

James hung his head.

"Six months in prison, James. I'm trying to be a friend here."

James raised his head and glared at the detective. "You're a liar. In Pennsylvania, you have to hit a point one zero to get jail time on a first offense. I would have had to drink five or six five-ounce glasses of wine at my weight in an hour to hit the blood alcohol you guys are claiming. Either Officer Emory is lying, or the machine was rigged. My money's on both. I want a lawyer."

The detective stared expressionless. He stood and exited without a word. Officer Emory and a tall, slender officer replaced the detective. They took James downstairs to a hallway with holding cells numbered one to six. The tall officer opened the last cell on the row. Once inside, Emory undid the handcuffs through the compartment on the heavy steel door.

"I need to make a phone call," James said.

The officers ignored him.

The cell was ten-by-ten with concrete walls and a stainless steel toilet, without a cover. A sink was over the toilet. A steel bed was built into the wall. It sat sterile and obstinate without a mattress or covering of any kind.

James paced in the tiny cell. *Is this payback for Harold? Why not arrest me for assault? I still don't think Harold said anything. If he didn't tell him about the assault, then why? Just to fuck with me. Was it just an opportunity that presented itself? Or did Officer Emory actually have faulty equipment? I don't believe that. They targeted me. But why? Because I'm not from around here? Because Harold doesn't like me? Because of Brittany? Brittany. Jesus, what if?*

James pounded on the door. He called out, "I need to make a phone call." He also tried yelling, "I'm really sick. I need to see a doctor." And "I need my medicine or I'll die."

There was no response. His eyes were heavy. He lay on the metal bed. Despite the discomfort, he drifted off to a fitful sleep. James awoke with a sharp pain in his hip. He rolled off his sore side onto his back. *What time is it? Is it morning yet? Have I been here an hour or ten? Definitely more than an hour. Maybe between four and eight hours.* He stood, his entire body ached. He yelled for a doctor and his medication again, but there was no response. He stretched and paced and stretched and paced some more.

After what seemed like days, the door slid open.

"It's your lucky day," a female officer said.

She was fortysomething, manly, with short brown hair, and a square jaw.

114

"What time is it?" James asked.

"Eight a.m." She led him to a metal desk. His things were on the desk, inside a clear plastic bag. "Have a seat," she said, motioning to the empty metal chair.

He sat.

She handed him a sheet of paper with a list of his things. "Check the list and double-check it to make sure all your personal possessions are accounted for."

James glanced at the bag. "Everything's there," he said. "Am I being released?"

"Yes, you are," she said. "You're a lucky man. The charges have been dropped."

James scowled. "Why?"

"You'd have to talk to Detective Warren."

James signed some papers and was shown out by the female officer. Outside, he dialed 4-1-1 and asked for the nearest taxi. He paced outside the police station for twenty minutes, freezing his ass off. The cab picked him up and took him to his cabin. His truck was parked in the driveway. He paid the cabbie in cash and sprinted to the front door. He turned the knob and pushed inside, surprised it was unlocked. "Brittany?"

He surveyed the one-room cabin. James's keys were on the dresser. Brittany's graduation cake was on the kitchen table where he had left it, but jagged pieces had been taken off, as if someone had grabbed handfuls of cake. Icing and yellow crumbs littered the floor. Her black dress and tights were in a heap by the love seat. Brittany was in the bottom bunk, curled up in the fetal position.

"Brittany," James said as he approached. "Are you asleep?"

She was tight to the back corner of the bed, close to the wall. She didn't move or speak. She wore white pajamas, patterned with tiny daisies. She had red marks on her neck.

"Brittany." James reached in and put his hand on her shoulder.

She jumped back as if his hand were a scorching cattle brand. He pulled his hand back. Her eyes were wide, her legs trying to push herself through the cabin wall. That's when he saw the brownish-red stain between her legs on her pajama bottoms. His stomach sank. He had a lump in his throat.

"It's just me," he said.

She blinked and gazed at James as if she were seeing him for the first time. Her eyes watered. She blinked again, and tears rolled down her face. He scooted closer, careful not to move too quickly.

"You said you would protect me," she said.

James wiped the moisture from his eyes with the side of his fist. "I'm so sorry."

"They were waitin' for me. They made me open the door."

"Brittany, who's *they*?"

"Harold and his brother," she said.

"The police chief?"

She nodded and bent forward, sobbing.

Tears collected in James's eyes and overflowed down his cheeks.

"I'm so sorry," James said. "I'm so sorry."

He reached out and put his arm on her back. She flinched but didn't move from his hand. He rubbed her back. James moved closer and wrapped his arms around her, rocking her like a child. Her sobbing subsided.

"Brittany, we need to go to the hospital now. They'll take care of you."

She shook her head rapidly. "We can't. They'll tell the police. They said they would kill me if I told."

James clenched his fists. "You don't have to tell anyone who did it, but we need to get you treated."

"We can never tell," she said, her eyes bulging. "Please, we can't tell. It's just gonna make everything worse. Promise me that you won't tell."

"I promise, but you still have to go to the hospital. I'll be right there with you."

James packed sweats, underwear, and socks for Brittany in his backpack. He grabbed her long jacket and helped her out of the bed. He wrapped the jacket around her. James placed her boots in front of her stocking feet, and she stepped into them. He walked her to the truck, his arm around her.

She leaned against the window, silent, as he drove.

# Chapter 12

## Into the Slurry

James sat in the waiting room, trying to distract himself with a magazine. Detective Warren waltzed past, with bags under his eyes. He was unresponsive to James's presence. The detective pushed through the swinging double doors. James stood and approached the reception window.

"Hello," James said to the heavyset young woman behind the glass. She looked up blank-faced.

"I would like to see my friend, Brittany Summers."

The woman picked up the phone and asked about Ms. Summers. She hung up. "They will call you when you can see her."

"I'd like to see her now."

The woman narrowed her eyes. "Please have a seat, sir."

James gritted his teeth and returned to his seat. He leafed through four issues of *Time*.

"James Fisher. ... James Fisher?" the tiny nurse called out. He stood, grabbed his backpack, and met the young nurse.

"Yes," James said.

"I can take you back now."

He followed her until the nurse tapped her small hand on the closed door.

"Come in," said someone in the room.

The nurse pushed in, announced James to the doctor, and shut the door behind her as she left. The walls were light blue, the floor linoleum. White curtains were partially drawn at a small window, and a television hung in the corner. The lighting was dim. The doctor was tall and thin with dark curls tight to her head. She was probably middle-aged, but she looked younger with flawless skin like coffee with cream. She wore large wooden hoop earrings.

James set his backpack on the chair next to the bed. He glanced at Brittany. She lay in the hospital bed, her eyes shut, and the blanket pulled to her chin.

"I'm Dr. Wiggins," she said, not offering her hand to shake.

"James Fisher," he said, his hands stuck to his sides. *Maybe it's a sanitation thing.*

"Ms. Summers said that you would be caring for her once she's released. Is that true?"

"Yes."

"She says you're a family friend?" The doctor pursed her full lips.

"Yes."

"She signed a release of information form, so that you can hear my treatment recommendations."

James nodded. They stepped away from Brittany, out of earshot.

The doctor said that physically, Brittany should make a full recovery. Brittany would not say what happened to her, but the doctor believed she was raped. Dr. Wiggins said she was obligated to call the police, but Brittany refused to press charges, and she refused any evidence collection. The doctor recommended counseling and warned of post-traumatic stress disorder. She said that a counselor would be by to talk to Brittany. The doctor gave James a few pamphlets about PTSD, sexual assault, and referrals for several counselors. Brittany was given the morning-after pill, and the doctor described the possible side effects. Dr. Wiggins also prescribed antibiotics, for the possibility of STDs. She said that the chances of pregnancy and STD contraction was much less likely because of the condom use, but she felt that it was better safe than sorry. She told James where they could fill the prescriptions. The doctor recommended that Brittany rest, eat healthy, and drink plenty of fluids.

"When can I take her home?" James asked.

"I'd like to keep her another day for observation," Dr. Wiggins said.

James walked with the doctor out of the hospital room. They stood in the hall.

The doctor asked, "You don't happen to be the same James Fisher who works over at the college?"

"I am," James replied.

"My son is Leon. He has such nice things to say about you."

"He's very bright."

She nodded. "Oh, he is. He just needs to figure out what he wants to do with his life. He was accepted to Penn, but I wasn't about to spend that kind of money if he couldn't decide on a major."

"Well, whatever he decides, I'm sure he'll be successful."

"He's wants to go pre-law. I'm not sure it's a good idea."

"I could see him as an attorney."

The doctor pursed her lips.

"Thank you for helping her," James said.

Doctor Wiggins narrowed her eyes at James. "I hope you take good care of that young lady."

"I will."

The doctor pulled a business card from her coat pocket. "Here's my card if she needs anything."

James put the card in his wallet and entered the hospital room, shutting the door behind him. He grabbed his backpack from the chair, set it against the wall, and sat next to Brittany.

She opened her eyes.

"I brought a change of clothes for you," he said.

She nodded, barely moving her head.

He scooted the chair closer to the hospital bed. "I was going to run down to the gift shop and get you some toiletries. I was thinking you'd need a toothbrush, toothpaste, and some floss. And maybe a brush. Is there anything else you want me to get?"

She shook her head, her eyes empty.

"Whatever you need, you just let me know, okay?"

She was unresponsive.

"I could get a book and read to you?"

She remained unresponsive.

He stood. "I'll be right—"

"No. Stay." She looked at him, her eyes red.

He sat down. "I'm not going anywhere."

She drifted off to sleep. Shortly thereafter, so did he.

He was awakened by a hand on his shoulder. His eyes popped open; he shot up straight in the chair, hoping it was all a bad dream.

"I'm sorry, Mr. Fisher," a young, slender nurse said. "Visiting hours are over."

James rubbed his eyes and looked at Brittany. She was sleeping, knocked out on meds.

"What time can I come back?" James asked.

"Eight a.m.," she replied.

James had déjà vu as he drove down the dark gravel road. He glanced in his rearview mirror expecting to see a cruiser. Nothing. He stopped at Harold's driveway. Harold's red Ford Ranger was parked in front of the trailer. The television cast jittery light in the window. He clenched his jaw and gripped the steering wheel. He took a deep breath and continued to his cabin.

He entered his cabin and surveyed the scene. James walked to the love seat and picked up her black dress from the floor. It was cut down the middle. The couch cushions were depressed. Images scrolled through his mind like a twisted slide show. The look of animal desire as they cut off her clothes. The grunting as they violated her petite body. Holding her down and spreading her apart on the love seat, on the bed. Taking their time to wear condoms. *Have they done this before?* Enjoying her graduation cake; eating it like conquering Vikings. He clenched his fists. *I lied to her. I said I would protect her.*

"Fuck!"

He rushed out of the cabin, still dressed in his rumpled suit and dress shoes. He started his truck and reversed wildly out of his driveway. The truck fishtailed and kicked up gravel as he mashed the accelerator. His heart was pounding, adrenaline coursing through his veins as he turned into Harold's driveway. He parked and ran to the front stoop, taking the steps two at a time. He banged on the front door. No answer. He banged louder. From behind the door, he heard *chik, chik*.

The door swung open, and Harold pointed a shotgun in James's face. James put up his hands, backpedaling. He stumbled down the steps but kept his balance. Harold moved forward, the gun barrel tracking James at point-blank range. James stood on the cold, hard ground, his hands up. Harold pressed the barrel to James's sealed mouth.

"Suck on it," Harold said.

James opened his mouth, and Harold jammed the barrel into the back of his throat. James gagged.

"Take it," Harold said. "I always knew you was a faggot." His eyes were alive as he pushed the barrel in and out. He pulled the shotgun out, and James gasped for air, his hands on his knees. Harold chuckled, pointing the shotgun vaguely to the left.

James lunged, grabbing the gun. Harold squeezed the trigger, the buckshot blasting past James. His ears rang as he wrenched the gun from Harold's grasp.

James dropped the shotgun on the ground. Harold turned to run, but James jumped on his back, tackling him to the ground. James pressed his knees into the old man's back as he squeezed his hands around his neck. Harold's limbs flailed as James tightened his grip like a vise. Thirty seconds later, the old man stopped fighting, but James held on, like a man possessed.

After a couple minutes, Harold clenched his fists and his body convulsed. James let go. He stood, breathless, watching the death throes. Once the convulsions stopped, Harold lay there, facedown on the frozen ground. James turned over the body. Harold's eyes and mouth were open, his fists clenched. He checked for a pulse on his neck. Nothing.

James looked around, listening. It was quiet ... dark. *I have to get rid of the body. Where? It won't work, the ground's frozen. It's been unseasonably warm. It's probably only the top inch or so. He won't fit. Sam said it had a manhole cover. Why would they call it a manhole if a man can't fit? The ground will be disturbed. The yard's covered in leaves. Just rake the leaves out of the way and put them back after.* He checked the time on his phone. *9:53 p.m. I have to get out of these clothes.*

James hopped in his truck and motored back to his cabin, leaving Harold in the front yard. *With the woods and the darkness, you can't see him from the road. Plus I need to stop getting my fingerprints on him.* He smacked the steering wheel. *Dumb ass! Why didn't you wear gloves?*

Inside his cabin, he changed his rumpled suit and dress shoes for canvas pants, a black jacket, black hat, gloves, and boots. He filled a spray bottle with concentrated oxygen bleach. He grabbed a handful of plastic bags, a rag, a flashlight, and a neatly folded tarp. He packed everything in his backpack and slung it over his shoulder.

He exited the cabin and opened the tool locker at the end of his porch. James set aside a pickax, shovel, and a leaf rake. He carried the tools to his truck and drove back to Harold's trailer. He parked off the gravel road, along the woods, one hundred yards away. *What if someone sees your truck? Like who? How often is there any traffic on this road at this hour? If someone does see the truck, it's better here than in Harold's driveway.*

He tied a few plastic bags over his boots and hiked to the trailer carrying his tools. The television flashed in the living room window. *I need to turn that off.* As he moved toward the front stoop, he looked at Harold. He was ghostlike, his face frozen with fear. *He must have been afraid in those last moments, when he knew he was going to die.* James half expected him to get up and attack him.

He set his tools on the ground. He climbed the stoop and walked through the open door, shutting it behind him. The dingy trailer smelled like mold, cigarettes, and body odor. He crept toward the flickering light of the plasma. A worn recliner with the stuffing spilling out of its arms faced the big-screen television. On the screen, a man forced his penis into a woman's mouth, while another penetrated her anally. The woman gagged and cried and grimaced, her pain adding to their pleasure. They called her a slut, a whore, a *cunt*. James felt nauseated. He turned off the television and departed the trailer.

James searched for the marker Sam had talked about. In the backyard, James found a piece of rebar with a pink ribbon attached to it. *Bingo*. He retrieved his tools and brought them to the backyard. He raked the wet leaves away from the site. James loosened the rebar by pushing it back and forth. He pulled it up and set it aside. He broke through the first few inches of frozen ground with the pickax. James dug down with his shovel for forty minutes until he hit the concrete manhole cover. He kept an eye on the plastic bags on his feet, adding another layer when the bags began to split. He dug for another half hour to fully expose the manhole. It was roughly two feet in diameter. His back ached as he heaved the cover off the cesspool. He shone his flashlight down the hole. The cesspool was nearly filled with a black slurry. Even in the cold weather, the rotten-egg-and-raw-sewage smell was overpowering.

He grabbed his backpack and walked to the front yard. With gloved hands, James fished out the rag and the spray bottle. He sprayed oxygen bleach on Harold's neck. James wiped the dead man's neck, hoping that the bleach would clean the oils from James's fingerprints and scrub away any DNA. He then wiped down Harold's face and hands, as well as the shotgun.

He spread out the tarp. James rolled Harold onto it, then dragged the body to the backyard. James stopped often to catch his breath. He positioned the tarp on the edge, with Harold facing the hole. His neck was red. His eyes and mouth were still wide open. His fists were still clenched. James pushed the body off the tarp. It barely budged at first, but, once hanging over the edge, gravity offered a helping hand. He pushed a little more, and Harold spilled into the black slurry. The body floated faceup near the open hole. James grabbed the rebar. He poked and prodded until Harold was wedged out of sight. James threw the rebar in with the body.

James spent the next few hours covering his tracks. He cleaned the stoop and steps to eliminate any footprints. He raked the area where the strangling had occurred. He dumped the shotgun inside the cesspool and replaced the manhole cover. James backfilled the soil and raked the leaves in place. He carried his tools to his truck and returned to his cabin. He put away his tools and took off his shoes on the porch. James placed his boots on the folded tarp and placed his gloves inside of them. He checked his phone—*2:48 a.m.*

James entered his cabin, added wood to the fireplace, and lit the insert. He took a deep breath. *She can't see this.* He cleaned the floor of icing and cake. The cake on the kitchen table was decimated, Brittany's name eaten entirely, only *Congratu* left. He put the cake in the trash. He pulled out the washboard and the wash bin. James washed the sheets and comforter on the bottom bunk. The top bunk appeared undisturbed. He strung the clothesline across the cabin, in front of the fireplace, and hung the bedding. He mopped the floor, cleaned the bathroom, and dusted the furniture, trying to get rid of the musty smell of body odor.

Afterward James showered and dressed. He checked the hanging sheets. They were still damp. He glanced at his phone again—*4:22 a.m.* He set the alarm on his cell and climbed into the top bunk. He dreamt of waking up in a cesspool, darkness all around him, the stench filling his nose and mouth. He shouted for help as he struggled to keep his head above the black slurry.

# Chapter 13

## Information Is Power

Help me! Somebody help me!" he said as he pounded on the concrete above him. He heard a phone. "Help me! Help me!"

His eyes fluttered; the cabin wall came into focus. He sat upright and looked around, trying to decipher truth from fantasy. His phone chimed on the dresser below. He felt the pangs of fear deep in his gut. *I murdered someone. That actually happened.* He climbed down the ladder from the top bunk, his back sore, his head pounding. James picked up his phone and turned off the alarm, confirming the time— *7:31 a.m.*

He staggered to the bathroom and rinsed with mouthwash. He threw on a pair of jeans and a fleece. James removed the trash bag from the kitchen, and he was out the door. He grabbed his boots, gloves, and the blue plastic tarp on the porch. He drove thirty minutes out of the way to a McDonald's. James discarded the tarp, his boots, gloves, and the trash bag in a Dumpster out back. He drove toward the hospital.

On the way his head was spinning with variables and scenarios and probabilities. *Did I leave any evidence in the house? I wore gloves, a hat. My body was covered. What about transfer of DNA? Maybe I had some hair on my pants or jacket? It's possible, but those canvas pants don't pick up hair, and neither does my parka. It's too slick.*

*And, if I did leave a hair, I can always say it was there from when I went to help Brittany. I would have to lie and say that I went all the way to the living room. Brittany's the only one who could say differently, and, even if they asked her that, and she answered truthfully, a lawyer could easily argue that she was stressed and not thinking clearly.*

*I think I'm okay on the evidence, but that doesn't mean the Stricklands won't pin it on me anyway. Shit, they might try to kill me. The timing's bad. I get locked up, Brittany's attacked, and the next day, Harold's dead. They'll know it was me.*

James exhaled and gripped the steering wheel.

*Yeah, that's a major problem. So what do I do? I could ask Yolanda to take Brittany, and I could leave, just get the hell out of here. But that'll look awfully suspicious. I'd be on the run for the rest of my life. What if the chief was out of the picture? Would I be worried about being arrested? Dale Strickland would pick up the torch.*

*What if Officer Strickland was also gone? Then, no, I wouldn't be worried. There wouldn't be enough evidence. There's the answer then. Chief Strickland and his son are the threats, and the threats have to be eliminated. I can't murder again. There's too much to cover up, too many chances for a mistake. I have to find another way.*

*How much time until someone finds out Harold's gone? I doubt the chief would come to Harold's anytime soon. I can't imagine they hang out in that shithole. The chief might call though. What about the firehouse? Harold's supposed to be there on Wednesday. If he no-shows, would they be worried? They are volunteers. Yeah, but I bet he never misses. He's probably been volunteering there forever. It's not like he had a lot going on in his life.*

*It's Monday, so I have roughly forty-eight hours until someone from the firehouse tries to call him. It'll go to voice mail. The firehouse guy may not be alarmed at first, or they may call his brother or nephew. The firefighters and police officers work together, so I'm sure any of the firemen would feel comfortable calling and asking.*

*This would probably result in Dale driving by and checking on*

*Harold at his trailer. He'll walk in the trailer. The door's unlocked. He'll call Harold's phone, and it'll ring in the house. Harold's truck's still there. There's no sign of a struggle, no broken windows or doors. Dale might think that someone Harold knew took him and did something to him elsewhere.*

*I can't imagine he doesn't have any other enemies besides me. The Stricklands will investigate the scene as a missing person's case. They'll find nothing, so they'll come to me. They'll force me to talk. They might hurt Brittany again. I can't let that happen. I can't let her down again. I have two days to turn the tables. If I can't, I better have a getaway plan for her and me.*

*What if I need more time?* James nodded. *I know how to get another week and an early warning device if it doesn't work.*

James parked in the visitor lot of the hospital and hustled inside. He knocked on the partially open door and entered the hospital room. Brittany sat on the chair, fully dressed in her sweats, watching television. Her arms were crossed over her chest. She had bruising on her neck. She scowled at the screen. He moved next to her.

"You ready to go?" he asked.

"Where were you?" she replied.

"I'm sorry. I overslept."

She glared, her eyes wet. "I didn't think you were gonna come back."

He bent over and wrapped his arms around her. "I'm sorry I was late."

She wrapped her arms around his waist and squeezed. Her tiny body trembled.

They filled her prescriptions at the pharmacy and walked outside.

James glanced at the concrete benches. "I can bring the truck around if you want to wait here. The truck is pretty far away."

"No," she whispered.

They trudged in silence, James looking over every few seconds, Brittany staring at her feet as if concentrating on moving each foot forward.

Inside the cab, James said, "We should probably tell Diane what happened before your next session. She might want to be prepared. I'm sure she would give you more time. I can call her if you want me to."

Brittany nodded, her head down.

They drove along a two-lane country road with farms in various stages of disrepair. Brittany gazed out the window. James glanced over often. He pulled into his driveway and cut the engine.

"There's something we need to talk about," James said.

She still stared out the window. "I don't wanna talk about it."

"Would you like to move?"

She turned her head to James. "Where?"

"Northern Virginia, where I used to live. It would be a fresh start. They have a good community college there, lots of jobs. You could stay with my friend Yolanda. She's really—"

"You're not comin'?" she said with a scowl.

James looked out the front windshield. "I can't."

Brittany crossed her arms. "Why not?"

James turned to her. "I'm sorry. I can't."

"You're not gonna just dump me with some lady I don't even know." Her face was red. "If you don't want me here anymore, just say so!"

"Brittany, it's not like that."

She opened the door and stepped out of the truck. "I'll be gone in ten minutes." She slammed the door and marched toward the cabin.

James exited the truck and caught up to Brittany, grabbing her arm. She whirled around and slapped him across the face. James let go. "It's not what you think," he said.

She glared at James and marched toward the cabin.

"I killed Harold," James said, condensation hanging in the air with his confession.

She stopped dead in her tracks.

James stepped toward her. "I promised you that I wouldn't let them hurt you." A tear slipped down his cheek. "I'm sorry, Brittany."

She turned around. Her face was tear-streaked. "No," she said, shaking her head.

"I just want you to be safe. I can't keep you safe here. I thought I could. I was so fucking stupid." He wiped his eyes with the side of his index finger.

She wrapped her arms around his waist and squeezed, sobbing. They stood in front of the crime scene, holding each other, sharing the guilt, the shame, and the pain.

After a few minutes, she stepped back and wiped her face with her sweatshirt sleeve. "What are you gonna do?" she asked.

"I have a plan."

"What is it?"

"It's better you don't know," he said.

"What if it doesn't work?"

"If it doesn't work, I get the hell out of here."

"Then would you come and get me?"

James took a deep breath. "If it doesn't work, you'd probably never see me again. But Yolanda's a good friend and a good person—"

"No."

James furrowed his brow. "What do you mean, *no*?"

"I mean no. I mean I won't do it."

"I think we can agree that it's not safe here."

"I'm not a kid."

"I know."

"I can make my own decision on stayin'."

"You have to trust me."

She crossed her arms over her chest. "Trust goes both ways. Tell me 'bout your plan, and I'll decide for myself."

They went inside, hung their jackets, and sat at the kitchen table. He explained in explicit detail, emphasizing the risks involved. He stated that, if she gets involved, she can't tell Diane, because she has an obligation to report felonies, which supersedes the doctor patient confidentiality. Brittany asked a few pointed questions.

"I'm stayin'. I wanna help," she said finally.

* * *

James and Brittany drove out of town to a shopping center forty-five minutes away. They used the cash James had hidden in the cellar for their purchases. At Lowe's, they bought rubber gloves, a disposable Tyvek chemical suit, Gorilla tape, several pairs of size eleven booties, and a tarp to replace the one he had used on Harold.

At Best Buy, he picked up a handheld MP3 recorder and a digital camera with a long-range zoom. They picked up a couple burner phones from a convenience store. At Staples they purchased five thousand white self-sealing envelopes, a folding machine, the first four hundred stamps, and a lint roller. They went to a half-dozen grocery stores and a Walmart to get the rest of the stamps they needed and the latest issue of *Autotrader*.

They sat at Chick-fil-A, perusing the *Autotrader* over chicken sandwiches and fries. Brittany wore a scarf to cover her bruising, yet no makeup to hide the dark circles under her eyes.

"How much can we spend?" she asked.

"We're looking for something in the $3,000 range. It has to be a private owner, no dealerships. We want the car to be reliable, no flashy colors, something nondescript. So I would say an older compact car—a Honda Civic or a Toyota Corolla or something like that."

She sighed. "All the Hondas and Toyotas are too expensive." She pointed to the magazine, tilting it so James could see. "Even this one with 130,000 miles."

They eventually decided on a white Hyundai Elantra with 75,000 miles that was close by. James called the number listed on the ad, from his new phone. He asked the man on the other end if the car was still for sale. When the man affirmed, James asked him if he could come and look at it, that it was a birthday present for his daughter. The man gave James his exact street address.

James and Brittany walked up to the one-story brick rambler, their cover stories already rehearsed. The grass was dormant, the trees leafless. A hefty bald man with pale skin answered the door. James wondered how he ever fit in the tiny car. The man let Brittany drive the car around the block by herself. When she returned, James checked the engine, even though he had no idea what he was looking at.

"How 'bout $2,600?" James asked.

The fat man winced. "I really didn't wanna go under three."

James frowned and spoke to Brittany. "We should prob'ly wait. I mean, I ain't sure I can even deal with the plates for a couple weeks." James turned to the man. "I'm a long-distance trucker. I'm leavin' t'morrow for two weeks."

"Come on, Dad. I really like this one." Brittany put her hands together as if she were praying. "Please, please, please," she said in rapid succession.

"It is nice," James said.

The man looked at Brittany, then back to James.

"Maybe it'll still be for sale in a couple weeks," James said.

"It prob'ly won't." Brittany pressed out her bottom lip and crossed her arms.

"We have had quite a lot of interest," the man said.

"Nothin' ever works out," Brittany said and stomped to the truck.

James sighed. "It's been tough since …" He shook his head. "You have kids?"

"Two boys. They're grown. The wife and I are hoping for some grandkids."

"Always wanted boys. Wasn't in the cards."

"Think you can do $2,800?" the fat man asked.

"Think you can give me a couple weeks with them plates?" James asked.

"Depends on how you're paying."

"Cash."

\* \* \*

James sneaked into Harold's trailer dressed in his Tyvek chemical suit and booties. He found Harold's cell phone and charger in the living room. He left the trailer.

Back in his cabin, James scrolled through Harold's text messages. Nothing since he was submerged in human sewage. James placed the phone in a Ziploc bag. Brittany emerged from the bathroom in her work clothes—black jeans, a white polo, and a scarf. She wore a long-sleeved shirt underneath.

"I got the phone and the charger," James said. "This goes without saying, but under no circumstances can we answer the phone. It'll be an early warning device. As soon as there's a text from the Stricklands that they're looking for him, we're out of here. So we have to keep this charged and monitored." He shoved the Ziploc-bag-covered phone into his pocket.

"Got it," she said.

"We need to get moving if you're going to make your appointment with Diane."

She bit her lower lip. "We should cancel it. She's gonna know somethin's wrong."

"We need to keep up appearances. Besides, you *should* talk to her about how you're feeling. Just attribute it to past events."

"Are you gonna take me to work? Or should I take the new car?"

"I'll drive you. We actually need to stow the Hyundai someplace. I don't want it seen more than it has to be." James took a deep breath. "I'm worried about you planting the MP3 recorder. I mean, I can do it if you want me to. I could cancel class and call the diner and tell them you have the flu."

She shook her head. "I thought we're supposed to be keepin' up appearances? How's it gonna look if you don't show up for class?"

He shook his head. "I'm just worried about you being there with him. I think it's too much, too soon."

"I'm scared. I'm not gonna lie, but I'm tired of bein' the victim."

"You do understand that it's illegal?"

She tightened her jaw. "The truly courageous are scared, but they go anyway."

James nodded and grabbed the tape recorder and the Gorilla tape. He handed her the recorder. "All you have to do is press the Power button and hit Record." He pointed to the buttons. "This is for Power. This is Record. It'll record for six hours, so you can set it up way before they get there."

She nodded. "Got it."

He pulled some tape from the roll and ripped it with his fingers. "This tape is really easy to rip. You don't need scissors. Here you try." He handed her the roll of thick black tape.

She pulled a bit of tape and ripped it with her tiny fingers.

"Good," he said. "I would suggest getting the tape on the recorder first and then sticking it under the table near the back wall. Act like you're cleaning under there." James took a deep breath. "Are you sure about this?"

"Like you said, I can set it up way before they get there. It's not my section, so I think I can stay away from them."

"Jessica knows the exact time and the exact booth, so you'll have to ask her. I think they show up around eight or nine."

After her therapy session, James dropped Brittany off at work and went to teach his night class.

\* \* \*

He parked in the lot at Dot's Diner. Brittany wore a poker face as she approached the truck.

"How did it go?" James asked, his heart pounding.

"I got it," she replied with a restrained grin.

"Are you okay?"

She nodded. "I took a long break when they came in. Rod didn't care. It was dead. They didn't even see me."

"Good."

After the jaunt home, they sat at the kitchen table. James pressed Play on the MP3 recorder. He forwarded through the first few hours of nothing except diner background noise and a couple of old biddies gossiping. The good part started with a groan as the chief sat in the booth opposite his son. Jessica took their order. The officers flirted with her.

"You sure are growin' up," Officer Dale Strickland said.

"They didn't make 'em like that in my day," the chief added.

Jessica ignored the comments. "What would you two like to drink?"

Once Jessica left with their orders, they continued, "Pretty girl," the chief said.

"What I wouldn't give to be young again," Dale said.

"Young? You are young. Have a little respect for the old man in front of you."

"Sorry, Pops."

The chief chuckled. "Doesn't matter how old you are. When you're sixty, you still want the eighteen-year-old just like when you were eighteen."

"Don't tell Mom that."

"I won't."

"So I heard Emory locked up that teacher who lives next to Harold."

"Prick needed to be taken off his high horse."

"How'd he do in lockup?" Dale asked.

"He was cryin' all night for a doctor," the chief said.

"These liberal faggots got no backbone."

The chief cackled. "What was the take from last week?"

"Kurt was light last Wednesday," Dale said. "I think he might be skimmin.'"

"He knows better than that."

Dale grunted. "When has he ever known better?"

"He wouldn't dare," the chief said finally.

Jessica brought their coffee. The men asked about her family and how school was going. Jessica's responses were polite but short. "Your food will be out soon," Jessica said.

"How's Margie and the girls?" the chief asked his son. "They must be itchin' for spring."

"I'll tell you what, Pops. Margie's not like Mom. It's never enough. The more money I make, the more she spends. The girls are little carbon copies."

"That's why you gotta marry an ugly woman."

Dale laughed. "Don't tell Mom that either."

Jessica brought their food. They thanked her and began eating. The conversation slowed to benign chitchat. Grunts and probably body language became acceptable forms of communication.

"You see what happened in South Perry the other day?" Dale asked.

The chief grunted.

"These cameras are lethal. Reputations ruined by the Internet. Should be a crime to film police."

The chief grunted once more.

Dale continued, "Nigger had it comin' if you ask me."

The chief swallowed and said, "People want the trash taken out, but they don't wanna *see it* bein' taken out."

"His family's hollerin' about excessive force and racial profilin'. It's liberal bullshit if you ask me, but they got some public support."

"Stats don't lie. Black males commit crimes at a much higher rate than any other group. We'd be stupid not to target 'em. You just can't say that."

After listening to ten minutes of mundane gossip, followed by silence, James stopped the recording.

"I'm not sure I understand what they're doing," Brittany said. "Can we get them in trouble?"

"Not exactly," James replied. "Recording someone without their knowledge is illegal, remember? It's inadmissible and would get us arrested."

"Then what's the point of all this?"

"Information is power."

# Chapter 14

## Preparation

James parked his truck in the small lot in front of the self-storage center. The morning sun was blocked by the trees. Frost clung to the edges of his windshield, where he'd neglected to scrape. The faded metal sign read Gil's Storage. Across the street was the entrance to the trail they had used to hunt mushrooms and pawpaws. James exited his truck and stepped toward the business.

The glass door to the office had the Open sign posted. James entered the cramped space. It was almost as cold inside as it was out. A white-haired man sat behind a metal desk in a parka, knit hat, and gloves.

"How are you doing?" James said.

"What can I do for you?" the man asked.

"I'd like to park my car here for about a month."

"Six months is the shortest lease we'll do."

"How much would that be?"

"What kinda car you got?"

"It's a compact car. It's small."

"Compact car will run you about forty a month, provided you got good credit. We do credit checks."

"What if I paid for the term up-front … in cash?"

He grinned. "Well then, I know you're good for it."

The old man gave James the combination to the front gate and pointed to a map of the storage center on the wall, showing him his space in the back corner.

"Number twenty-two, marked on the asphalt. You can't miss it. Don't be parkin' in someone else's space. It's a pain in the ass when that happens."

James left the office, removed the burner phone from his pocket and dialed.

"Hello," Brittany said.

"It's ready," James said. "Come right through the gate, and drive all the way to the back. Don't park in front. I'll be waiting in back."

James walked through the gate, toward his parking space. Brittany drove through a few minutes later. She stopped next to James and powered down her window.

"Park in number twenty-two," James said, pointing to the tight space.

They left the car and hiked to James's truck. He cranked the engine and looked at Brittany.

"Get comfortable," he said.

* * *

They drove a few hours southeast, into Maryland. The traffic was heavier, the cars more expensive. James parked in front of a three-story brick-and-glass office building.

In the lobby, they read through the directory to locate Direct Data in Office 212. They took the stairs to the second floor. Inside, James told the receptionist that he had an appointment with Stephanie. An attractive thirtysomething emerged from a back office.

"Mr. Miller," she said to James.

"Please call me Ray," James replied.

James paid the woman in cash, and she produced four boxes of Avery labels. James opened one of the boxes. Names and addresses were printed on every label as specified. He shut the box.

"Thank you, Stephanie. I appreciate it."

"Next time, if you give us a week, we can mail the lists. Save you the trip."

On the way home they stopped for lunch at a deserted Subway. They sat at a corner table, eating their subs with the wax paper as makeshift plates. James bought them chocolate chip cookies for dessert.

"The chocolate chips are always melty," he said. "I don't know how they do that."

After their sandwiches and cookies, James made a phone call with his burner phone.

"North Schuylkill Township Police nonemergency line," a female said.

"Hi, my name is Ray Miller," James said. "Could I speak to Dale Strickland, please?"

"I'm sorry, sir, but he's not in at the moment."

"Do you know what time he'll be in?"

"He'll be here tonight from four to twelve. Would you like to leave him a message?"

"No, thank you. I'll call back."

James put the phone in his pocket. "I figured it was four to twelve. I'd like to see what he does, where he goes."

"Aren't we supposed to keep up appearances? Aren't you gonna teach tonight?"

"My class is six to nine. I'll tail him for an hour and a half and then go to class. I'll drop you off at work a little early in the truck, if that's okay. I don't want anyone at the diner to see the Hyundai."

"We still have a lot to do," she said.

"We do, but we need more information. We get one shot. I don't want there to be any doubt."

"We need more time then."

"I figured we would. I'll send the text in the morning, before they get worried."

* * *

James dropped off Brittany at the diner an hour early for her shift. He drove to the storage center and parked in the lot. The chain-link gate was open. He hopped into the Hyundai and drove to the police station. He parked on a neighborhood street across from the one-story brick building. James sat and watched, his camera in the seat next to him.

Officer Dale Strickland pulled up to the station in a black Yukon Denali. Dale entered the station wearing his uniform. Fifteen minutes later he departed in his cruiser. The officer sped down the road. James kept a safe distance behind. They drove on a two-lane road that was wooded on either side. Officer Strickland pulled off at a small clearing. James drove past, shielding his face with his arm. *Shit.*

*He's probably setting up a speed trap.* James pulled off the road six hundred yards away. The ground was frozen and dry. The last snowstorm of a few weeks ago had melted in a short stretch of above-freezing weather. He parked the car tight to the woods, out of plain view. He took out his camera and exited the Hyundai. With the zoom cranked up, he could see Dale with his radar gun. James watched Dale for an hour. The officer flagged down cars without moving from his spot. He nabbed four cars for speeding.

After the fourth car drove away slowly, Dale drove in the opposite direction. James ran to his Hyundai and spun the front wheel as he gunned it back on the road. He pressed the accelerator to the floor, trying to gain ground. He saw the cruiser turn off the two-lane road into a rural trailer park.

James followed. Most of the trailers were well cared for, with small leafless trees and empty flowerpots. *Maybe he's here for the money. No, they said Kurt picks up the money.* The cruiser stopped in front of a single-wide trailer with white vinyl siding. A young woman ran from the trailer to the cruiser and hopped in the front passenger seat. Dale made a three-point turn. *Shit, he's coming back this way.* James backed into an empty driveway and ducked his head. He listened as the V-8 rumbled past. James lifted his head to see the cruiser driving back toward the main road. He followed.

They drove farther away from town, fifteen miles maybe. The cruiser turned down an asphalt road into a wooded housing development. The community was sparsely populated with cabins and single-family homes. James allowed a healthy distance between him and Dale. The police car pulled into a gravel driveway of a small stone house. The front yard was mostly dormant grass. James edged a little closer to get a better angle on the cruiser. He rolled down the passenger window and turned on his camera.

With the zoom, he had an excellent view of the back of the police car. The exhaust was still spewing smoke. *They're still in the car.* He pointed the camera at the back window. He snapped photographs of Officer Dale Strickland kissing and groping the young lady. The officer cut the engine, and the couple exited the vehicle. The woman ran around the car and jumped on Dale. She straddled him. They kissed. James continued to snap photographs as she unclenched her thighs and let her feet drop to the ground. He snapped a nice shot of her face as Dale smacked her on the ass. *I guess there really is no honor among thieves.*

\* \* \*

James and Brittany entered the cabin, looking like death. Brittany had dark circles under her eyes, and James didn't look much better. They were running on fumes after two nights of little-to-no sleep.

"You gonna show me the pictures now?" she asked.

They sat at the kitchen table. James scrolled through the camera screen, showing Brittany the pictures he had taken.

"Who's the girlfriend?" Brittany asked.

"It's Heather Davenport," he said, flipping to the shot with a good view of her face.

Brittany leaned into the picture. "She looks familiar."

"It's Kurt Strickland's girlfriend."

She cackled.

James nodded with a grin.

\* \* \*

The phone rang. His eyes fluttered. He smelled bacon and eggs. He blinked in rapid-fire fashion. The cabin came into focus. He rolled out of the bottom bunk, stood, and stretched his arms high over his head. He grabbed his phone from the dresser and cut the alarm. Brittany glanced back from the stove. Her blue eyes were bright, the dark rings faint. She wore black sweats.

"Breakfast is almost ready," she said.

"Smells really good," he replied. "I should send that text real quick."

He grabbed a pair of latex gloves from the box and slipped them on. He pulled Harold's phone from the plastic bag. He checked text messages and missed calls.

"Nothing since those two calls from yesterday," he said to Brittany.

"But you said those were telemarketers," she replied.

"I'm pretty sure they were. One was from Minneapolis and the other Los Angeles. I have telemarketers calling me from Minneapolis all the time. And I doubt Harold knew anyone from L.A."

He double-checked the text he had prepared. He had researched Harold's past text messages to make this one seem authentic. He showed the text to Brittany.

I got the flu bad must be the wether. I wont be at the firehouse today or Friday.

James pressed Send. "There it goes," he said. "That should give us some breathing room."

"So what's next?" she asked.

"They said Kurt does the pickups on Wednesday. I want to see for myself and get some pictures."

"Where are you gonna follow him from?"

"He takes a night class. I've seen him leaving campus in his jacked-up truck."

"How do you know he doesn't do the pickups in the mornin's? They didn't say when exactly. They just said *Wednesday*."

"He doesn't seem like a morning person. Besides, if he's doing something shady, like I suspect, I think he would be more likely to do it at night."

"What else?"

"I need to learn how to mix videos and set up a blog. There's an Internet café type place about half an hour from here. I don't want this stuff to point to my IP address. I was thinking I should also wear a disguise, just in case they have cameras there. Maybe at least a hat pulled low."

"What do you need me to do?"

James grinned. "You could start putting those labels on the envelopes."

She groaned. "There's five thousand of 'em."

"Don't touch anything without gloves."

# Chapter 15

## If You Ain't First, You're Last

"That's it for class tonight," James said.

The students packed their bags and started for the door. James put on his jacket, knit cap, and gloves. He slung his laptop bag over his shoulder. Leon and Jessica approached. Leon wanted to debate; Jessica wanted to talk about her project.

"Next class, guys," James said. "I have to go."

James hurried his students out the door. He locked the classroom and jogged to the parking lot, his computer bag bouncing on his shoulder. The lot was well lit by the street lamps. He spotted Kurt and Heather climbing into a red lifted Dodge pickup with vertical exhaust pipes. James broke into a sprint toward the back of the lot, where the Hyundai was stowed.

He shoved his computer bag under the seat, cranked the engine, and headed for the exit. He searched for the red truck. Post-class traffic was clustering in front of him. *Shit.* He pulled the Hyundai onto the shoulder and zoomed past the traffic, eliciting a few honks. In the distance, he saw Kurt's pickup turning left from the college.

James ran out of shoulder, so he drove with one wheel on the frozen grass and one on the sidewalk. At the end of the sidewalk, he drove off the curb, the front end of the Hyundai scraping the asphalt. He made a left, cutting off a Toyota truck. The truck pitched forward as the driver slammed on his brakes and laid on the horn.

James saw taillights shaped like a ram, stopped at a red light a few hundred yards ahead. The traffic light went green. James mashed on the accelerator. The four-cylinder engine whined, the speedometer rising despite the complaints. The quick light went yellow as he crossed the intersection. He was gaining ground on the truck. He eased off the gas pedal, careful not to get too close.

Kurt turned into an industrial park. There was a single warehouse as big as a football field, with roll-up garage doors for the dozens of businesses contained therein. The front lot was mostly empty, except for a fleet of water delivery trucks. James stopped at the entrance, watching Kurt motor around back. James drove into the lot and parked tight to the side of the building.

His camera and flashlight sat on the front passenger seat. He grabbed the camera, exited the Hyundai, and peeked around the corner. The rear of the building had docks high enough for tractor trailers to offload. The lot and the building were well lit. Each dock had a set of concrete steps that led to a metal door. Kurt's truck was one hundred yards away. A black car was parked next to the pickup, visible under the Dodge's lifted frame. James was partially shielded by the concrete steps in front of him.

He turned on his camera and pointed it over the steps toward the truck. Kurt hopped down from his pickup and climbed the steps in front of him. He pressed a buzzer and waited. A few seconds later, he opened the door and entered the building. Heather, still in the Dodge, blew cigarette smoke out the passenger window.

A few rigs and trailers were parked along the back of the lot. James ran across the asphalt to a big rig. He crouched next to a truck tire and pointed his camera at the loading dock and door. The metal door had vinyl lettering that read All-American Auto Parts. He snapped a few pictures. He had a better view of the black BMW M5 that was parked next to Kurt's truck. He took pictures of both license plates.

Kurt departed the building with a white envelope. He stopped just outside the door and flipped through the contents. James took rapid-fire pictures as Kurt took a few hundred dollar bills and shoved them in his front pocket.

*Chop shop maybe?* James ran across the lot to the Hyundai as Kurt and Heather drove the opposite direction around the building.

James followed the truck across town to an older development of homes built in the early 1900s. The single-family homes were mostly brick foursquares, two-and-a-half stories tall, with dormer windows and expansive front porches. The neighborhood was a mixed bag— some houses well maintained, while others were falling apart. Kurt pulled up to a well-cared-for brick foursquare, lit by porch lights and a streetlight. A small purple neon sign glowed in an upstairs window. In cursive it read Spa Appointment Only. James chuckled to himself and parked a few houses away.

He took photos as Kurt entered without knocking. A few minutes later Kurt exited with another envelope. This one yellow and shaped like a greeting card. Again he took a few bills and shoved them in his pocket.

Kurt and Heather were on the move again. James followed them out of town to a familiar trailer park. Kurt kissed Heather, dropped her at her trailer, and drove back to the main road. He continued farther away from town. Kurt turned down a gravel road not far from James's cabin. The road was potholed. The suspension of the old Hyundai squeaked and groaned and banged as James tried to avoid the hazards. The lifted truck rolled over the holes like they weren't there.

After a few miles, Kurt turned onto a dirt and gravel driveway. He parked in front of a vinyl-sided double-wide trailer that looked new. Security spotlights shone from each corner of the trailer. A Ford F-350 dually pickup truck and a Ford Expedition SUV were parked in front. An enormous covered trailer, almost as large as the house, was parked at the end of the driveway. On the side of the trailer was a vinyl cartoon version of a sprint car with a huge boxy wing on top. Underneath was the slogan If You Ain't First, You're Last.

James pulled off the gravel road and parked, the drive wheel slipping into a ditch caused by erosion. He crept closer on foot. He took photos of Kurt entering the trailer and exiting with another envelope. James hurried back to his car and tried to get back on the road. The car engine whined, and the front tire whizzed, spinning in the ditch. He was stuck. Kurt was coming his way. James ducked in his seat.

The red truck motored past. James sat up and watched the truck moving away from him. The pickup stopped. It sat still for ten seconds, ... then it reversed. *Shit.* James ducked down again. Kurt hopped out of his truck and shone a flashlight in James's passenger side window. Kurt tapped on the window with the flashlight. James looked up. Kurt had a smirk on his pudgy face. James powered down the window one-quarter of the way.

Kurt pointed the flashlight in James's face. "Mr. Fisher, what the hell are you doin' out here? I was wonderin' who'd be parked out here at this time a night." He wore a black puffy North Face jacket and a backward-facing baseball hat.

"I have a friend who lives down here," James replied. "I guess I was tired and veered off the road."

Kurt narrowed his eyes and grinned. "Oh, yeah? Who you know over here?"

"Paul Richards."

Kurt cackled. "Paul Dicks, huh? Sounds made up, like a porn name or somethin.'"

James laughed. "I never thought of it that way. I'll have to tell him that."

Kurt shook his head, reached behind, and pulled a Glock 9 mm from his lower back. He tapped on the glass with the boxy muzzle, still shining the flashlight at James. "Now why don't you tell me the real reason why you're here, hidin' like a little *bitch.*"

James nodded, his mouth flat. "I'm here for meth. I heard I could score some down here. I got scared when I saw your truck. I could get fired."

He pursed his lips. "How'd you know it was my truck?"

"I've seen you leaving campus. It's hard to miss."

He chuckled. "That is true."

"Do you think maybe we could keep this a secret, between you and me?"

"I could do that, but what're you gonna do for me?"

"What would you like me to do?" James replied.

"How much cash you got?"

James exhaled and opened his wallet. He leaned over and handed Kurt a couple hundred dollars through the passenger window. "Are we straight now?"

Kurt took the money, peering into the Hyundai.

"Gimme your phone," he said.

"Seriously?" James replied.

"Did I fuckin' stutter? I know you got one. Everyone does."

James handed over his Droid.

Kurt took the phone and shook his head. "You ain't got an iPhone? Cheap bastard." He shoved the Droid in his pocket.

"That's enough, Kurt. I have to go."

He cackled. "I don't know where the fuck you gonna go. This piece of shit's stuck." He peered in the Hyundai, his eyes searching. "And I'd like that camera right there. That shit is tight."

"Come on, Kurt. The camera's not mine. I have to return it."

"I don't give a fuck whose it is. It's mine now, motherfucker. Hand it over." Kurt pointed the Glock at James's face.

James frowned and picked up the camera on the passenger seat. He opened the memory card slot and popped out the tiny plastic disk.

"What the fuck you doin'?" Kurt asked.

"Do you really need this?" James asked. "It has pictures from my friend's wedding."

"But then I gotta take *my* time and *my* money to get another one."

"Fine." James handed the camera to Kurt in his right hand. As he handed him the camera, he motored down his driver's side window with his left hand, still holding the memory card.

Kurt snatched the camera. "Don't touch the window. What the fuck you doin'?" The memory card slot was open. "I said gimme that fuckin' memory card."

James chucked it out the window into the woods.

Kurt shook his head. "Dumb motherfucker. You better bring me a memory card on Friday. I'll stop by your class to pick it up."

And he was gone. James bent over the steering wheel and rubbed his temples. He lifted his head and pounded on the steering wheel. "Fuck!"

He grabbed the flashlight from the passenger seat and opened the door. He shone the light on the ground in front of him before he stepped out, in the unlikely event that the memory card had bounced back. He used a systematic approach to his search, moving inch by inch, starting at the car and working toward the woods. After three hours of fruitless, freezing-cold searching, he saw a flash of purple. James snatched it up with a huge smile and shoved it in his pocket. "Yes!"

He grabbed his laptop from under the seat, slung it over his shoulder, and started walking. He hiked close to the woods, to lessen the possibility of being spotted from the road. This was unnecessary as he didn't see a single car. An hour later, he walked up his cabin driveway, his face and feet numb. The lights were on. He unlocked the deadbolt and entered the cabin. Brittany rushed to the front door, her eyes bloodshot.

"Oh, my God," she said. "Are you okay?"

"I'm fine," James said, as he stepped into the warm cabin. "What time is it?"

"It's after three." Brittany checked her burner phone. "It's 3:25. I was freakin' out. You said you'd be back by one at the latest. You left your burner phone here, so I couldn't call you. I almost called your regular cell, but I knew you'd freak about leaving evidence."

Stacks of envelopes and Avery labels were on the kitchen table along with James's Buck knife. Brittany made James some tea while he explained what had happened. Brittany sat down, her hand on her chest, her eyes wide.

"We're fine," he said. "Everything's still on track."

"But he saw the Hyundai."

He exhaled. "I know, it's not good, but it was dark, and he didn't take down the license plate. The car is pretty nondescript, besides I'm not sure we have time to get rid of it and find another car. We'll have to risk it."

"What if he goes through your phone?"

"There's nothing there. That's why we have the burners. I do need to get another burner to call Yolanda. I don't want her to be connected to the ones we've been using."

"Do you think he believed that you were really there for meth?"

"I don't know. I think so. I think if he knew I was watching him, he would have killed me."

She put her hand over her mouth.

"It did teach me a valuable lesson," he said. "We need a good backup copy of our data. I almost lost the pictures. He didn't know about my laptop under the seat. What if he would have stolen that? I need to make a copy of everything. The information, the audio, the pictures, everything. I'm going to keep a copy hidden on me at all times. That way, if they catch on and raid the cabin, we'll still have everything."

"Information is power," she said.

He nodded and glanced around the table at the stacks of envelopes. "You didn't touch these without gloves, did you?"

She frowned. "Of course not. I spent about seven hours on 'em today, and I'm only maybe halfway through. And that's just stickin' on the addresses. We still have to prepare the paper with all the information that we wanna send. *And* we have to copy it, fold it, seal the envelopes, and put all the stamps on … five thousand times. I'm worried that we don't have enough time."

"Let's do the math. If each one takes a minute, that's five thousand minutes, divided by sixty gives us about 83.33 hours. If we divide that by two, we each need to put in about forty hours."

"That's in addition to everything else. We only have six days until they realize Harold's missing, and you never know, they could figure it out sooner."

"I think a minute each is probably too long. If we get a good system down, with the folding machine, we could probably cut that by one-third at least. Worst-case scenario, we'll take the letters with us and mail them from the road."

# Chapter 16

## Chucky

James and Brittany slept until noon. They returned to the scene of the robbery. They used a piece of plywood stuck under the drive wheel to get the Hyundai out of the ditch. They stowed the car back at Gil's Storage.

They spent the next four days working, tying up loose ends and completing mundane, but crucial, chores. Brittany wore latex gloves as she affixed addresses and stamps to 5000 envelopes. She listened to music on James's laptop, humming along as she worked on the assembly line. The Buck knife sat on the table within her reach.

James followed Chief Strickland on two occasions, but he never left the police station and went straight home after work. James spent the majority of his time on a computer at an Internet café thirty minutes away. He learned how to podcast and mix videos. He set up an e-mail account, a YouTube channel, a Facebook page, and a website. He hosted his podcast on Libsyn.com. Hosting and domain names were paid for with a prepaid credit card, purchased with cash.

On his way home from the Internet café, he made a phone call with his new burner phone.

"Hello?"

"Hey, Yolanda. Sorry to bug you on a Sunday night," James said.

"James, where the hell have you been? I tried calling you. Your phone—"

"My phone was lost. I'm in a bit of trouble up here, and I need some help."

"What's going on? Are you okay?"

"I'm fine. I can't really tell you everything, but I'm in a jam that I'm not sure I can get out of."

"What kind of jam?"

"The kind you don't want to be in."

"How can I help?"

"Do you know any coyotes?"

"What?"

"A coyote. You know, the people who help you cross the border."

"I know what a coyote is, but what the hell do *you* need one for?"

"To get into Mexico without papers."

"What is going on, James? You're scaring me."

"I'm sorry, but it's better I don't tell you the specifics. Do you know a good coyote? One who won't rob me blind and leave me for dead?"

"You think because I'm Mexican I know a coyote?"

There was a pause. "Well, yes."

She exhaled. "Well, I don't, … but Cesar does. I'll talk to him."

"Thank you. You've always been a good friend to me. Can I ask you for one more favor?"

"You're lucky I like you."

"You remember the girl I told you about?"

"The one you helped with her GED?"

"Yes, her name's Brittany. She may have to leave here, and she has no family. If that happens, I was wondering if she could stay with you for a month or two until she gets settled? She's really nice and helpful. She won't be a burden."

"That's fine. I just have to ask Cesar, but I doubt he'll care."

"Thank you. Can I call you tomorrow for the information on the coyote?"

"Yes."

"Talk to you then."

James pulled into his driveway and turned off his phone. He entered the cabin, his head dusted with ice pellets. Brittany looked up from her assembly line on the kitchen table.

"You didn't get the copies?" she said with a frown. She wore frilly slippers and sweats.

"I'm sorry," James said as he hung his coat on the rack next to the front door. "I've been racking my brain, trying to figure out how to setup the letter so that it'll cause an uproar. Not just around here but nationally. The problem is, I don't think we have enough on them." He ran his hand through his hair and sat across from her at the kitchen table.

She set down a book of stamps and raised her eyebrows. "We're cuttin' it close on time, don't you think?"

"I know, but I have an idea. I think we should set up the MP3 recorder again at the diner tomorrow. Do you think you can do it one more time?"

She nodded. "I think so."

"Just set it up early and stay away from them."

"I know. You think we'll get somethin' new?"

James grinned. "If we give them something to talk about."

* * *

"You want to take a look before I send them?" James asked. "This one's to Dale."

Brittany set her book facedown on the kitchen table and scooched her chair next to James. She peered into the tiny screen on the burner phone.

Kurt's been a very bad boy—stealing from the family business. He must not have much respect for you or your dad. What's this world coming to? You can't trust anyone, not even family. I suppose the apple doesn't fall very far from the tree. As bad as Kurt's been, you and I both know you've been worse ... much worse. And soon the world will know too.

Hugs and Kisses ☺

Charles Lee Ray aka "Chucky"

Underneath the text were three pictures of Kurt shoving bills from an envelope to the front pocket of his jeans. In the background, vinyl lettering spelled out All-American Auto Parts on the door.

Brittany laughed. "That'll get 'em talkin'. Who's Charles Lee Ray anyway?"

James smiled. "It's from the *Child's Play* movies. You know? Chucky, the homicidal doll?"

"I never saw that one."

"It's actually pretty scary. That doll used to freak me out—I hope they don't actually know someone named Charles Ray."

"I like how you signed it, *hugs and kisses*, with a smiley."

"Do you think they'll appreciate the irony?"

She giggled. "Do you have their cell phone numbers?"

"I pulled them off Harold's cell." James tapped on the burner phone. "This is the other one, to the chief." He put the phone in front of Brittany.

"Fathers shall not be put to death for their sons, nor shall sons be put to death for their fathers; everyone shall be put to death for his own sin." There are plenty of sins hanging around the Strickland family tree—hanging like dirty laundry that needs to be aired. Wait a second. I thought we weren't supposed to air our dirty laundry? Don't worry. You won't have to. I'll do it for you. It won't be long now.

Hugs and Kisses ☺

Charles Lee Ray aka "Chucky"

Underneath the text were pictures of Heather running into Dale's cruiser, her vinyl-sided trailer in the background.

"Are you gonna send 'em now?" Brittany asked.

"I thought about waiting until right before they have their meeting at Dot's, but they might get suspicious. I could do it now, so they're less likely to realize that the diner's unsafe. What do you think?"

"That makes sense. Can they trace the phone? Are you gonna go someplace?"

He nodded. "You read my mind. Thought I'd drive to the river, send the texts, and, as soon as they've gone through, I'll ditch the phone. I'll pick up another burner phone on the way back. In the meantime, we need to get our stuff packed and ready."

\* \* \*

His heart pounded in his chest as he pulled up to Dot's Diner. The lot was deserted except for a couple employee vehicles in back. Brittany pushed through the metal-clad door with a frown. *Shit.* James's heart pounded. She hopped in the truck.

"Are you okay?"

"I got it," she said.

His shoulders slumped in relaxation. "How did it go?"

"They were mad when they came in. Even from across the diner, I could tell."

James nodded.

Brittany continued. "I went in the back and had dinner. Rod let me have a long break again." She frowned. "He made sure I understood that I was off the clock. Like our hourly wage is so awesome. I asked Jessica about the Stricklands. She said they stayed longer than usual, and, at one point, they were arguin'. Jessica told me that she had never seen them like that. Officer Dale didn't even finish his food."

James glanced at her as he backed out of the parking space.

She pursed her lips and gazed out the window.

"What's wrong?" he asked.

"I think Jessica's mad at me," she said to the window.

James drove out of the parking lot. "What happened?"

"Jessica keeps wantin' to hang out, and I keep tellin' her that I'm busy. I told her that I have to study to get into college. I could tell she thinks I'm blowin' her off. I just feel bad. I really like her."

James glanced over again. Brittany had her arms crossed over her chest.

"I know. I'm sorry," he said.

She took a deep breath. "It's not like I can tell her the truth."

"No, you can't. But she'll know soon enough."

They entered the cabin, hung their coats, and rushed to the kitchen table.

"You ready?" James asked.

She nodded. He forwarded through the first few hours of diner noise. The good part started with a banging on the table, what sounded like one hard fist slamming down like a gavel.

"Somebody's gonna fuckin' pay," Officer Dale Strickland said.

"It's sloppiness, pure and simple," the chief said.

"Fuckin' Kurt. I told you that he was a problem."

"No more of a problem than you."

"Me? I never took a dime from you."

"You've been takin' somethin' worse from your brother."

There was silence.

The chief continued, "And what do you think shit like this does to business? You can have any goddamn whore you want, but you gotta fuck your brother's girlfriend."

"Pops, I, uh—"

"Shut your fuckin' mouth. You will stop seein' that little whore immediately, and you will make sure she understands how important it is that she keeps her trap shut. You got me?"

"Yes, sir," Dale said.

"Where you been takin' her?"

"Motel 6 on the interstate."

"You ever take her to the stone hut?"

"Come on, Pops. I know better than that."

"When was the last time you were there?"

"Last week. Everything was where it should be."

"I'm thinkin' we should move the money. This Charles Ray character knows too much."

"Pops, I told you. It's from a movie."

"Goddamn it, I know that. We gotta call him somethin'."

There was silence, followed by Jessica taking their orders. They were curt and short and did not flirt.

"Where's the stone hut?" Brittany asked James, while the Stricklands were still quiet.

James smiled. "I caught Dale there with his brother's girlfriend and have the photographs to prove it."

"Any ideas who it might be?" Dale asked his dad.

"It has to be someone local, someone who knows us well."

"One of our clients?"

"I don't think so," the chief said. "We haven't taken on a new client in years. What would they have to gain anyway? Without us, they'd have to deal with a department that might put 'em out of business."

"You don't think Harold might try somethin' like this?" Dale asked.

"I don't see the motive."

"Maybe for a ransom to stay quiet. Maybe Harold's tired of livin' in a trailer."

"Harold knows he could take a bigger role in the business if he wanted to. He's never given two shits about money."

"Maybe Kurt saw the guy?" Dale said.

James's stomach turned.

The chief grunted. "If he knew he was bein' followed, you think he'd be stealin'. Hell he didn't even try to conceal it. Your brother's dumb, but he ain't *that* dumb."

"You want me to handle Kurt?"

"I don't want you anywhere near your brother until you have some distance from that fuckin' whore. I'll handle it."

The men were silent.

"Here are your drinks," Jessica said as she set the drinks on the table. "Your food will be out shortly."

After Jessica left, Dale said, "I tell you what, whoever it is, is fuckin' *dead* when we find out."

"I keep thinkin' about that nigger doctor," the chief said.

"You think she'd dredge all that up now, after all these years?"

"She was just another broke nigger back then. She can afford a good lawyer on her salary now."

"You think he was innocent?" Dale asked.

"Hell no," the chief replied. "Nigger was guilty as sin. He was escalatin'. Hell, I busted him for vandalism when he was a kid, assault a few years later, and breakin' and enterin' a few years before the first rape and murder. You were just a little shit at the time, so you might not remember, but, when the second woman was killed, people got crazy. We were havin' a tough time denyin' that we had a serial. An eyewitness placed Frank at the scene, and another placed a black man at the first murder but couldn't ID Frank in the lineup. We thought we had the right guy and so did the public."

"What about that murder we had when I was a rookie?"

"What about it? Had nuthin' to do with Frank."

"The MO was the same as Frank's. She was raped, strangled, and the techs found water-based lubricant in her throat."

Brittany gasped, on the verge of tears.

James paused the recorder, his eyes wide. "Harold?"

A few tears slipped down Brittany's face.

"Do you want me to listen to this alone?" James asked.

She wiped her eyes with her sleeve and shook her head. "Keep playin' it. But who's Frank?"

"I'll have to look it up to be sure, but I bet his last name is Wiggins."

"Is he related to Dr. Wiggins?"

"Husband, I think." James pressed Play.

The chief exhaled. "Unfortunately, those things are commonplace for the sick bastards who do this shit."

"She was worked over pretty good. The first thing I thought when I saw her was that there had to be more than one guy."

"There's a big difference between thoughts and evidence. There was no evidence of a second perp."

"What about the murders in Northumberland and Columbia? Again, same MO."

"We were gettin' close. That's prob'ly why he moved on. Still don't have shit to do with Frank."

"Did you guys find any DNA?" Dale asked.

"We found some hairs," the chief said, "but they were too degraded for a DNA profile."

"Nigger hair?"

"We got the right guy."

"You gonna talk to the doctor?"

"I'll have to remind her that she still has a son to keep out of trouble."

"Did you hear that Harold's been sick?" Dale said. "Bill told me that Harold called in sick last week. I can't remember him ever bein' sick."

"Hmm. I'll have to give him a call tomorrow," the chief replied.

Brittany's eyes were like saucers.

"What do you think about the teacher?" Dale said. "He could be behind this."

"I doubt he has the stones for somethin' like this, but it wouldn't be a bad idea to pay him a visit. You could check on Harold while you're out there."

"Shit," James said.

Dale and the chief spent the rest of the conversation discussing the particulars of covering their tracks. They talked about destroying documents and possible places to move the money.

James pressed Stop on the MP3 recorder.

"We are so screwed," Brittany said.

James stood and paced.

"James?"

"Let me think," he said. After a minute of pacing, he stopped and sat at the table across from Brittany. "Here's what we know. They don't know that I sent the texts, but I'm on their radar now. Dale's coming here tomorrow to check on Harold *and* to pay me a visit. He won't find anything at Harold's, but he would probably start a missing person's investigation, and I would be a prime suspect. The other issue is Kurt. He's a moron, but I'm pretty sure he can put two and two together if Wade shows him the pictures I took. He did steal my camera."

"Do you think he's gonna show Kurt the pictures?" Brittany asked.

"I'm not sure. If he does, we better be long gone."

"How much time do you think we have?"

James rubbed his chin. "I have a hunch that he'll give him a chance to confess before revealing the evidence. Could be weeks, could be days. The bottom line is we need to work fast. The more immediate issue is Dale coming here tomorrow."

"Do you think they know about you beating up Harold?"

"I don't think so. They would have mentioned it when they were talking about me. I do think, if an investigation into Harold's disappearance starts, that would be very bad. I imagine they'd be watching us or worse."

"We need to make sure Officer Dale doesn't come here then."

James exhaled. "I don't think we can stop that, but maybe we can stop him from going to Harold's."

"How?"

"Did Harold ever go away? Like on a vacation or a hunting trip?"

"I wish. He barely went anywhere but to the firehouse, the ABC store, and some bar in town. I'm assumin' it was a bar because he came back smellin' like alcohol." She shivered at the thought. "He talked about goin' huntin', but he never did."

"Do you think he went hunting in the past?"

"I think he did a lot when he was younger."

"What about any friends?" James asked.

She tapped her lips with her index finger. "There was this guy when

I first moved in. Harold went to help him move with his pickup. He said his name was Buzz. I only remember that because I loved *Toy Story* when I was little. You know, the Disney movie?"

"Buzz Lightyear."

"Yeah."

"Do you remember where this guy lived?"

She shrugged. "It was up north somewhere."

James opened his laptop and turned it on. Once loaded, he typed *county map of PA* in the search engine. "Any of these counties sound familiar? Carbon, Luzerne, Columbia?"

"Lycoming," she said, pointing at the screen.

James typed *Lycoming PA map* into the search engine. He tilted the screen toward her. "Any of these towns sound familiar?"

Her blue eyes scanned the screen. She frowned. "I don't remember. He may never have said exactly."

"That's okay. I think we have enough to be believable. First we need to get rid of Harold's truck, and then I want to take a closer look at that stone house."

They retrieved the Hyundai from Gil's Storage and drove to Harold's. James pulled off the road, near the single-wide trailer.

"I don't think we'll see anyone at this time of night," James said, "but, if we see headlights, we need to hide behind the car. It would be really bad if anyone sees me in the chemical suit."

She nodded.

They exited the car, and he put on his hooded chemical suit, latex gloves, and booties. James held out his arms as if he were being frisked, and Brittany rolled the lint roller over his gear. He put on his jacket over the chemical suit, and Brittany repeated the process with the lint roller. She "cleaned" his knit hat too, before he put it over the chemical suit hood.

"I think you're good," she said. "I went over the jacket three times at the cabin. The hat, like ten times."

James crept to Harold's trailer, his flashlight cutting a swath through the darkness. He retrieved the truck keys from Harold's bedroom and returned to the driveway. The Ford Ranger was unlocked. James climbed inside, his legs cramped. He adjusted the seat back and started the truck. He pulled out of the driveway and drove down the gravel road. He checked his rearview mirror, but he knew from the headlight glare that she was back there.

James drove the red pickup for ninety minutes, with Brittany following close behind in the Hyundai. Traffic was nonexistent. They drove past Harrisburg International Airport toward the Long Term Parking sign. James motored beyond the entrance to the lot. He parked on the shoulder. Brittany pulled up behind him. He told her to wait, that he'd be right back.

James slipped on sunglasses and turned the truck around. He stopped at the gate and leaned out the window, pressing the button on the machine. He grabbed the ticket that the machine spit out, and the gate arm lifted. He drove into the enormous parking lot. Rows and columns of cars lit by streetlights with signs denoting the section that most travelers would forget.

He thought about how many arguments the lot caused. Couples weary from travel, arguing over who was supposed to keep track of the car. *Lori would write down the section and put it in her purse.*

He parked in the first empty spot he could find. He leaned over the seat, pressed the passenger lock down, and adjusted the driver's seat forward. James opened the driver's side door, pressed the lock down, and threw the keys under the seat. He shut the door and fast-walked toward the lot entrance. He slipped off his booties and carried them with him, once he had made some distance from the truck.

Brittany climbed over the center console into the passenger seat, as James entered the Hyundai. She slept on the way home, while James recalculated variables and scenarios.

He cut the headlights of the Hyundai as he pulled off the asphalt onto the frozen shoulder. Brittany's eyes fluttered.

"Where are we?" she asked.

"The Stricklands' stone house. I'll just be a minute. I want to see what the security's like. Wait here."

James slipped his booties back on and crept up the gravel driveway. No cars, as he suspected. The house was a single story with a rubble foundation, similar to his cabin. The stone walls were thick, well built. *They don't make them like this anymore.* Two small windows in front were covered with burglar bars. *I wonder if those are up to code.* He crept around the house, found an electrical panel and a phone line and a few more small windows—all covered with burglar bars. He peered inside and saw a queen-size bed and a black bearskin throw rug. The stone fireplace had an insert, with a deer head hanging over it. A blinking light came from the corner, halfway up the wall. *Alarm system.* The back door was solid oak, like the front—no windows. He inspected the hinges. *It opens in—good.* He worked his way around to the front. A sticker in one of the front windows read Protected by Spartan Security.

James slipped back into the Hyundai.

"What do you think?" she asked.

"They have thick stone walls, an alarm, burglar bars on the windows, and two solid oak doors."

She frowned.

He grinned. "I have to call Spartan Security."

# Chapter 17

## I Love YouTube

After checking the security on the Stricklands' stone house, James and Brittany stopped by their cabin and grabbed some blankets and pillows. Brittany climbed into the backseat of the Hyundai and lay across the bench seat, wrapping her blanket around her. She was asleep before they reached the highway.

James drove north toward Lycoming County. His eyes were heavy. The dark empty roads were hypnotic. He occasionally slapped himself and cracked open the window, letting the cold air in to revive him. He pulled into the back of a Walmart parking lot. He glanced at the clock on his burner phone—*5:58 a.m.* He cut the engine and set the alarm on his phone for 7:30 a.m. He tilted his seat back and grabbed his blanket.

In the blink of an eye, his phone chimed. His body shot upright. His head pounded; his heart raced. He fumbled with the phone, jabbing buttons until the racket finally stopped. Brittany stirred in the back, her hair a tangled mess.

"What time is it?" she asked, stretching her arms.

"Seven-thirty," he replied, rolling his neck. "Was Harold a morning person?"

"He didn't usually get outta bed until ten, but I think hunters get up really early."

James rubbed the stubble on his chin. "I'll send the text around ten. You want to grab some breakfast? We need to be quick, so I was thinking McDonald's. I have a couple things I need to do before making the call."

They had breakfast on Styrofoam. Afterward they drove to the Lycoming Public Library. The one-story brick building had a pole in front with a limp American flag. They parked and marched to the front door. James pulled on the door, but it was locked. He checked the time on his phone again: *8:03 a.m.*

James frowned. "They're supposed to open at eight."

They peered through the glass door. An elderly woman approached with a fast walk. She unlocked the door and pushed it open.

"I'm sorry," she said. "I don't move as fast as I used to."

James and Brittany entered the library. The woman showed them to the computer room. They sat in the corner and logged onto a chunky desktop computer.

James typed *YouTube* into the search engine. In the YouTube search box he typed *how to break down a door.* They watched several videos showing the weak points of doors and the proper placement of kicks, sledgehammer strikes, and pry bars.

James typed *how to open a safe* into the search bar.

"You think they have a safe?" Brittany asked.

"They said they keep money there. I'm guessing they have it hidden or in a safe."

They watched a video of a stocky man pry open a heavy-duty safe in sixty seconds.

James cleared the cache on the computer just in case the slow-moving woman was suspicious of strangers, then he and Brittany left the library and drove across town to a Home Depot. James purchased a sledgehammer, a mini–pry bar, and a sixty-inch pry bar. They drove out of town, toward the nearest Pennsylvania State Game Lands. They drove on a deserted gravel road, the sun blurred by gray skies. The car slipped as they moved over the slushy surface. They pulled into a driveway of a deserted hunting cabin. James hopped out, holding

Harold's phone in a Ziploc bag with latex gloves. He sent the text message to the chief.

Im up in lyco with buzz. He got a new hunt camp. Found some fun up here thats worth sticking around for. Dont tell bill. He thinks Im sick. Be back next week.

He sent another text to Bill at the firehouse.

I still feel like dog shit. Be back next week.

James suspected that Harold wouldn't be missed. James checked that the ringer on Harold's phone was turned off, returned the cell to the Ziploc bag, and sealed it. He stepped through four inches of wet snow to the woods behind the cabin. James hid the phone behind a tree, under some leaves, and returned to the car.

"Let's go home," he said.

"You think they'll track the phone?" she asked.

"I hope so. It gives legitimacy to the two texts I sent."

* * *

After returning the car to the storage center, James staggered into their cabin, bleary-eyed, Brittany behind him. She shut the door and flipped the dead bolt as he hung his coat. He dropped his keys on the kitchen table and turned around.

"You look tired," she said. "Why don't you take a nap?"

"We have to get ready for Dale," he replied.

James stowed the boxes of envelopes under the bed. Brittany carried the box of latex gloves, the burner phones, and the chemical suit down to the cellar. James adjusted the curtains so the windows were completely covered. Brittany shut the cellar hatch and covered it with the mat.

"As soon as you hear the driveway alarm," he said, "I want you in the cellar. If you hear the cellar hatch open, you know what to do."

She nodded. "Got it. Now go to bed."

"I have to make a call first." James dialed the number he found online.

"Spartan Security, this is Tricia. How can I help you?"

"I was interested in your security service," James said, "but I had a technical question to see if your system would be a good fit for my home."

"I'll have to put you through to Roger," Tricia said. "He deals with the technical stuff."

"That's fine."

"Hold please."

"This is Roger. How can I help you?"

James repeated the sentence he had rehearsed in his mind. "I'm interested in your security service, but I had a technical question to see if your system would be a good fit for my home."

"What's your question?" Roger asked.

"My old house has a phone line that cuts out every now and again. If you guys lose the phone line signal, would that trigger an alarm automatically? That would, of course, amount to a lot of false alarms at my place."

"You don't have to worry about that. We don't call the police for phone signal losses."

*Bingo.*

"Would you like to make an appointment to send a tech out to give you a quote?" Roger asked.

"I'll be traveling the next few weeks. I'll call back."

James crashed on the bottom bunk, falling asleep shortly after his head hit the pillow. He was awakened by the driveway alarm.

"Alert zone one. Alert zone one," the mechanical voice said.

James rolled out of his bunk. The cabin was dim, one floor lamp lit, the afternoon sun waning. He glanced at the hatch to the cellar. The mat was off to the side. He straightened it.

"Alert zone two. Alert zone two."

He turned off the monitoring box. There was an impolite pounding at the front door. He moved to the door, took a deep breath, and opened it.

Officer Dale Strickland stood in his puffy police jacket, with his big beak nosing over the threshold.

"Can I help you?" James said.

"Mr. Fisher, can I come in?" the officer said.

"Not without a warrant." James stepped onto the porch, shutting the door behind him.

The officer glared. "You got somethin' to hide?"

"You guys locked me up for no reason. Hassled me about my property. I have ample reason not to trust you guys."

The officer crossed his arms. "That right?"

James's face felt hot. "Yes, that is right."

"We've had some burglaries in the area."

James's stomach turned. He resisted the urge to break eye contact. He feigned concern. "Anyone hurt?"

"Not yet." The officer glared at James for a few slow seconds. "Have you seen anyone suspicious?"

"I haven't. Sounds pretty serious."

Dale nodded, his jaw set tight. "It certainly is. I can assure you that we'll find him and the justice will be swift and *severe*."

"Well, good luck. I'll call if I see anyone suspicious."

Dale placed his hand on his Glock. "Most people around here invite me in. It's suspicious when they don't."

James nodded, his heart pounding.

"Where's that little girl you got?"

"Out with friends."

"I don't need permission," Dale said, stone-faced.

"Permission for what?"

"To enter your house whenever I damn well please. I can pull probable cause out of my fuckin' ass."

"I don't doubt that," James replied.

The officer scowled. "Move the *fuck* out of my way!"

James stepped aside, and Dale entered the cabin. James followed, leaving the door open. Dale strutted around the cabin. He opened dresser drawers, rifled through them, leaving them open. He looked under the bed and pulled out a box of envelopes. He opened the box and flipped through, looking at the addresses.

He glared at James. "What the fuck you doin' with all these envelopes?"

"The girl got a job working for a junk mail company. She stuffs envelopes."

He chuckled. "Fuckin' junk mail. That shit should be illegal." He dropped the box on the floor and marched into the kitchen. He opened the refrigerator. "No beer?" He smirked at James. "You look like a wine drinker." He went through the kitchen drawers and their contents. He knocked over some spice containers on the counter. He swaggered to the back door and stood on the mat covering the cellar hatch. He inspected the hinges on the door. He turned to James. "What's all this?"

"Brackets to make the door stronger," James replied. "Probably a good idea with all the burglaries we have around here."

The officer stood silent, staring at James.

James stood expressionless, matching his stare.

"All right then," Dale said finally. The officer marched past James to the front door. He turned around at the threshold. "Next time just let me in, and I won't be such a dick."

James shut the door behind Dale and breathed a sigh of relief. James parted the window curtains, watching the cruiser drive away. He walked over to the mat and pulled it aside.

"He's gone," he said. "You can come out."

\* \* \*

James pulled the Hyundai into the gravel driveway of the Stricklands' stone house. He was dressed in his chemical suit, booties, jacket, gloves, and knit cap. He glanced at his burner phone—*3:12 a.m.* James took the duffel bag from the passenger seat and stepped out of the vehicle. He slung the bag over his shoulder and opened a rear door. The sixty-inch pry bar was laid diagonal, barely fitting in the compact car. He grabbed the pry bar in one hand and the sledgehammer in the other. The house was pitch-black, the moonlight guiding his way. His arms felt immediate relief as he placed the heavy tools and bag next to the back door.

He unzipped his duffel bag and pulled out a pair of wire cutters. He snipped the phone line and placed the wire cutters back in the bag. He took a deep breath and shook his arms. Condensation blew from his mouth as he picked up the sledgehammer. He held on to the fiberglass handle and positioned the steel head just beneath the doorknob. He stepped back and tried a few practice swings, using his legs, hips, and back to give the tool the most striking power.

Comfortable that he had found the right technique, he stepped toward the door and took a deep breath. James swung the sledgehammer, connecting just beneath the doorknob. It bucked but held. He swung again and again and again. The door was warped, but still it held. He set down the sledgehammer and shook his arms, his breathing elevated. As he caught his breath, he listened. He heard leaves shuffling and wind whistling. He picked up sledgehammer and swung repeatedly. Finally, the wooden door frame cracked; the door flew open, and the alarm blared.

His heart pounded as he pulled his flashlight from his jacket pocket and hurried inside. He shone his light on the breaker box. James opened it and turned off the main breaker, cutting power to the house. The alarm still screamed. *Shit!* He glanced at the metal alarm box beneath the breaker box. *Battery backup.* It was locked. The earsplitting siren made it difficult to think. He felt queasy. He ran to his bag and grabbed his mini–pry bar and hammer. He returned and shoved the pry bar into the edge by the lock. He hammered the bar into the edge and cranked on the pry bar, bending the thin metal. After a minute of cranking, the box was deformed, the lock impotent. He opened the box and ripped out the batteries, dropping them on the floor. The noise ceased. It was quiet, his heavy breathing now audible. He stepped outside and put his tools back in the bag. He moved to the corner of the house and surveyed the road, listening for signs of life, listening for sirens. Nothing. James went back inside, slinging his duffel bag across his chest.

He started at the fireplace and searched toward the kitchen. He moved methodically, touching and shining his light, looking for crevices, compartments. A cellar hatch was underneath the bearskin rug, similar to the one in his cabin. He opened the hatch and descended the ladder. The cellar was cramped with a dirt floor and stone rubble walls. Rusted metal racks stood with a few hundred old empty mason jars. Empty plastic crates were lined along the wall. One of the crates was turned upside down. Gray metal glistened in the flashlight beam. James picked up the crate to find a small safe underneath.

He went upstairs and exited the open back door. He heard a twig snap. His gaze flicked toward the sound. He peered into the black woods, listening, afraid to shine his flashlight. He stood still and heard nothing. James retrieved the long pry bar and returned to the cellar. He turned the safe faceup and wedged it under a large stone that jutted out from the wall. He used the mini–pry bar and hammer from his bag to get a corner bent just enough for the big pry bar to fit. He cranked on the door for a couple minutes until it opened. *Damn, I love YouTube.* Inside were a few bound stacks of fives, tens, and ones. *This can't be more than a thousand dollars. This has to be a dummy safe.*

James shoved the cash in his bag and climbed the cellar ladder, the pry bar in hand, his duffel bag still slung across his chest. He leaned the pry bar against a recliner in the living room. He continued to search— drawers, cabinets, closets, every nook and cranny. Nothing. *Maybe they've already moved it.* He paced back and forth across the wood floor. He stopped and looked at the painted drywall ceiling. *There has to be an attic.* He shone the flashlight on the ceiling, searching for a hatch. He found it in the kitchen, eight feet above the floor. He pulled the kitchen table under the hatch and stood on top of it. James pushed the hatch up with his arms but didn't have the leverage or the strength to pull himself up. *I should have brought a ladder.* He moved a chair on top of the table.

Standing on the chair, he could stand with his head through the hatch. He shone his flashlight around. Dust motes hung in the air, suspended in the light. Pink fiberglass insulation was rolled between each joist with a hump of fiberglass in the corner. With the extra height the chair provided, James pulled himself into the attic. He walked on the joists toward the hump. James pulled the fiberglass off the hump, revealing another safe the size of an old microwave, this one bolted to two-by-fours that were in turn bolted to the joists. He set his duffel bag next to the safe.

He climbed back into the kitchen and fetched his big pry bar from the living room. James climbed the table and chair and pushed the pry bar into the attic. He pulled himself up again. He cranked on this safe like he did the other one, bending and warping the metal until the door opened. James gasped. It was nearly filled to the brim with stacks of one-hundred-dollar bills. *Jackpot.*

He hurried back to the Hyundai and tossed the sledgehammer in the backseat. He placed the pry bar diagonally to fit. James dumped the contents of his duffel bag, and slammed the door in haste, the thud reverberating through the woods. He heard a low rumble and gravel crunching, then saw headlights and a vehicle rounding the corner. *Shit.* James scurried behind his car, peering out from the back corner. He waited as the rumble grew louder and the lights grew brighter. His stomach turned as he saw a lifted truck cruising down the gravel road. *Kurt.* The truck and its driver were obscured by fog lights perched on the roll bar and the grill. *I need a weapon. The tools!* The big truck rumbled past. It was a beautiful shade of green. James put his hand over his chest, catching his breath.

He rushed to the attic, his duffel bag empty. Full of adrenaline, James opened his bag and stuffed it with stacks of cash. With the safe bare and his bag bulging with Benjamins, he retrieved a solitary hundred-dollar bill, and a Sharpie from his jacket pocket. James wrote *Hugs and Kisses* ☺ on the bill and placed it at the bottom of the empty safe. He had to press down on the money to get the duffel's zipper to shut. He coughed, tiny fiberglass particles irritating his throat and lungs. James slung his bag over his shoulder and climbed down from the attic. He hustled to the Hyundai with a wide grin.

James glanced at his burner phone as he pulled out of the driveway. *3:41 a.m. Not bad for a beginner.*

He returned to his cabin, dimly lit by a single floor lamp. Brittany was curled up on the love seat, distracting herself with a book. The Buck knife sat by her side. She popped up as James entered with a bulging duffel bag slung over his shoulder.

She stood. "How did it go?"

He frowned. "Not great."

Her mouth turned down. "Are you okay?"

He dropped the duffel bag on the kitchen table. She walked over.

"I'm fine," he said. "They don't have much of value there … anymore." He grinned as he unzipped the bag, revealing the endless stacks of C-notes.

She put her hand over her mouth. "Oh, my God. Is that what I think it is?" She picked up a stack and flipped through the bills. "They're all hundreds. How much is here?"

"I don't know. I didn't count it, but I would estimate somewhere between half a million and a million."

"Holy crap." She put the stack of bills back in the bag. "What do we do now?"

"We need to get the hell out of here."

"What about the envelopes?" she asked. "We're not done."

"We'll take them with us. We can mail them from anywhere."

They spent the next several hours covering their tracks and getting ready to leave. James took his burglary tools down to the river and threw them in, while Brittany packed. When he returned, they packed the Hyundai with the envelopes, latex gloves, folding machine, bag of cash, laptop, MP3 recorder, memory cards, USB flash drives, and two small suitcases. Brittany shut the trunk. James stood next to her.

"I think that's it," she said.

The morning sun was peeking over the horizon.

"I have something for you," he said. He pulled out two letters from the inside pocket of his jacket. One was labeled Brittany, the other Yolanda. "If we ever get split up, open the letter with your name on it. It'll explain what to do and where to—"

"James, no." She frowned. "I told you. I'm stayin' with you."

"Brittany, listen to me. This is important. It could be the difference between life and death. If we split up, open the letter with your name on it and take the other one unopened to Yolanda. All the instructions are inside."

She crossed her arms over her chest. "Won't need it."

"Will you just take them please? It'll make me feel better."

She snatched the letters and shoved them in her jacket pocket. "Is that it?" she asked.

"I have one more thing," he said, "but we have to get this car out of here first. I don't like it being here in the light."

She threw up her hands. "Why can't you just get it done now? How long can one thing take?"

He deadpanned, "I have to dig it up."

# Chapter 18

## A Tangled Web

They parked the Hyundai at Gil's Storage and drove back to the cabin in their truck. James checked his unused burner phone—*7:07 a.m.*

James opened the tool locker on his porch and pulled out a shovel. He tightened his work gloves. He heard the throaty roar of a V-8 in the distance. His heart pounded.

"Go to the cellar," he said to Brittany as he threw the shovel back in the locker.

They hurried into the cabin. He locked the front door behind them. She pulled the mat from the hatch and opened it. James tossed his gloves on the kitchen table and fished his car keys from his pocket. He grabbed her hand and put the keys in her grasp.

"If something goes wrong," he said, "you know what to do."

Her blue eyes were glassy. "Let's just run now, together. We can make it."

"We need more of a head start. Besides, it's only one car, no siren. They'd send the cavalry if they knew. Let me take care of this, and we'll get the hell out of here."

She nodded.

The alarm monitor chimed, "Alert zone one. Alert zone one."

"Go," he said.

He shut the hatch and covered it with the mat.

"Alert zone two. Alert zone two."

He knew from the short time span between the alarms that the person had moved from the vehicle quickly. His stomach churned. Someone pounded on the front door. He parted a corner of the curtains. Officer Dale Strickland stood on the stoop in jeans and a heavy coat. James opened the door. Dale marched inside. He had dark circles under his beady eyes. They stood in the middle of the cabin, the front door wide open.

"You don't mind if I come in, do you?" he said.

"Can I help you, Officer?" James asked.

Dale smirked. "I don't know. Can you?"

James shrugged. "Depends on what you need."

"What do I need? What do I need?" Dale said in a singsong voice.

Dale moved into James's personal space and punched him in the stomach. James doubled over, falling to one knee, coughing. Dale pulled his Glock from the holster under his jacket and pressed the barrel to James's forehead. James's eyes were wide, his eyebrows arched.

Dale said, "I need you to tell me if you know my brother, Kurt. If you lie, it'll be the last lie you tell."

*He knows I know him.* "He took one of my classes last summer."

Dale nodded. "What about Heather Davenport?"

"She was in the same class."

"What do you know about them?"

"I think they're dating. He drives a red truck with big tires."

He pressed the square barrel harder into James's forehead. "How the *fuck* do you know that?"

"I see them sometimes in the campus parking lot. The truck's hard to miss."

He pulled the Glock from James's forehead, leaving an impression of the barrel. He narrowed his eyes. "Charles Lee Ray mean anything to you?"

"No," James said with a poker face.

"Did you send me a text message?"

"No."

Dale chuckled. "You know, most times when you jam a gun in a man's face, he cowers and begs. My dad doesn't think you have the stones to fuck with us, but I can see now that you do."

He walloped James across the head with the butt of his gun. James grunted, still on one knee. He held his head, blood pouring from a gash just above his hairline.

"Why did you send those texts?"

"I don't know what you're talking—"

Dale reared back and struck James again, knocking him off his knees and opening another gash on his head. Blood gushed down his face, blurring his vision. Dale cackled. James crawled away, vaguely in the direction of the open door. He felt the cold air on his face. Dale grabbed James's foot and twisted it. James grimaced as Dale pulled him back into the cabin by his twisted ankle.

Dale dropped James's foot.

James turned and looked.

Dale reached behind his back. He exhaled, his breath spraying blood droplets from his mouth and nose. He wobbled and dropped to his knees. He wheezed and sprayed more blood.

Brittany backed away, her hand over her mouth.

Dale collapsed on his side, sucking in air and exhaling blood. James's Buck knife was stuck in his back. James struggled to his feet and wiped the blood from his eyes. He limped over to Dale, pried the Glock from his hand, and set it on the floor out of reach. He hobbled to his dresser and grabbed an old T-shirt. James tied it around his head to stem the tide of blood.

He struggled past Brittany to the kitchen table and grabbed his gloves. He put them on as he limped back to Dale. James clasped his gloved hands around Dale's neck and squeezed. Brittany stood like a statue, her eyes wide, her hand still over her mouth. James held tight until the death throes came. James staggered back, careful not to drip his blood on the body. He removed the T-shirt headband and wiped his face.

He looked at Brittany, his eyes wide, his head still bleeding. "I have to clean this up."

She remained frozen.

"You need to go," he said. "Take the Hyundai and drive south on I-15 for half an hour, then pullover and open the letter I gave you."

She was silent.

He limped closer. "Brittany, get moving. Now."

Her eyes were saucers. "I killed him."

"No, you didn't. *I* did. *I* choked him to death. Do you hear me?"

"You're bleeding," she said.

"Head wounds bleed, *a lot*. They look worse than they are."

"And your leg. You can't clean this up on your own."

"Go. I'll be right behind you."

She shook her head. "I told you. I'm stayin' with you." She went to the sink and opened the cabinets.

"Brittany, this is not the time to be obstinate."

She pulled out the first aid kit, holding it up. "We have to clean you up first, right?"

He exhaled, shaking his head. "First we need a tarp. He's bleeding on the floor."

James told her where to find a fresh tarp. With gloved hands they laid out the tarp next to the body. James pulled the knife from Dale's back and wiped the blood on the man's jacket. James took the knife to the sink. Brittany grabbed the oxidized bleach jug from under the sink and washed the murder weapon. She put it back in its sheath.

"Could you give me that?" James said. "I don't want to forget it."

She handed the knife to him, and he attached it to his belt.

They returned to the body. James took Dale's car keys and cell phone from his pocket, and shoved them in his. The Glock was on the floor a few feet away. They rolled the body on the tarp, stopping when he was facedown. They tucked the tarp around and under his body, like a Dale burrito.

"Could you grab the gorilla tape?" James said. "It's in the bottom drawer, to the left of the sink."

Brittany hustled to the kitchen and picked up a half-used roll of tape.

"Not that one. There should be a brand new roll, covered in plastic."

She looked at James with her brow furrowed.

"No fingerprints," he said.

Brittany retrieved the new roll of tape. James pulled off the plastic wrap, and they taped the tarp tight around Dale's body.

Brittany helped James clean his face and head in the kitchen sink. She disinfected his head wounds and wrapped a bandage around him like a mummy. James placed his knit hat over the bandage.

"I'm actually more worried about my ankle. It's swelling. Feels tight in my boot."

She bit the lower corner of her lip. "Do you think it's broken?"

He winced as he tried to move his ankle. "I think it's a bad sprain." He glanced at the gun on the floor. "Shit, the gun. Could you bring me that handgun? Fingers nowhere near the trigger please."

James washed his blood and fingerprints off the butt of the Glock. He set the handgun on the counter. She stared at the blue tarp.

"I need you to drop me off at Harold's, so I can get rid of the body," he said. "Brittany, did you hear me?"

She turned to James and nodded, her face blank. "You need me to help you with the body?"

"I just need you to help me get it in my truck and into Harold's backyard. I can handle putting it in the cesspool. It'll take a few hours to dig up the manhole cover. I don't want you there."

"I can help. It'll go quicker."

"No. Someone has to drive my truck back here. We can't park at Harold's for hours in broad daylight. It's too risky. I need you to come back here and start the cleanup. There's a lot of blood."

He instructed Brittany on cleaning. He told her to mop the floor with a heavy amount of bleach, letting the sanitizer soak into all the crevices of the wood. He told her to wipe down the furniture and walls as well, because of the blood spray that had come from Dale's mouth.

"Check the cellar ceiling," he said, "and wash it if you see any sign of blood that may have seeped through the floor. You'll have to move furniture to get all the crevices. Also inspect every item in this house. Leave nothing uncleaned. When in doubt, wash it again."

She nodded.

"Let's get this piece of shit out of here."

Outside, Dale's black SUV was parked tight behind James's truck. James turned into the leaves and brush and backed up his truck across the yard, next to the front porch. He dropped the tailgate and limped into his cabin. James put booties over his boots. He gave a pair to Brittany. They were big, but they stayed on. Brittany put her hair up and placed a knit cap over her head. They wore slick puffy coats and gloves. They took turns being frisked by the lint roller.

Dressed for success, they dragged the Dale burrito outside to the truck.

"This'll be the hard part," James said between heavy breaths.

James had the head. Brittany had the legs, but they were having trouble getting the saggy middle high enough to clear the tailgate. They dropped him and stood, condensation spilling from their lips. James shook his arms, trying to recover.

"Let's try something different," James said.

They heaved Dale upright and bent him over the tailgate. They grabbed his legs and shoved him into the truck bed.

"Could you grab some tools from the locker?" James asked. "I need the pickax, a shovel, and the leaf rake."

Brittany hurried to the locker, retrieved the tools, and dumped them in the truck bed. They sped to Harold's with the blue burrito bouncing in the truck's bed. James backed into the driveway.

"I didn't want my tire tracks here," James said, "but it's too far to drag him from the road. And someone might see us."

They dragged Dale around back. Brittany left James with the tools and drove back to their cabin to cleanup.

James surveyed the area, his rake in hand. *I wish I had left that rebar in place.* James raked leaves from the approximate area, finding fresh, loose soil. He hobbled around the cleared area, feeling for a soft spot. His boot sank into the ground. James grabbed his shovel and began to dig. Despite the loose soil, his throbbing ankle slowed the process. *I would have left it open if I knew this was going to happen.* His shovel thudded off the concrete manhole cover. He hopped around on one foot, excavating the soil from the manhole. He estimated that the digging took three times as long as the first time. James reached down and grabbed the handle on the cover. He braced himself with his good leg and heaved. Shooting pain reverberated through his ankle as the cover slid off the hole. The raw sewage smelled like rotten eggs.

He struggled to drag Dale the short distance to the hole, stopping several times for the searing pain in his ankle to subside. James positioned the burrito close to the hole and gave it a few pushes. The tarp-covered body leaned over the edge. He helped it along with another big push, and now Officer Strickland joined his uncle, slipping into the black sludge. A bit of tarp was visible through the manhole. James hobbled to the woods and picked up a sturdy stick. James pushed on the body with the stick, tucking it out of sight. He threw the stick in the cesspool and lugged the cover back over the hole.

He spent the next couple hours backfilling the hole, raking the soil, and replacing the leaves over the site. He glanced up at the sun and checked his burner phone—*12:38 p.m. Shit, it's been almost six hours.* He dialed Brittany's burner phone.

"I was getting worried," she said.

"I'm all done here," he said. "Can you come pick me up?"

James peered out from behind the back corner of Harold's trailer, waiting for Brittany. She pulled into the driveway, stopping near the house. James gimped toward the truck, his tools in hand. He tossed the tools in the truck bed and climbed into the driver's seat. Brittany scooted over. He adjusted the seat and put the truck in Reverse. He heard the rumble of an engine, not his own. It was faint at first. James stopped his truck in Harold's driveway. He glanced at Brittany. Her eyes were wide. She'd heard it too. He watched in his rearview mirror as an old Jeep Cherokee lumbered past.

"Do you think they saw us?" she asked.

He backed out of the driveway. "Unless they know Harold, it's probably fine."

He limped into their cabin behind Brittany. His eyes burned from the bleach fumes. The entire place was wet and shiny.

She turned to James. "I still have to check the cellar."

They climbed down into the cellar. James pulled the string on the lightbulb. The bulb cast a dim glow. They scanned the ceiling with flashlights, looking for blood. Blood dripped between the floorboards on to the cardboard boxes of freeze-dried food.

"Shit," James said. "We have to clean the ceiling, and we have to use heavy bleach on this cardboard."

They spent the next two hours cleaning the cellar. James struggled up the ladder after Brittany.

"I think everything's clean," she said.

James checked the time on his phone—*2:14 p.m.*

"Let's get Dale's truck out of here," he said. "Follow me in the Ford but don't follow close."

"You don't wanna get the Hyundai?" she asked.

"I do, but Dale's supposed to be at work at four, and we're running out of time. Just keep your distance. I'll drive slow to make sure I don't lose you."

James drove the black SUV wearing his jacket and hat over his chemical suit. Brittany followed in the Ford. They drove to the next town over. James parked the GMC Yukon in a rundown residential area, leaving the doors unlocked and the keys in the ignition. Brittany waited a block behind. He hobbled back to the Ford pickup, and they drove toward the river. James parked his truck on the shoulder, the river just beyond an edge of trees. James gave her Dale's cell phone. Brittany hiked through the trees, looked around, and chucked the phone into the water. James and Brittany drove on toward the cabin and storage place. He turned down the gravel road toward their cabin.

"We're not going to the storage place?" Brittany asked, her eyes bulging.

"I still have to dig up something," James said.

"James, come on. I have a bad feeling. We have to go."

"I'm not going to leave it now after everything. I'll be quick."

He heard it before he saw anything. He looked in the rearview mirror—nothing. He glanced at Brittany. She bit her lower lip. *She had heard it too.* It was getting louder. He turned around and caught a glimpse of red and blue lights. He mashed on the accelerator, the V-8 roaring to life, the truck's back end fishtailing on the gravel. The sirens were getting louder. He saw her out of the corner of his eye. She gripped the armrest, her knuckles white, as the speedometer hit ninety. He slowed as he approached his cabin. James swung the truck into the driveway and drove over the garden, parking directly in front of the porch. Brittany hopped out, her door facing the cabin. She waited at the front door, bouncing on the balls of her feet as James hobbled around the truck. She turned around, facing the house, too afraid to look at the onslaught coming. James hopped up the steps on one leg, holding his keys, as a caravan of four cruisers and an SUV turned into the driveway.

"Barricade and evade," James said, his hands shaking as he slid the key into the dead bolt.

Brittany nodded.

He opened the door, letting her in first.

"Stop right there" James heard from the driveway.

He entered the cabin, not bothering to see if a gun was pointed at him.

The monitoring box chimed and said, "Alert zone one. Alert zone one. Alert zone one. Alert zone one ..."

He slammed the door and locked the reinforced dead bolt. Brittany moved the mat and opened the cellar hatch. James struggled down the ladder, hopping down with one foot, his arms controlling his descent.

Brittany positioned the mat over the open hatch and closed it as she climbed down the ladder, hopefully with the mat still in position over the hatch.

The monitoring box was going crazy. "Alert zone two. Alert zone two. Alert zone two. Alert zone two …"

"Shit!" James said, limping toward the ladder.

"What?" Brittany asked.

"The gun's in the kitchen."

Brittany turned and sprinted for the ladder.

"No!" James said as she blew past him.

She scaled the ladder and pushed open the hatch. He heard pounding on the front door and a constant invader alert from the monitoring device. A hard bang on the door shook the cabin. The door held. Brittany scurried down the ladder, shutting the hatch over her head, the Glock in hand. She handed it to James. He put the handgun in his jacket pocket and zipped it up. The house shook again, the doorjamb armor giving them extra time.

A two-by-two piece of plywood hung from hinges at the top of the back cellar wall. It opened outward. Brittany lugged a forty-pound bucket of rice and positioned it on the floor under the hinged plywood. James opened the tiny door. Brittany stepped on the bucket and climbed into a twenty-four-inch-diameter tunnel made of black corrugated pipe.

The house shook again, this time followed by a crunching sound, deep voices, and a dog barking. *They're in.* James stood on the bucket with his good leg and squeezed into the pipe headfirst, letting the plywood door shut behind him. He was prone, his elbows jammed against the pipe walls. He felt like he was in a coffin. He looked ahead, with his eyes wide open, but there was only darkness. Brittany was gone, her tiny body fitting with ease.

James struggled; he felt claustrophobic. The voices grew louder.

*They found the cellar hatch.* James closed his eyes and thought of the woods. He thought of the places they'd hiked. He pulled himself forward, with no reference to the distance he was traveling. The voices grew quieter. He was making progress. He heard her groaning ahead.

"It's stuck," she said, groaning again. "I can't get it open."

He was close now. He touched her foot, but he couldn't see anything but black.

"There's a few inches of soil on top," he said. "Squat underneath it and push up, using your legs for power."

"I'm tryin'. I'm not tall enough."

"Can you turn around?"

"I think so."

"Climb over me, and I'll try."

She wiggled her body over his, barely squeezing past. James inched forward, reaching the end of the pipe. He pushed himself up on his knees, the drain pipe elbow allowing vertical space. He stood, hunched, on one foot, his knees bent toward the open pipe. James put his hands on the hatch above him. He heaved, grunting. The hatch pushed open, and light filled the tunnel. He stood, his head peeking out of the ground. He was behind a brush pile. James couldn't see the cabin through the pile, but he knew he was only eighty feet from the back door.

"They went through here," a man said, his voice reverberating through the tunnel.

James climbed out and helped Brittany from the pipe.

"We need to hurry," he said.

James leaned on Brittany as he hobbled along the trail. Rocks and tree roots made the hike especially difficult and painful. The police dog barked in the distance. James's ankle was getting worse. His boot was tight from the swelling. Any weight on his bad foot sent shards of pain through his body. They soldiered on. The dog barked again; Brittany flinched. It was closer, much closer. James grabbed his keys from his pocket.

"Meet me at the car," he said.

"We're almost there," she said.

He slammed the keys in her hand. "Wait ten minutes. If you don't see me, go."

"No, I'm not leavin' you."

James pushed her, a lump in his throat. "Go, you stupid fucking bitch."

She looked at him with glassy eyes for a moment, the keys in her hand. She ran, disappearing down the trail in the blink of an eye.

The barking grew closer. He took off his jacket and turned around. *Here it comes.*

# Chapter 19

## Melty Chocolate Chips

Brittany sprinted through the woods like an experienced trail runner. She reached the fork at the end of the trail. She followed the trail downhill to the small empty gravel parking area. Brittany looked left and right and ran across the street to Gil's Storage. She ran through the open gate to the Hyundai. She unlocked the door and sat in the driver's seat. Brittany put the key in the ignition and started the car. She looked at the clock on the radio—*3:36 p.m.* She climbed over the hand brake and automatic shifter to the passenger seat. *He'll be here.*

She glanced at the clock—*3:42 p.m. Come on, come on, come on.* She tapped her foot on the floor mat and watched the cracked asphalt lane in front of her. *Any second he'll be here. Come on, James.* She glanced down at the clock—*3:44 p.m. Eight minutes. Come on, James. Don't do this to me.* She watched the asphalt lane, biting her lower lip. Her eyes flicked to the clock—*3:46 p.m. Ten minutes. Come on, James. Hurry up. I'm not leaving you.* She jumped at the gunshot in the distance. The clock read *3:49 p.m.* Tears welled in her eyes as she climbed into the driver's seat. She sped out of the storage lot.

Brittany drove south on US 15 for half an hour. She peeked at the gas gauge—three-quarters of a tank. She heard his voice in her head. *This is enough gas to get down there. We'll stay in the right lane and drive slow but not too slow.* She saw signs for a Subway. She pulled off the exit and followed the signs for the restaurant. A Sheetz gas station was across the street. The Subway was next to a grocery store. She parked away from the restaurant, in an empty part of the lot. She pulled the two envelopes from her jacket pocket. Brittany put the one for Yolanda back in her pocket and opened the letter for her. It contained two pages; one was a double-sided printout from Google Maps. The other was handwritten in James's neat cursive.

Brittany,

If you're reading this, something went wrong. But something also went very right, because you <u>are</u> reading this. First, know that if we're separated, I will do everything in my power to find you, but, if it is too dangerous for either of us, I will stay away. Under no circumstances do I want you to seek me out. You need to distance yourself from me and absolutely do not go back to that town. Further, do not contact Jessica or Denise. I know they're your friends, but it is best that they do not know where you are. It is possible that the police will question them.

You're the strongest person I know and the most important person in the world to me. I know you're probably scared right now. That's a perfectly normal reaction. If you follow my directions listed below, everything will be fine. Just follow the directions, like a recipe for freedom and happiness. It'll work out. I promise.

1. Take a deep breath. You did it!

2. Follow the Google Maps directions I printed for you. They will take you to Yolanda's house. There's likely to be lots of traffic. Don't freak out. The driving rules are the same. Just be extra careful when changing lanes.

3. When you get to Yolanda's house, park in a spot clearly marked Visitor. People in northern Virginia can be really snooty about their parking spaces.

4. Ring the doorbell. If it's after five, she'll be home. She knows who you are and that you might show up on her doorstep. After you introduce yourself, ask her if you could talk to her in private. It's best if as few people know as possible. In private, give her the letter addressed to her.

5. Let Yolanda help you. She's my second-favorite person in the world.

6. Destroy this letter. Yolanda has a shredder.

Love—Your Best Friend,
James

Brittany burst into tears, her chest convulsing in sobs. She leaned her head on the steering wheel and cried. It all poured out—the stress; the trauma; her mother; her mother's boyfriend; Harold and the chief touching her, taking her, choking her; wanting to curl up in a ball and die; the knife in Dale's back; James. *The man who gave me everything without asking for anything in return.*

She sniffled and pulled a tissue from the glove box. She wiped her face and went into the Subway. She ordered a turkey sub, recreating the one he had ordered for her, the one that was better than what she would have picked for herself. She bought two chocolate chip cookies. She smiled to herself, thinking of what he had said. *I don't know how they get the chips to stay melty.* She ate by the window, keeping an eye on the car, not that would-be-burglars would think a three-thousand-dollar Hyundai would be carrying close to a million dollars in cash. After a long overdue meal, she was back in the car. She went through the Google Maps directions, making sure she understood them.

She took a deep breath and headed for the highway. Brittany drove south, the traffic getting a little bit heavier with each passing mile. There was gridlock near Dulles. She tried to relax and listen to the radio. Brittany enjoyed the variety of music. She eventually arrived at Crescent Cove in Woodbridge, Virginia. She searched for a few minutes, finding an empty spot marked Visitor. The town house community was jam-packed with cars. The parking lot was well-lit.

She fixed her hair in the rearview mirror, brushing it with her fingers and tucking it behind her ears. She frowned at her reflection. Her eyes were red and puffy with dark circles. She stepped from the Hyundai, locked the door, and marched up to house number 8817. It was a vinyl-sided middle unit townhome with a red door and a mat that read *Bienvenido.*

She rang the doorbell.

A boy yelled, "Door! … Mom, door!"

A female said, "Are your legs broke? *Ay dios mio.*"

The door opened. A brown-skinned preteen boy with big dark eyes answered with a bright smile.

"Hi," he said with a wave.

"I was lookin' for Yolanda."

The boy turned and yelled down the hall. "Mom, it's for you!"

He was replaced at the door by a heavyset Latino woman in scrubs. She had dark curly hair, round cheeks, and a wide nose. She looked down at Brittany; her eyes narrowed. "Hello," she said. "May I help you?"

"I'm a friend of James. He told me to come here and talk to you."

She smiled. "You wouldn't happen to be Brittany, would you?"

Brittany nodded. "I am."

"Why don't you come inside?" Yolanda said, stepping back from the door.

"Can we talk in private?"

Yolanda led Brittany into a tiny cluttered office, with a desktop computer and an enormous monitor.

Yolanda shut the door and offered Brittany a seat. She sat in the wooden chair, Yolanda in the computer chair. Brittany pulled the letter for Yolanda from her jacket pocket and handed it to the woman.

Yolanda furrowed her brow and opened the letter. She pulled out three handwritten double-sided pages in James's neat cursive.

"This might take me a while to read this," Yolanda said.

"That's okay," Brittany replied.

Brittany took off her coat and hung it on her chair. She watched the woman read James's letter, alternately angry and sad, shaking her head, her jaw tight, gasping, and dabbing the corners of her eyes with the side of her fist. Then her eyes were as big as quarters. At the end she stood and stepped to Brittany. She bent forward and gathered her in her arms. Brittany laid her head on her chest.

Yolanda let go and said, "Everything'll be fine, honey. Don't you worry."

"What now?"

"First things first. James brought you down here after your shift on Monday. Do you understand?"

She nodded.

"And you are not to talk to anyone without me and a lawyer present. Do you understand?"

She nodded.

"Let's get you moved in then," Yolanda said. "You can have Marco's room for the time being. He can sleep on the couch in the basement. He usually ends up there anyway. My husband can help you with your things. Make sure you bring that bag inside."

Brittany furrowed her brow.

Yolanda winked. "You know the one I'm talking about. Just put it in Marco's room for tonight. I'm taking off tomorrow so we can take a trip to Ashburn. In James's letter, it said that you should store the money at the Commonwealth Vault & Safe Deposit Company."

"Is that a bank?"

"I'm not sure, honey, but, knowing James, I bet it's not." Yolanda opened the door and called out to the living room where the television flickered. "Cesar, I need your help."

A middle-aged Latino man with a weathered face and thick fore-arms stomped down the hall in construction boots.

Yolanda frowned at the man. "What did I tell you about your boots in the house?"

He smiled, exposing two gold teeth. "I was inside today."

"This is Brittany." Yolanda motioned to the tiny white girl in their office. "She's the friend of James's who needs a place to stay for a while."

"It's nice to meet you," Cesar said to Brittany with a thick hand held out.

Brittany held out her tiny hand. Cesar shook it gently with a smile. Brittany smiled in return.

"Let's get your things," Cesar said.

Cesar and Brittany carried her stuff in from the Hyundai. She held tight to the duffel bag. Marco had already taken the clothes he needed for the next few days. Cesar left her alone in Marco's room with her belongings. She shut the door and shoved the duffel bag under the bed. The bunk beds reminded her of the cabin. Marco had a small desk and posters of soccer players. Her boxes of envelopes were stacked in the corner, stamped and addressed, awaiting the letters. She opened James's suitcase, stared at his neatly folded clothes, and cried. She heard a soft knock at the door. She sniffled, wiped her tears on her sleeve, and opened the door. Yolanda stood with a folded towel, a washcloth, soap, and a travel-size shampoo bottle.

"I brought you some shower things," Yolanda said, handing the toiletries to Brittany. "You can use the shower across the hall whenever you're ready."

"Thank you," Brittany said, her eyes wet. She placed the toiletries on the desk near the door.

"What's wrong, honey?" Yolanda stepped into the room.

"I left him."

Yolanda frowned. "I'm sure you did what you had to do."

Tears spilled over Brittany's eyelids. "He was hurt. He couldn't run. He told me to wait ten minutes, but he never came, and there was a gunshot. He's gone. I know it." She sobbed.

Yolanda stepped forward and hugged her tiny houseguest. "Honey, you don't know that."

Brittany let go.

"Can I tell you something about James?" Yolanda asked.

Brittany nodded.

"He's a very smart man." Yolanda smiled. "Something tells me that you already know that. So if anyone could have figured a way out, he would have. Don't count him out, okay?"

"Okay."

"Cesar and I have to take a trip to Pennsylvania tonight to return that car of yours."

"Are you going to the airport parking lot?"

Yolanda shook her head with a smirk. "I don't even want to know why you would think that. He gave me the address of the person he bought the car from. It just says we're supposed to drop it off with the note he prepared and to not let the previous owner see us."

"What does it say—the note?"

Yolanda chuckled. "It says something about his daughter using the car to go out and party and buy drugs, so he took it away. It says that he's sorry for the inconvenience, and he doesn't want a refund. It also says that he was too embarrassed to drop the car off face-to-face." Yolanda took a deep breath. "Will you be okay by yourself for a while?"

"I think so."

"You can help yourself in the kitchen if you get hungry. I'll see you in the morning." Yolanda turned to walk away.

"Yolanda?"

She turned back around.

"Thank you ... for everything."

# Chapter 20

## Take a Bite out of Crime

*Here it comes.*

His heart pounded; his breath was heavy. James tied his thick winter coat around his shin on his bad leg. He pulled the knife from his belt. He stood on his good leg, bending into an athletic stance, bracing for impact. James pressed his bad leg out in front, like a lamb to the slaughter. He held the knife in both hands, the blade facing down. He heard the rustling of the leaves, then he saw it—the German shepherd with its teeth bared, racing toward him. In the blink of an eye the dog clamped on his leg, sinking its teeth into his jacket, and shaking loose some white feathery goose down. James rammed the knife into the back of the dog's neck. There was a yelp and a whimper as the dog let go of the jacket. James held on to the knife as the police dog lay on the ground, whining.

He placed the bloody knife back in the sheath and hobbled down the trail. He struggled forward, each step taking away his breath, powered by pure adrenaline. James heard men behind him on the windy path. He pushed forward, the voices getting louder. He saw the fork at the end. A single shot fired in the distance that made him flinch. He continued downhill toward the small gravel parking lot. Through the trees, he saw the Hyundai motor past. He waved his arms and hurried into the street, but she was gone. He hobbled across the street, not bothering to look for oncoming traffic. James burst into the office at Gil's Storage, his jacket still attached to his leg, bleeding goose down. The old man sat behind his desk, glaring at James.

"I need to go to the hospital," James said. "Can you take me? I can pay."

The man stood in the cold office, wearing his parka and gloves. He grabbed his keys. "Let's go then."

James hobbled out the door. The old man locked the office and helped James into his rusted Chevy pickup. The man cranked the ignition and tore out of the gravel lot. They turned left, toward town, toward the hospital. James bent forward as he saw men in uniform between the trees, coming down the trail. He glanced in the side-view mirror. He saw them run across the street with guns drawn.

The old man's face was weathered with white stubble. He glanced at James and back to the road. "What happened to you?"

"Hiking accident. I hurt my ankle," James said. "I think it might be broken."

The old man chuckled. "Prob'ly a sprain. You wouldn't be able to walk at all if it were broke. You do look like death warmed over."

"It's been a rough day."

"How's that parkin' spot workin' out?"

"I won't be needing it anymore."

They made small talk about the weather, business, and the Steelers. The old man stopped his truck short of the emergency room entrance, an ambulance offloading precious cargo.

"I'll get out here," James said, opening the door.

Once standing on his good foot, he reached in the back pocket of his canvas pants and pulled out his wallet.

"Don't even think about it, young man," he said.

James pushed his wallet back in his pocket. "Thank you. I just realized that I don't know your name."

"Name's Gil," he said.

"Makes sense. Thank you, Gil."

"You need help gettin' in there?"

"No. Thank you."

The old man nodded and drove toward the exit.

James gimped toward the parking lot labeled Employee Parking. He found a concealed place between a six-foot-tall holly hedge and a couple of SUVs. He removed his shredded jacket from his calf and stuck his hands inside the tears, rearranging what was left of the goose down. James put on the jacket, pulled his wallet and burner phone from his pocket, and sat on the curb. He removed a white business card from his wallet that read Cynthia Wiggins, MD. He dialed her cell phone number.

"This is Dr. Wiggins," she said.

"This is James Fisher. I'm not sure if you remember me. I brought my friend in who was attacked."

"Yes, of course I remember. How's she doing?"

"She's fine, but I need your help."

"Mr. Fisher, is it an emergency?"

"Yes."

"Then hang up and dial 9-1-1."

"Not that kind of emergency." James took a deep breath. "I believe Frank Wiggins is innocent, and I have information that might get him a new trial."

The line went silent.

"Dr. Wiggins?"

She exhaled. "You think I don't know my husband's innocent? I've been down this road, had my hopes up and my heart broken too many times. Frank, bless his heart, is where he is, and that's where he'll be until the day he dies."

"All I'm asking is that you hear me out. If you don't like what I have to say, I'll walk away."

The line was silent.

"Dr. Wiggins?"

"Where are you?"

"I'm in the employee parking lot of the hospital."

"I get off at five," she said. "I'll meet you by my car then. It's an old Mercedes. It's in the back of the lot."

"I'll be there."

She hung up.

James checked the time on his burner phone—*4:23 p.m.* He staggered behind the bushes. His bladder ached as he peed. He hobbled along the cars at the back of the lot, keeping his eyes and ears open for sirens, lights, and police cruisers. He groaned and sat down with his injured leg straight out in front of him. James sat on the curb between the old Mercedes and a Cadillac Escalade. Periodically he heard sirens and saw flashing lights zoom past the main road adjacent to the hospital. A couple cruisers pulled into the emergency room parking lot with flashing lights. His mouth was dry, his stomach hollow. His heart raced, and his head pounded from lack of sleep. He closed his eyes.

"Mr. Fisher," a female said.

His eyes fluttered and opened. Dr. Wiggins stared down at him with a frown. She wore a pencil skirt, flats, and a gray pea coat.

"What happened to you?" she asked. "You look dreadful."

"Hiking accident," he said with a groan as he stood with his good leg.

She shook her head. "I don't think I want to be a part of whatever it is you're selling." She marched around the car to the driver's side.

"Please, Dr. Wiggins. I need your help. Please."

She ignored him, opened the driver's side door, and sat down, her eyes forward. She cranked the engine.

He felt for the Glock in his pocket. "The Stricklands have been harassing Leon," James said loud enough for Dr. Wiggins to hear through the car window.

She turned toward James, her eyes wide.

"He didn't tell you, did he? Did Wade Strickland threaten you?"

She powered the passenger window down. "How did you know that?"

"I've been taping them."

She exhaled and unlocked the passenger door. "Get in."

James removed his hand from the butt of the Glock and entered the Mercedes. He powered the window up.

"Do you have a computer at your house?" he asked.

"We can go to the library."

James looked at her, his eyes bloodshot, his face pale. "Please. I can't show you what I have in a public place. It's not safe. I need your help."

"I can't have you in my home."

"One hour, Dr. Wiggins. Just listen to me for one hour. If you don't want to help me, I'll walk away."

She pursed her lips. "One hour," she said.

Dr. Wiggins pulled out of the parking lot. He dipped down in his seat as she passed the police cars near the emergency room. They drove through town in silence, James sitting low. Dr. Wiggins turned into an upper-middle-class neighborhood of homes made from vinyl and particleboard. She stopped the Mercedes in the driveway of a two-story colonial. She hit the garage door opener on the visor and pulled the Mercedes inside. James staggered behind her through the garage door into the kitchen. She turned on the lights and dumped her purse on the center island. Dr. Wiggins walked out of the kitchen toward the front door.

"Where are you going?" James asked, struggling to keep up.

"You said you needed a computer," she responded without looking back.

She made a right turn near the front door into an office with a laptop computer. She flipped it open, turned it on, and sat in the desk chair. James stood next to her, on one leg.

"Pull up a chair," she said. "You don't look too comfortable."

He dragged a wooden chair from the corner. He winced as he sat next to her.

"Let's hear it," she said with an edge in her voice.

"My friend Brittany was raped by Harold and Wade Strickland."

She put her hand over her mouth. "That's why she wouldn't talk about it."

He nodded.

She narrowed her eyes at James. "How did you become involved?"

"Brittany was living with Harold. I live two miles away on the same road. I saw Harold yelling at her, and it appeared he was hitting her."

"Appeared?"

"I couldn't see everything from the road."

She nodded.

"My cabin's just off a trail that she hiked. She was watching me garden."

Dr. Wiggins frowned. "She was watching you?"

"Yes. The houses are far apart, and a lot of people use the cabins as hunting camps, so very few people are around. I think she was desperate to talk to someone. I caught her watching me, and I talked to her. She helped me with my garden and showed me how to forage in the woods. We became friends."

She pursed her lips. "Just friends?"

James was stone-faced. "There was never anything physical between us."

"How did she come under your care?"

"I suspected she was being abused. She'd always have some bruise she couldn't explain, and she covered her neck with a scarf. One day we had plans to meet halfway between my cabin and Harold's trailer to pick persimmons. On that day, I walked toward Harold's, but I never saw her on the path. I ended up walking all the way to Harold's trailer. That's when I figured out why she didn't meet me. I heard shouting and glass breaking. I ran to the door and knocked. Harold answered and threatened me. Brittany's face was beaten. She had a black eye and a bloody lip. I asked her to come with me, and she did."

"What about her family?"

"That was my first question for her. I thought I could just drive her home. She was a runaway. And for good reason. Going home wasn't an option."

"How does this have anything to do with Frank?"

"I'm getting there."

She nodded.

"Brittany was doing really well. She passed her GED. She got a job. She was in therapy at the campus. We went out to celebrate, and, on the way home, I was pulled over. I was arrested for drunk driving."

Dr. Wiggins scowled. "How much did you have to drink?"

"I had one glass of wine. They put me in the township jail for the night and released me in the morning. They dropped the charges. When I returned to my cabin"—he swallowed—"that's when I brought her to the hospital."

"I'm sorry," she said. "Where is she now?"

"Someplace safe." He took a deep breath. "I wanted justice for her, and I knew it wouldn't come from the police. Chief Strickland and his son Officer Dale Strickland would meet every Monday night at Dot's Diner in the same booth. I taped a few of their conversations."

Her eyes were wide.

"They talked about Frank. They talked about something that your lawyer could use to get him a new trial. Based on what they did to Brittany, and what I heard on the tapes, I think Frank is in prison for crimes committed by Wade and Harold."

"Do you have the audio?"

James pulled the USB flash drive from his wallet. "Can I get in there?" he asked motioning toward the computer.

They switched seats, and James played the conversation. Dr. Wiggins leaned in, listening. She asked James to pause and rewind the recording at certain points. She took notes on a yellow pad. At the conclusion of the recording, he turned to the doctor. Her eyes were glassy.

"Are you okay?" he asked.

She shook her head. "You know, a tiny piece of me always had my doubts. In the back of my mind I thought, maybe he did do it. They had an eyewitness who placed him at the scene. Frank had had a few brushes with the law when he was younger. Eleven years he's been in prison." She wiped her eyes.

"Unfortunately you can't use the recording. It's illegal to record someone without their knowledge. That doesn't mean your lawyer can't look into those murders that happened while Frank was in prison. He should reopen the evidence. I don't know how that works, but I have a feeling they tampered with it. Frank could get a new trial."

She exhaled. "It's a long road—the legal system. May I have a copy of that?"

"On one condition," James replied.

She scowled. "Nothing's free in this world."

"I need a place to hide out for a few weeks. The Stricklands know I've been snooping around. They're looking for me now."

"So you're asking me to harbor a fugitive?"

"If we get caught, I'll tell them that I broke in and threatened to kill you if you didn't help me."

"I'm not sure I even need the recording. I wrote down the details that my lawyer would need."

"That's true," he said, "but, if you help me, I can guarantee that the Stricklands are going down for good. Do you want to live in a town where Leon's harassed by the cops, the same cops that put away your husband for life?"

She pursed her lips. "There's something you're not telling me. If you expect me to help you, I have to know the whole truth."

James took off his knit cap, revealing bloodstained bandages wrapped around his head. Her mouth was open.

"Dale Strickland figured out it was me," James said. "He beat me with the butt of his gun. He would have killed me, but … I can't tell you what happened. It's best you don't know. All I can say is I did what I had to out of self-defense."

She exhaled and closed her eyes for a moment. She looked at James's ashen face. "I can't believe I'm doing this."

"You're literally saving my life."

"I'll have Leon stay with his grandparents while you're here. I think it's best that nobody knows."

Dr. Wiggins gave James a large bottle of water and took him upstairs to the guest bathroom. James sucked down the water. The guest bath had a toilet, sink, and a shower with a tub. He sat on the toilet as she cleaned his head wounds, added a few stitches, and applied fresh bandages. She rolled up his pant legs. He grimaced as she pulled the boot and sock off his hurt foot. She examined the ankle. His foot and ankle were swollen and puffy. He winced as she manipulated it.

"Good news is, I don't think it's broken," she said. "Bad news is, you should stay off your feet for a week or so. I'll bring some crutches home tomorrow."

She grabbed a fresh bar of soap from under the sink and some shampoo. She put the toiletries in the shower and hung a fresh towel and washcloth on the rack.

"You can wear some of Frank's clothes," she said. "You're a little thinner than him, but you two are about the same height."

James looked up at the doctor. "After everything they did, why did you stay?"

She sighed. "Frank's parents, I guess. I don't have a relationship with mine. His folks became my surrogates. We talked about moving. The Wiggins name was pretty well destroyed around here. Frank's dad wouldn't have it. He said we weren't going to hang our heads in shame and let them banish us. He said we would stay and fight for ourselves and for Frank." She half smiled, her eyes dead. "That was ten years ago, and people around here have pretty much moved on … except for us."

# Chapter 21

## Time to Go

James buttoned Frank's flannel shirt. He parted the blinds in the guest bedroom. The late-afternoon sun warmed his face. He saw the Mercedes pull into the garage. James bounded down the steps to the kitchen. Dr. Cynthia Wiggins entered from the garage.

"How was your day?" James asked.

She sighed and put her purse on the center island. "Not too bad," she said. "What did you want to do for dinner?"

"I was going to cook burgers and mushrooms with parmesan asparagus, if that's okay with you."

"Sounds great." She sighed. "Are you sure you won't stay? It's been nice having a live-in maid and cook."

"It has been nice." James smiled. "Leon must be bugging you to come home."

"Not a peep out of him. His grandparents treat him like royalty."

They sat at the kitchen table, eating dinner with the shades drawn.

"Have you decided where you'll go?" she asked.

"Yes, but …"

"I know you can't tell me. I don't know why I keep asking. I guess I want to be able to picture you somewhere." She half smiled. "I meant what I said earlier. I've enjoyed your company."

"The past few weeks … what you've done for me … what you've

risked for me ..." James paused, his eyes on her. "Thank you."

\* \* \*

James drove Cynthia's Mercedes to the small gravel lot across the street from Gil's Storage. He wore gloves, a dark jacket, and a knit hat. He pulled a shovel from the trunk. James hiked up the trail to the fork. He followed the path toward his cabin, the moonlight providing just enough light to stay on course. He felt for the flashlight in his pocket. *Only if I really need it.*

He slowed down and listened as he neared the cabin. All was silent. He crept behind the brush pile. Police tape marked the exit of the escape tunnel. He sneaked to the back of the cabin. Police tape covered the back door. It was dark inside. He tiptoed to the front. More police tape was strung across the cabin driveway like the finish to a track event. He surveyed his surroundings, listening—nothing.

He walked to the middle of his garden, the shovel in hand. The pinkish-white quartz rock glowed in the moonlight. He set down the shovel and flipped over the rock, moving it aside. The leaves rustled behind him. He whirled around, listening—still nothing. James started digging. He moved the loose soil quickly, until he hit something solid. He dug around the oblong-shaped object, a twenty-four-inch section of PVC pipe capped at both ends.

He heaved the pipe out of the hole. He knew the contents weighed exactly forty pounds. James backfilled the hole and reset the rock. He groaned as he placed the pipe on his shoulder. He stepped on the shovel, so the handle popped up within reaching distance. James grabbed hold of the shovel and hiked back to the trail. He put the shovel and the pipe in the trunk of the Mercedes and headed back toward Cynthia's. He drove on a lonely two-lane road with fallow fields and leafless trees as scenery. Closer to town, he approached an intersection, with a cruiser parked on the grassy median. He held his breath as he approached. He laughed. The police car was empty, sitting there as a passive deterrent to would-be speeders.

\* \* \*

The late-morning sun warmed the interior of the Mercedes. James glanced over at Cynthia. She drove like she practiced medicine— precise, nothing left to chance. Her hands were at ten and two. She looked off in the distance, scanning for hazards, the car straight and true. They took the Hanover exit off US 15. James navigated the doctor to a strip mall. She parked in front of a coin shop.

She turned to James, her coffee-colored skin shining in the sun. "I'm just supposed to leave you here?"

James nodded. "I can't ever repay you for what you've done for me. Thank you, Cynthia."

She smiled. "Will I receive one of your letters?"

"Everyone in the township will."

He opened the passenger door of the Mercedes and stepped out. Cynthia exited and walked around the car. James opened the back door and pulled out a rolling suitcase, heavy from the PVC tube inside.

"Thank you for the clothes," James said, setting the suitcase on the asphalt.

Cynthia wrapped her arms around James. He reciprocated, a lump in his throat.

"Maybe one day you could send me something to let me know you're okay," she said.

"I will." He walked toward the coin shop. He stopped at the door, turned around, waved, and entered.

A glass case filled with collectible coins had a fat man behind it. James showed the man a few one-ounce gold American Eagles. James gave the man five ounces of gold. The man paid in cash, the price they agreed to over the phone. The cash was denominated in hundreds. James put $4,000 in an envelope and $2,400 in his wallet.

He walked across the street, pulling his suitcase. He entered a

Dunkin' Donuts, ordered an egg sandwich and a coffee. James sat in a booth by the window. He glanced at his new burner phone—*10:47 a.m. Almost time.* He ate his sandwich and sipped his coffee. A black Honda Civic and a Ford F-250 pickup with a toolbox pulled into the lot. Two burly men wearing thick canvas jackets and work boots exited the vehicles. They marched into Dunkin' Donuts, their heads on a swivel. James waved and stood as the men stomped over to his booth.

"James?" the bushy-bearded one asked.

"You must be Greg," James said as he shook the man's hand.

"This is my friend Chris," Greg said, referring to the stubbly faced man to his left.

They exchanged pleasantries and sat down at the booth.

"You guys want anything to eat? Coffee?" James asked.

"We need to get back to work," Chris said with a frown.

James pulled the white envelope from his pocket and handed it to Greg. "The amount we agreed upon."

Greg opened the envelope. "With the extra for the plates?"

"Yes."

"You don't mind if I count it, do you?"

"By all means."

James sipped his coffee while Greg counted out four thousand dollars in hundreds.

He pulled the Honda keys and the title from his jacket pocket. "Here you go," Greg said. "I put the spare on the ring for you too."

"I appreciate that," James said.

"And you'll mail my plates in two weeks?"

"You have my word."

"It's in great shape," Greg said. "Do you wanna drive it around?"

"You drove it here, so it must run okay."

After the two men left, James finished his coffee and drove the Honda around the corner to a FedEx store. James parked in front and opened his suitcase. He removed a manila folder, locked the car, and walked into the office. Inside were copiers, boxes, packing materials, and a counter against the far wall. He approached the young female employee behind the counter.

"I'd like to make five thousand single-sided copies," James said.

"I can do that for you," she said with a smile.

"Would it be okay if I did it myself on one of the self-serve copiers?" James asked. "The letter is private."

"I can set it up so it will do five thousand, then you can put the paper in." She winked at James. "I won't look."

She took James to a self-serve copier, keyed in her employee number, and punched in *5000* for the amount.

She said, "You just have to put your paper in facedown and hit Start. Check them as they come out. If they look wrong, hit Cancel here." She pointed to a button with a red *X*. "It would be a bummer to print so many and not like them."

"Thank you," he said.

"I'll just be at the desk if you need me."

James removed the single typewritten sheet of paper from the manila folder, placed it facedown inside the copier, and shut the lid. He smiled to himself and pressed the button. He asked the woman if he could have a pen, a piece of paper, and a letter-size envelope. He said she could add it to his total. While he waited, he wrote a letter in neat cursive and sealed it in the envelope marked Brittany.

James drove south on US 15 in the Honda with his suitcase, PVC tube of precious metals, and the twenty-five-pound box of paper. He hit a little bit of lunch traffic near Dulles. He drove into a middle-class town house community. The stone sign in front read, Crescent Cove. He parked in the empty space in front of a middle unit townhome. He left the car running as he hauled the box to the front door and dropped it on the *Bienvenido* mat.

# Chapter 22

## Exodus

Yolanda parked in front of the two-story brick building. The sign over the front door read, Prince William County Police Department. A man in a dark suit waited outside under the sign. Brittany sat in the passenger seat, her palms sweaty, her face flushed. The sun shone into the front window of the Toyota Camry.

"You ready?" Yolanda asked.

"I can't do this," Brittany replied.

"It'll be fine, girl. It's better to face it now than to worry all the time."

Brittany looked down at her hands.

"Mr. Matthews is waiting for us," Yolanda said. "He'll be right there. He won't let you say anything that could hurt you."

Brittany nodded. *Courage is being afraid but doing it anyway.*

They met Mr. Matthews in front of the building. He was fit for someone north of sixty. He wore a tailored three-piece suit. He was clean-shaven with a full head of salt-and-pepper hair.

"Brittany," he said with a wide smile, his hand outstretched.

"Hi, Mr. Matthews," she said as she put her tiny hand in his.

"Don't worry," he said with a wink. "We're prepared."

They signed in with the receptionist just inside the building. They were led upstairs via an elevator. On the second floor, they were greeted by a petite female detective in a pantsuit. She was in her mid-forties, with short hair and a boyish face.

"I'm Detective Morgan," she said. "I'll be sitting in with Detective Warren from North Schuylkill Township." They exchanged brief pleasantries. She led them to a windowless room. Video cameras were mounted in the upper corners, and a rectangular table with six chairs filled the room. "We'll be with you in a moment."

She shut the door and left Mr. Matthews, Yolanda, and Brittany alone in the room. They sat on one side of the table, Brittany sandwiched between her muscle.

"I know we went over this," Mr. Matthews said to Brittany, "but do not answer any questions unless I say it is okay to answer. Do you understand?"

"Yes," she said.

"We're doing this as a courtesy. You're under no legal obligation to be here. If they get out of line, we'll walk," he said with a grin.

Detective Morgan entered the room, followed by Detective Warren. Warren was of medium height, stocky, with pale skin and blond curls cut tight to his head. They stood across the table from Brittany and her posse.

"This is Detective Warren from North Schuylkill Township," Morgan said, motioning to the man standing next to her in a suit that was too loose on his legs and too tight on his barrel chest.

Mr. Matthews and Yolanda stood and shook the man's hand, making introductions. Brittany remained seated with her arms crossed over her chest. Everyone sat down.

"I appreciate you taking the time to meet with me, Ms. Summers," Detective Warren said to Brittany.

Brittany nodded, not making eye contact.

"As you probably know," Warren said, "we're looking for James Fisher in connection with the disappearance of Harold and Dale Strickland, as well as felony burglary and theft."

Brittany's jaw was set tight.

"When was the last time you saw him?" Warren asked.

Brittany looked at her lawyer. He nodded.

"A little over three weeks ago," Brittany said. "He dropped me off at Yolanda's house really early."

"Do you remember the exact date?" Warren asked.

Brittany looked at her lawyer. He nodded.

"February twenty-third," Brittany said.

The detective narrowed his eyes and pursed his lips. "The twenty-third, huh? Would it surprise you to find out that we have an eyewitness that places a petite female with James Fisher on the afternoon of the twenty-fourth?"

"Don't answer that," Mr. Matthews said. "Mrs. Mendez has already vouched for Brittany's whereabouts on the twenty-fourth, and, since you do not have a positive identification, I suggest you move on, or we will cease our cooperation."

Detective Warren cleared his throat. "After Mr. Fisher dropped you off with Mrs. Mendez, did he say where he was going?"

Brittany glanced at her lawyer. He approved.

"No," she said.

"Do you have any idea where he may be?" Warren asked.

Mr. Matthews nodded.

"No," she said.

"Can you describe your relationship with Harold Strickland?" Warren asked.

"Don't answer that," Mr. Matthews said.

Detective Warren frowned. "Can you describe your relationship with Dale Strickland?" Warren asked.

Mr. Matthews affirmed.

"I never met him," Brittany said, "but I did see him when he came to inspect James's cabin."

"Did you have a romantic relationship with James Fisher?"

Brittany scowled at Detective Warren.

Mr. Matthews said to Brittany, "You are welcome to respond, but you are under no obligation to so."

"We were just friends," Brittany said.

Detective Warren asked a dozen more questions. Some were answered; some weren't.

"I guess that's it," Warren said. "I was hoping you would be more helpful."

"You knew what you were getting into, Detective," Mr. Matthews said. "We told your department over the phone that Ms. Summers did not have any information that would be helpful. Let me remind you that *your department* sent you down here on a wild goose chase."

Detective Warren frowned.

Mr. Matthews stood. "If there are no further questions, we will be leaving."

Yolanda and Brittany stood.

"Thank you for coming," Detective Morgan said.

They said their good-byes. Mr. Matthews made it clear that, if they wanted to contact his client in the future, they should contact his office. He handed them his card.

In the parking lot Brittany thanked Mr. Matthews and gave him a hug.

Brittany felt light, like a weight had been lifted from her shoulders. On the way home, she sang with Yolanda to a pop hit on the radio. During a commercial, Yolanda turned the sound down and glanced over at Brittany with a smile.

Brittany said, "I've never seen anyone talk to the police like that."

Yolanda looked over. "Me neither."

Brittany gazed out the window. *They fought for me.*

Yolanda parked her Camry in front of the town house. A brown box the size of a microwave oven sat on the front stoop. They approached the box to find a white envelope taped to the top that read *Brittany* in James's neat cursive. Brittany's eyes widened.

"He did it," she said with a smile.

Yolanda grinned and gave Brittany a hug.

Brittany lugged the box upstairs to her room. Yolanda offered to help, but Brittany declined. She shut Marco's bedroom door and tore into the envelope.

Brittany,

I'm sorry that I haven't contacted you until now. Unfortunately, it's not safe.

I hope you're settling in nicely with Yolanda and Cesar. I know, at some point, you'll want to get a car, an apartment, and go to school. You cannot under any circumstances use the money for these things or anything that can be tracked. You must get a job to pay for these types of expenses. I know that won't be a problem for you. I admire what a hard worker you are. You can spend the money on things that can't be tracked. So, if you want to go out and have a nice dinner and pay cash, by all means, have fun. Just make sure you can pay cash in person. If you have to give a credit card or a debit card or give your name for the transaction, you must use the money you earned from working. (By the way, you should stay away from credit cards. They're for debt slaves.)

Another thing in regard to the money. I would like you to go to YouTube, type The American Dream full length into the search box and watch the thirty-minute cartoon. This video is enter-taining and will explain why I would like you to do something crazy. I want you to gradually convert one-third of your cash into gold and silver coins at a 50:1 ratio. That means you buy one gold coin for every fifty silver coins.

I suggest you go to Cavalier Coin Shop. It's in Woodbridge, only a few miles from you. Talk to the owner. His name is Herb Greenwood. Tell him that you're a friend of mine and that you would like to buy metals at a 50:1 ratio, like me, with cash and no names. Tell him that you would like to do $9,000 a month. I suggest you do this for three years. Each month you will give him $9,000 in cash and then transport the metal to your storage facility in Ashburn. You may have to get a bigger box, but they will be happy to accommodate.

Last thing about your finances. This is _very important_. Make sure that you file your taxes every year. Yolanda can help you with this. The last thing you want is the IRS poking around. The deadline is next month, April 18. You will have to call the diner and give them Yolanda's address to mail your W-2.

If you decide to go college, Northern Virginia Community College has a Woodbridge campus. That would be a good inexpensive place to start. Yolanda can help you with the application process. You can go there for two years and then transfer to a four-year school. Just make sure you're going to school for a job that <u>requires</u> college. Stay away from liberal arts degrees—total waste of time and money. I have complete confidence in your ability to be successful in whatever endeavor you choose.

I suppose we should talk about the box of papers. I would like for you to stuff the envelopes and mail them. Make sure you wear gloves at <u>all times</u> when you are handling the papers. I hope you still have the folding machine. After the envelopes are sealed, drive out of town at least an hour away and find a few post office boxes. You know the blue ones they have outside?

Do not dump all the letters in one box. Put one thousand letters in each of five different blue boxes in five different towns. Do not park next to or pull up to the mailbox. Park at least four hundred meters away and walk to the box with your head and face covered. You can wear a hat and scarf. It's still cold enough.

There will be a postmark from which town the letters came from, so someone could conceivably watch security videos from all the mailboxes around town. I know it's doubtful, but better safe than sorry. I'm pretty sure there is some inflammatory rhetoric in the letter. The truth tends to get people in power upset.

*I should get going. I've got a long trip ahead of me. I'm not out of the woods yet. I don't want to lie about my situation. It's too dangerous for us to see each other and that makes me sad. I miss you terribly. On the other hand, I am extremely happy that you're free. You have a fresh start, and I know you'll make the most of it.*

*Oh, I almost forgot. And that would have been bad! Please put the envelopes in the mailboxes on Monday, March 28, after 7:00 p.m. I need to make sure things are "live" as people receive the letters.*

*Love—Your Best Friend,*
*James*

Brittany put the letter back in its envelope, put on a pair of latex gloves, and opened the box. The stack of documents was facedown. She picked up the top sheet of paper and turned it over.

Dear North Schuylkill Township Resident,

I'm writing to inform you of the biggest threat to this township's safety, security, and prosperity. Chief Wade Strickland, his sons Officer Dale Strickland and Kurt Strickland, and his brother Harold Strickland are the culprits. The depth of their depravity knows no bounds.

I have proof of a protection racket run by the Stricklands to allow criminal enterprises to exist in the township without prosecution. The criminals pay the

Stricklands, and the police look the other way. Take a drive past the home of Chief Strickland at 136 Eagle Drive and ask yourself if his salary could afford such a monstrosity. While you're at it, take a look at Dale Strickland's house at 12 Regal Drive. Dale has been with the police department for seven years, yet lives in a half-million-dollar home and drives a sixty-thousand-dollar vehicle.

If this were their only crimes, you would not have this letter in your hand. I have proof that Chief Wade Strickland tampered with evidence to convict an innocent man, Frank Wiggins, of a string of rapes and murders. These murders were committed by Chief Strickland himself, along with his brother Harold.

If you or anyone you know has been attacked by these men, please contact attorney Gerald Matthews at 703-555-3578. His firm will be handling cases on a contingency basis, so there will be no upfront cost, and payment is only rendered if there is a settlement. Alone we are powerless; together we can fight these men.

Detailed evidence of their crimes can be read at www.StricklandCorruption.com. You can view a video compilation on YouTube at www.youtube.com/user/StricklandCorruption. The audio can be found in podcast form at www.StricklandCorruption.libsyn.com. Please visit our Facebook page at www.facebook.com/StricklandCorruption.

I expect this information to be taken down by the powers that be, so please copy, like, and share with as many people as possible before that happens.

Sincerely,
Charles Ray

# Chapter 23

## *48 Hours Mystery*

James sat at a dented wooden table, the ocean breeze blowing through the barred windows. Waves crashed in the distance, one after the other. He wore baggy khaki shorts and a T-shirt. His skin was tanned. He heard a knock on the metal screen door.

"Jaime, Jaime, you want fish?" someone called out.

James stood and took a few strides to the front door of the one-room bungalow. He stepped outside with a smile. A stocky Mexican man stood with bare feet and frayed jean shorts.

"*Hola*, Jaime," he said. "You want fish?"

"*Hola*, Efrain," James replied. "I do want some fish."

"*Tengo fruta, vegetable, tambien.*"

James followed Efrain to the back of the bungalow to find a Toyota pickup loaded with coolers and a toolbox.

"I have a good one," the man said, smiling as he opened the cooler. He pulled out a neon-green fish with a fat round head and a long dorsal fin. He held it up with two hands. It was almost three feet long. "Dorado."

James grinned, his eyes wide. "Wow, that's a fish. What the hell's a dorado?"

"You dice mahimahi."

"That's mahimahi?"

"*Sí*. I cut for you. Twenty dollars."

"*Sí*," James said. "You have fruit?"

Efrain opened two more coolers—one filled with a variety of fruits and the other with vegetables.

"You want?" Efrain asked.

James nodded. "A little of everything."

"Twenty for fish *y* twenty for *fruta y vegetable*."

"*Esta bien*," James said, handing Efrain forty dollars from his wallet.

Efrain heaped produce into plastic bags. There were avocados, limes, strawberries, bananas, a melon, tomatoes, carrots, tomatillos, mamey, onions, corn, and jicama. It took James two trips to carry the produce into his kitchen. He returned to watch Efrain debone his fish and cut it up into individual steaks. He packed it in plastic and handed James two bags filled with mahimahi. Efrain washed his hands in the outdoor spigot.

"Next week?" Efrain asked.

"*Sí*."

James hauled his fish into the bungalow and packed it in the freezer. He put one steak in the fridge for dinner. He sat down at the kitchen table, his laptop in front of him. He scanned the headlines.

Russia and the United States Fight Proxy War in Syria

China Condemns US Actions in the Middle East

Dead Zone in the Gulf of Mexico Expanding

The City of Sin Is Running out of Water

Silver and Gold Gap Up at the Open on Proposed Silver Standard in Mexico

Baltic Dry Index at Another All-Time Low

James finished his reading and made dinner. He listened to the waves as he ate. He thought about Lori. He thought about what Brittany had said. *Maybe you don't get second chances. Maybe you can only give them*. He smiled to himself.

After dinner and dishes, he logged on to Hulu. Customer Support said the episode would be available today. He had checked three times already but nothing. He clicked on *48 Hours Mystery*. There it was. "The Cesspool Murders." He pressed Play.

A male voiceover spoke while crime scene images flashed across the screen. "'The Cesspool Murders,' tonight's *48 Hours Mystery*." A school picture of James flashed on the screen. "He was a mild-mannered teacher by day, but the police claim a criminal mastermind by night."

The pensive intro music continued, with graphics of chalk lines, bullets firing in slow motion, and police lights turning. A picture of a balding man appeared, identified by a caption as Richard Schlesinger. An image appeared of a Mercedes smashed into a telephone pole.

Richard spoke over the pictures. "Some say it all started with this accident. An accident where James Fisher lost his wife, Lori." There was an image of Lori, smiling next to her bicycle. "She didn't die alone. Her boss, Ronald Powers, was driving under the influence when they crashed."

They cut to a picture of a plump middle-aged woman with a caption that read Janice Powers.

"I knew he was having an affair with her," Janice said. "I caught them at our lake house. He said he would stop."

"But he didn't," Richard Schlesinger said.

Janice shook her head, her eyes wet.

They cut to a school picture of James, smiling with his class. They zoomed in on his face.

Richard asked, "Did James Fisher know that his wife was having an affair? If so, did he care?"

Lori's sister, Rebecca, appeared. "I think he knew," she said, "and I don't think he cared one bit for my sister. He walked out in the middle of her funeral. I never did like him. He was flat-out crazy."

"In what way was he crazy?" Richard asked.

"He thought the economy was going to crash, worse than the Great

Depression. And he used to say that our money was worthless, yet I buy things every day." She shook her head. "Crazy."

A stocky man in a gray suit was identified as Officer Jeff Koch.

Officer Koch said, "He didn't hardly react at all when we told him the news about his wife's accident."

Vernon Dixon and Maurice Hawkins appeared on the screen sitting side-by-side. They were dressed nicely in button-down shirts. Vernon's mustache was a little thicker, and he was growing his hair out in an afro. Maurice still looked young, with a tight fade, high cheekbones, and a nice smile.

"What kind of teacher was Mr. Fisher?" Richard Schlesinger asked.

"Mr. Fish was cool," Vernon said.

"We learned a lot in his class," Maurice added.

"What kinds of things did you learn from Mr. Fisher?" Richard asked.

"White people make terrible slaves," Vernon said.

"They get sunburnt," Maurice added. "And we learned school doesn't teach us stuff to be successful. It teaches us to follow the rules, so we can be part of the machine."

"They just want obedient workers," Vernon said.

"And who's *they*?" Richard asked.

"Bankers and the government," Vernon replied.

They cut to Dr. Paul Richards aka Dr. Dicks. He wore a dark suit. His flat top was crisp; he was clean-shaven. A caption with his name and title flashed on the screen for a moment.

"Would you describe James Fisher as an effective teacher?" Richard asked.

"He could have been," Dr. Dicks replied. "He had trouble following the rules. His students became very unruly because of the ideas he put in their heads. It was almost like a cult. We finally had to fire him."

"How did he react?"

"Not well. He was very angry. He shouted and used foul language."

Richard spoke over a photo of James's cabin. "After losing his wife and losing his job, James Fisher moved to the wilderness of Pennsylvania to this tiny one-room cabin, without indoor plumbing." They cut to an image of the college. "He took a job teaching at the Community College of Central Pennsylvania. Here he would be up to his old tricks."

An attractive young woman in a conservative dress appeared. The caption on the screen read Heather Davenport, former student.

"He was paranoid," she said. "He thought the police were out to get everyone."

They cut to Kurt Strickland, with his pudgy frame and pencil-thin beard. "He had the whole class hating the police. It was hard for me. I tried to be the voice of reason in debates, but he always cut me down because of my dad and my brother."

Richard narrated over images of Dale and Chief Strickland. "Kurt's brother Dale was a decorated officer of seven years, and his dad, a thirty-year veteran and the chief of police. What comes next involves a young girl and the unthinkable."

The program returned with photographs of Brittany as a young girl on a swing in faded jeans and as a young woman with Jessica and Denise at New Year's in Philadelphia.

Richard said, "Brittany Summers, by all accounts, was a troubled young woman. She ran away at the age of sixteen. She ended up in a coal-mining town in Pennsylvania, eating out of a diner Dumpster."

They cut to a fortysomething woman with perm-curly hair and a tight blouse. The tag below her read, Tracy Wilkerson, Brittany's mother.

She said, "Britt refused to follow the rules. She was always makin' trouble. One day she just up and left. She didn't want no rules." Tracy pursed her lips. "We looked everywhere."

"Did you call the police?" Richard asked.

"We knew she left on purpose, so no."

"Did you ever meet James Fisher?"

She scowled. "Yeah, I met him. He was actin' like he was a lawyer.

He demanded Britt's birth certificate and social security card. I thought he *was* a lawyer, so I gave him the stuff. I think he was holdin' her hostage."

Kurt appeared. "I knew she was trouble," he said, "but my uncle wanted to help her."

Old smiley photographs of Happy Harold the Outdoorsman scrolled on the screen. He showed off a trout and turkeys, and posed behind a dead buck, holding up the antlers.

Richard said, "Harold Strickland took care of Brittany Summers for two years, until James Fisher took control."

They cut back to Kurt. "I saw him with her on campus. I thought it was weird."

Jessica appeared looking beautiful with her wavy blond hair and light-blue blouse. She said, "It was strange, but I thought it was innocent. I think he just wanted to help her. I was friends with Brittany. I would have known if something bad was going on. She loved James and not like a boyfriend, but like a father or a big brother. He helped her get her GED and asked me to help her get a job at the diner."

Richard narrated while images of Dot's Diner filled the screen. The shiny metal exterior, interior, and finally the Stricklands' favorite booth. "Brittany Summers worked at this diner, the very same diner that Officer Dale Strickland and Chief Wade Strickland would frequent."

Chief Strickland appeared in a blue suit with his big shiny forehead and mustache. His chin hung like a chicken wattle. The chief said, "I knew he was gonna be a problem the first time I met him. It was just a simple code violation, and he acted like we were persecutin' him." Pictures of the cabin flashed on the screen. "He was tryin' to live full-time in a cabin with an outhouse. You gotta have a septic for that. That's when it all started—his vendetta."

They showed a dramatization of a Ford F-150 driving erratically, followed by a police car with rotating red and blue lights. They cut to a clean-shaven man with dark hair, light eyes, and a fat face, identified as Officer Matt Emory. He wore a large suit jacket that wasn't large enough to contain his gut.

"What happened on the night before Valentine's Day of 2016?" Richard asked.

"James Fisher was driving erratically, so I pulled him over," Officer Emory replied.

"Did you know who you were pulling over?"

"I had no idea."

"Bullshit," James said to his laptop.

"What happened when you pulled him over?" Richard asked.

"I looked in the truck, and a young girl was with him. She was dressed in a fancy black dress, and he was in a suit. It was Saturday night. A lot of couples went out for Valentine's Day on that night instead of Sunday. I thought it was odd. She looked like a little girl, and he was … too old for her. I asked if she was okay. She looked like she was upset."

"Do you think she wanted to be there?"

"No, sir." The officer shook his head. "I could smell alcohol on Mr. Fisher's breath, so I gave him a breathalyzer."

"What was the result?"

"It was a .082. He was over the legal limit, so I took him to the station."

"What was he like at the station?"

"Unstable. He kept yelling for a doctor, saying that he was dying and needed medication. So we kept him overnight, hoping he would sober up."

"Did you let him out in the morning?" Richard asked.

"I didn't. Another officer did."

"Were there any charges?"

"The charges were dropped. I guess the chief felt that it was so close to the limit. He was giving the guy a huge break. I think he figured that Fisher had learned his lesson spending the night in a holding cell.

We're not interested in ruining the lives of our citizens. We're interested in keeping them safe."

Chief Strickland appeared. "That was a mistake. That was my mistake. We should have followed through. I felt bad for the guy at the time. If I knew what I know now, I would have handled that differently. I suppose hindsight's twenty-twenty."

Richard spoke over a photograph of Harold with his big smile and big fish. "A few days later, Harold Strickland, beloved brother to the chief, texted the firehouse where he worked that he'd be out because of illness." Richard Schlesinger appeared. "Was it like Harold to miss work?"

They cut to a pudgy man in a light gray suit with a thinning head of salt-and-pepper hair. Underneath his image was the caption Fire Chief Bill Moran.

Bill said, "No, it wasn't, but the text looked genuine, and I figured anyone's bound to get sick eventually."

"So you didn't do anything?"

Bill frowned and shook his head. "No, I didn't, and I wish I had. I was trying to get a million things done before my vacation. The wife and I go to Key West in the winter for a week. You just don't think of these things ever happening to your friends."

"When we return," Richard said, "Fire Chief Bill Moran receives a distressing text message."

After the commercials, they returned with a dramatization of a plane landing. Richard Schlesinger said, "Fire Chief Moran landed at Harrisburg International Airport, fresh from his Key West vacation on February 24, 2016." They cut to a dramatization of a man checking his phone in an airport. "He was immediately concerned by another text message he received from Harold Strickland."

The fire chief appeared. "It said Harold was still sick and would be out another week. I got concerned then, because, even if the text was legitimate, maybe he needs medical attention. So I called Chief Strickland and let him know my concerns. Wade said he would check it out."

They cut to Chief Wade Strickland. "I was concerned about the text message, but my brother's a grown man. Harold sent me a message sayin' that he was up in Lycomin' County, huntin' with a friend that he mentioned by name. I did think it was unlike him to shirk his duties, so I was concerned. I called him, but it went to voice mail. I traced the phone, and it was near a huntin' camp in Lycomin', so everything checked out as far as I was concerned. Then I spoke with Kurt."

Richard narrated as images of the Community College of Central Pennsylvania scrolled across the screen. "When we return, James Fisher takes a special interest in his former student, Kurt Strickland."

After the commercials, a dramatization was shown of a compact car on the side of a road, and a man taking pictures with a long-range lens.

Richard said, "James Fisher was caught following Kurt and photographing him with sophisticated equipment."

Kurt Strickland appeared. "I was in my truck, and I saw him with this camera. I got out and asked him what he was doin', and he told me that he was lookin' for meth."

"But you don't think he was there for meth?" Richard asked.

"No, sir. I was seein' friends, and that neighborhood is a nice neighborhood. I don't know where you would go for meth, but it wouldn't be there. Plus, it messes you up. Have you ever seen *Faces of Meth*? He didn't look like that."

"Why do you think he was there?"

"I think he was watchin' me. I think he was plannin' to kill me. If I didn't have that conversation with my dad, maybe he would have."

They cut to Chief Strickland. "I called Kurt, just to see how he was doin'. I was always so busy with work that Kurt sometimes got lost in the shuffle. I guess I was feelin' guilty." The chief looked down for a moment. "I asked him how his classes were goin'. That's when he told me about James Fisher spyin' on him. I didn't even know my son had him as a professor. That's when I called Dale." Tears welled in the chief's eyes. The camera pulled in tight on the chief's face, holding for a moment.

Richard spoke over photos of Dale in his dress blues. "Officer Dale Strickland never answered his father's call."

A red-eyed Chief Strickland appeared. "I had a bad feelin'. I dispatched damn near the entire department to James Fisher's cabin, myself included." They cut to a dramatization of police cars chasing a Ford F-150 down a gravel road. "When we got to his road, we saw his truck. He must've been goin' about a hundred."

"Was he alone?" Richard asked.

"He had a small young woman with him," the chief replied.

"Was it Brittany Summers?"

"I believe so, but the first officer on the scene was the only one to see her, and her back was turned, so he couldn't make a positive ID. But I believe 100 percent that it was her."

"What happened when you pulled up to the cabin?"

"They barricaded themselves inside. The cabin was like a fortress. He had an alarm, motion sensors, bars on all the windows, and the doors were reinforced. It took the guys a couple minutes to break through the front door."

Richard narrated as images of the cabin flashed on the screen. "James Fisher and presumably Brittany Summers are locked inside the one-room cabin, surrounded. What happens next, stunned Chief Strickland. When we return, the pair make a dangerous and dramatic escape."

The show returns with the camera on Chief Strickland. He said, "When we got inside, they were gone, vanished into thin air. It's a small cabin, only one room. There's no place to go. Then we found the hatch. It was hidden under a mat." They cut to footage of the hatch and the cellar. "We thought we had 'em dead to rights in the cellar, but it was empty." They cut to footage of the escape tunnel. "That's when we found the tunnel. It was a black drainpipe about two feet in diameter. It was tight."

Richard spoke over photos of the hatch at the end of the tunnel. "The escape tunnel led here, only eighty feet from the cabin." Footage of the trail flashed on the screen. "They escaped down this hiking path, but the police were hot on their trail."

Chief Strickland appeared. "We chased 'em down the trail, but we never saw 'em."

"But Sarge did," Richard said.

The chief nodded, his mouth turned down. "We let our canine loose, and Sarge caught up to him."

Richard narrated over a dramatization of a German shepherd running through the woods. "What happened next sounds like it was taken from a Hollywood script."

They cut to Chief Strickland. "When we got to the scene, Sarge was dying, stabbed in the back of the neck, and there was what looked like white cotton everywhere." A dramatization played of a dog biting a puffy jacket and tearing the stuffing out of it. "The cotton was actually goose down. We think James Fisher tied his jacket around his leg and let Sarge bite down on it. When that happened ..." The chief shook his head. "Fisher plunged a blade into the back of the dog's neck. I heard Sarge yelp. It was the one of the worst sounds I've ever heard."

"Did this kill Sarge instantly?"

"No, sir." The camera zoomed in on the chief's face. His eyes were wet. "We had to put him out of his misery."

Richard spoke over footage of the trail fork and the small gravel parking lot. "James Fisher and possibly Brittany Summers came to this lot at the end of the trail."

The camera cut to Chief Strickland. "They must've had a car ready to go, because, when we got there, they were gone. Kurt said James Fisher was in a white compact car when he saw him, so we put out an all-points bulletin for a white compact with a man and a woman in the car. State police pulled over hundreds of cars, but we never found 'em."

Richard narrated over images of the chief's stone house. "They escaped, but it wasn't over. This quaint stone house was owned by Chief Strickland as a hunting camp and weekend getaway."

They cut to the chief. "That same day I found out my house had been broken into. I had a good security system, burglar bars, and a very secure safe hidden in the attic and bolted to the floor."

They showed footage of the stone house.

"Do you think it was James Fisher who broke in?" Richard asked.

The chief appeared on-screen. "Definitely, and I'll tell you another thing. There is no way an inexperienced thief could've done what he did. It was a professional job."

"What was taken from the home?"

"A few thousand dollars in cash, and my wife's jewelry. Her jewelry had been handed down in her family for centuries. It was worth a fortune, but it was worth much more to us in sentiment."

Richard spoke over pictures of Dale Strickland and his black SUV. "On the same day of the dramatic escape, Officer Dale Strickland went missing along with his GMC Yukon. When we return, the police begin to uncover the crucial pieces that would lead them to their worst nightmare."

Upon returning, they showed a dramatization of a police officer picking up a phone in a Ziploc bag in the woods.

Richard narrated over the video. "Police tracked down Harold's cell phone in Lycoming County, but they didn't find Harold. The phone was planted there to give legitimacy to the texts previously sent from Harold's phone. Who was doing this and why?"

Chief Strickland appeared. "It had to be James Fisher, and I think Brittany Summers helped him. I think he was buyin' more time for himself. He didn't want us to think Harold was missin'."

Richard's voiceover corresponded with photos of a black SUV on blocks, its interior shredded. "Two weeks later police found Dale's GMC Yukon, stripped and abandoned in Pottsville, about half an hour from James Fisher's cabin. There was no sign of Dale. A few days after that, the police were alerted by airport authorities in Harrisburg that they had found Harold's red Ford Ranger in their long-term parking lot." They cut to security footage of James walking out of the lot, his head covered with a knit cap. "Police believe this grainy image to be James Fisher. He's wearing a chemical suit under his jacket, which would be perfect for keeping his DNA out of a crime scene."

Chief Strickland appeared. "He was careful but not careful enough. We found hair follicles that matched James Fisher's DNA in both vehicles."

"Bullshit," James said to his laptop.

The chief continued, "When we found the trucks and the DNA, we knew it brought us closer to findin' Harold and Dale, but I also knew it meant that we were closer to findin' out that they were gone." The chief shook his head, his eyes puffy. "As a father and a brother, I prayed and tried to have hope, but as a police officer I knew what the odds were."

Richard narrated over pictures of Brittany. "At this time Brittany Summers resurfaced in Virginia, with an alibi for her whereabouts on the day of the escape."

They cut to Richard Schlesinger holding a sheet of paper in front of him.

"Ms. Summers refused to be interviewed," Richard said to the chief. "She did make a statement through her attorney. She said, 'I have no knowledge of the events that transpired on February 24, 2016. James Fisher is a kind and decent man. He is not a criminal.'"

The chief appeared, chuckling. "That alibi she's got is paper-thin. I know she was involved. That Yolanda woman is an old friend of James Fisher."

Richard spoke over a school photo of Yolanda. "School nurse, Yolanda Mendez worked with James in Virginia at Woodbridge Middle School. Mrs. Mendez vouched for Brittany's whereabouts on February 24."

The camera cut to Dr. Dicks. "Mrs. Mendez is an excellent nurse. I never understood why she was friends with someone like James Fisher."

Richard narrated over images of James and Brittany. "A few weeks later, with James Fisher in the wind and Brittany with a solid alibi,

James strikes again. When we return, the story takes a dramatic and surprising twist."

The show returned with Richard narrating over a dramatization of stacks of letters being dumped into blue post office boxes. "A letter was mailed to every single resident of North Schuylkill Township that created a firestorm of controversy. It was signed Charles Lee Ray aka 'Chucky.' This is a nod to the horror movie franchise, *Child's Play*, that featured a homicidal doll." Richard appeared holding up a letter to the chief. "Do you believe this letter to be the work of James Fisher?"

"Yes, I do," the chief replied.

"This letter claims that you, Dale, and Kurt took money from local criminal organizations in exchange for safety from police prosecution."

They cut to the chief. His neck was red, his nostrils flared. "That's trash. All lies."

"What about the allegations of convicting an innocent man, Frank Wiggins, of serial rape and murder?"

The chief shook his head, his jaw set tight. "I said, they were lies."

Richard held up another sheet of paper. "I have a statement from attorney Daniel Nelson who says there were at least seven murders that fit the exact same MO that Frank Wiggins was convicted of, *after* he was put away. Do you think it's possible Frank Wiggins is innocent?"

"Absolutely not."

"Do you think the letter from Charles Lee Ray harmed your reputation?" Richard hung air quotes with his hands when he said, *Charles Lee Ray*.

"Of course it did." The chief's face was red. "It's sick that you can slander a man like that, after all the sacrifices I've made for my community, my country."

They displayed images of Harold's trailer. Richard said, "After the letters, you went back to Harold's home."

They cut to the inside of Harold's trailer. The chief said, "I felt like I was missin' somethin', that there was a clue that I had overlooked. I went back to Harold's house and looked through every nook and cranny." The camera cut to the chief. "When I got to the bathroom, it smelled like raw sewage. I flushed the toilet, and it backed up. His cesspool was clogged. I thought it was odd because I knew he had had a contractor drain it the year before. I went outside. I wasn't sure exactly where the cesspool was, but I had an idea, because he used to have a stake to mark it."

They portrayed a dramatization of a police officer walking on leaves. "I was walkin' and one area felt soft, and my first thought was that someone had been diggin'. You gotta compact the ground after you dig or it'll sink. I grabbed a rake from Harold's shed to move some of the leaves. It was obvious that someone had been diggin' there recently." They showed helicopter views of Harold's backyard, with police vehicles and construction equipment digging up the cesspool. "So we opened up the cesspool." The camera cut back to the chief. He looked down, rubbing his temples.

"What did you find?" Richard asked.

The chief looked up, scowling. "We found Dale and Harold."

Richard narrated over video of the bodies being hoisted from the cesspool. "When we return, the North Schuylkill Police Department continues to mount a case against James Fisher."

They returned with the camera on Chief Strickland. He said, "We found hair follicles that matched James Fisher's DNA on Dale's body. At that point, we knew we had the evidence. We just needed to find James Fisher."

Richard spoke over pictures of James. "Unfortunately for the North Schuylkill Police Department, James Fisher was never found, and the pressures and allegations began to mount." They cut to images of Facebook and YouTube. "The letters, presumably sent by James Fisher, provided web addresses where people could check the validity of the claims made by the author. One of the most damning pieces of evidence is an audiotape illegally obtained in Dot's Diner, the very same restaurant where Brittany Summers worked."

Chief Strickland appeared. "She was in on the whole thing. He's some kind a cult leader."

"But you couldn't prove it," Richard said.

"No."

"Going back to the letter and the websites, what about the allegations that you and Harold were in fact the perpetrators of the serial rapes and murders?"

The chief stood up, his fists clenched. "I told you that I wasn't gonna talk about this slander."

"We have four women who claim that you and Harold raped them and threatened to kill them if they didn't keep their mouths shut."

The chief yanked out his mic and stormed off the set.

The camera cut to Richard Schlesinger. "Chief Wade Strickland declined to be interviewed further after we asked him questions about the women you are about to meet."

The screen showed a blacked-out silhouette of a woman. She spoke with an altered voice. She described how the chief and Harold raped her at the stone house, how they choked her almost to death, revived her, and did it again. Three other women had similar stories. Two of them were brave enough to show their faces. The women were middle-aged, their attacks happening twenty to twenty-five years ago. They were beyond the twelve-year statute of limitations for rape in Pennsylvania.

Richard Schlesinger appeared again. "Here we are six months since the great escape and the cesspool murders, and James Fisher is still out there somewhere." The show displayed pictures of James smiling with his students. "Was this mild-mannered teacher a cold-blooded killer or, as some claim, a Robin Hood taking out the trash?" The camera showed the chief covering his face as he entered his SUV. "Chief Wade Strickland retired amid controversy. He is facing multiple civil lawsuits. As of this taping, nine women have accused Wade Strickland of rape." They cut to Kurt being escorted by men with DEA jackets. "Kurt Strickland was recently arrested by the DEA for distributing methamphetamines." They showed Frank in an orange prison uniform. "Amid national uproar, Frank Wiggins has been granted a new trial by the Supreme Court of Pennsylvania." The camera cut to pictures of Brittany at New Year's, with a big smile. "Brittany Summers is attending Northern Virginia Community College and working as a waitress." Richard Schlesinger appeared. "One of our producers was able to get a comment from the previously silent Ms. Summers. She asked if we would give James Fisher a message over the television. Her message was simply … thank you."

# Chapter 24

## Math and History

G ood morning, Mr. Hamilton," she said in a singsong voice.
"Hi, dear. How are you?" he asked, his leg elevated.

She smiled. "I think I'm supposed to ask *you* that question. How did you sleep?"

"Okay."

She glanced at the half-full container filled with urine hanging off the bed railing. "I see you were able to urinate. That's good. Sometimes after anesthesia it can be hard."

She took the container to the bathroom, dumped the urine, and flushed the toilet. She returned and replaced the container on the bed railing.

"How about some sunlight?" she asked. "It's gonna be a beautiful day."

"That'd be great," he replied.

She opened the curtains, and sunlight streamed into the hospital room. The room overlooked a courtyard. Brittany watched as the early birds got their worms. She turned around and grinned at Mr. Hamilton.

"They should be by with your breakfast soon. Do you need anything else?" she asked.

"I'm fine," he said. "Will you be back around?"

"I will, in an hour or so. If you need me before that, just buzz me."

She pulled off her latex gloves at the door and dumped them in the red bin.

Brittany spent the next four hours making her rounds. At noon she received a text message. She glanced at the clock on her phone. *Shoot.* She hustled to the nurse's station. A middle-aged woman sat behind the counter.

"I'm going to the cafeteria for lunch," Brittany said to the woman.

In the elevator, her thumbs moved rapidly. She typed *Sorry, lost track of time. I'll be there in five minutes.*

In the cafeteria, she grabbed a tray and ordered a chicken salad. She pushed her tray along the stainless steel counter, adding a bottled water along the way. Brittany paid at the register and entered the dining area with her head on a swivel. She saw him and made a beeline to his table. He sat alone, his sandwich almost gone. She sat down, with her bottom lip pressed out.

"I'm sorry I'm late," she said.

He smiled, his teeth white and straight, his skin dark and smooth. "It's okay. I just miss you."

"Me too. We've both been working too much."

A lanyard hung around his neck with his image and his name, Dr. Rene Gautier.

"One more week," Rene said.

"I know. I can't wait."

"For which part?"

"All of it."

He pursed his full lips. "It's not like here. You'll see suffering that …" He shook his head.

"Rene, we've been through this."

"I don't want you to feel obligated."

"It's not obligation. It's love."

He smiled.

* * *

"Do you think he'll come?" Brittany asked.

They sat poolside, nursing iced teas. They were protected by beach cover-ups and the large umbrella that shielded their table.

"If he saw the advertisement, he'll be here," Yolanda replied. "I don't want you to get your hopes up though. Cesar's guy only knew where he dropped him off. It's been six years. He may not even be in Mexico at this point."

Brittany exhaled. "I know. I guess I just built up this fantasy all these years." She frowned. "You know, I think I see him all the time. At the hospital, at the grocery store. I keep thinking one day he'll just … be there. I don't even know for sure if he's still alive. The world hasn't exactly been a stable place."

Brittany gazed at the breaking waves in the distance, her straw hat casting a dark shadow over her face. Rene and four Mexican men were bodysurfing. "They look happy," Brittany said.

Yolanda turned to the sea and laughed. "Look at Cesar. He's just a big kid."

"I like seeing him with the boys, how they interact." She took a deep breath.

"Are you okay?"

She nodded and turned to Yolanda, stone-faced. "I'm fine. Everything's fine."

Rene shouted and waved his arms at the women. Brittany shook her head. He held out his palms. Brittany pushed her arms forward as if she were pushing him away. Rene ran and dove into a breaking wave.

"I've had enough sun," Brittany said.

"I think everyone's seen enough of *my* beach body," Yolanda replied.

Brittany scowled. "Yolanda."

Rene jogged away from the surf, toward the pool. Water flicked from his body as he moved. He was tall and well-built.

"Speaking of beach bodies," Yolanda said.

Rene approached with a wide grin. He bent over and kissed Brittany on the lips, dripping salt water on her cover-up. She smiled through the kiss. He pulled out a metal chair and sat down next to Brittany and across from Yolanda.

"You two are missing all the fun," he said.

"I don't wanna get burnt on the first day," Brittany replied.

Yolanda stood from the table. "I'm going to take a nap. I'll see you two love birds at the rehearsal dinner."

Rene stood from the table and smiled at Yolanda. He sat back down as she walked toward the hotel. Brittany watched Cesar with his sons, lost in her own thoughts.

"Is something wrong?" Rene asked.

Brittany shook her head.

"You're not getting cold feet are you?"

"I've never been more sure about anything in my entire life."

Rene smiled. "I love you."

"I love you too." Her smile faded before it could bloom.

"You thought he'd be waiting for you?"

"I should have never gotten my hopes up."

He grasped her hand. "Hope is a good thing. Sometimes it's the only thing."

She smiled for a moment.

He squeezed her hand.

"I'm still a little wiped from the flight," she said. "Do you mind if I go back to the room and take a nap?"

"Of course not. I'll wake you up for dinner."

They stood from the table. He kissed her on the cheek and jogged toward the ocean. Brittany walked into the lobby, her flip-flops snapping. She stopped at a bank of shiny elevators and pressed the up arrow. She turned around. A family was checking in at the front desk. Their backs were turned. A shapely Mexican woman held the hand of a little boy. A man with salt-and-pepper hair paid in silver coins. *James was right about that.* The elevator door opened. Brittany turned around and stepped inside. She pressed ten on the panel and leaned against the back of the elevator. She glanced up to see the man pulling a large suitcase toward her. She reached out to hold the door, but she was too late. He wore sunglasses, but she knew.

Her heart raced as she stopped the elevator on the second floor. She stepped out and watched the numbers above the elevator next to hers. It stopped on six. She took off her flip-flops and held on to her hat as she ran to the stairwell and hustled up four flights. She was out of breath as she spilled into the hallway and ran down the empty corridor. The hallway formed a big square with rooms on either side. She heard laughing around the corner. She heard the click of a door. Brittany turned the corner in anticipation. It was empty. She stopped, breathless. *This is crazy.* She turned around and started for the elevators. She stopped dead in her tracks.

"Brittany," he said.

She turned toward the voice, his voice. He took off his sunglasses and stood with a broad grin, his face tanned. She ran toward him and threw her arms around him. They hugged for a long while.

"I can't believe you're here," she said.

"I wouldn't miss it for the world." He smiled. "Why don't you come in and meet Veronica and Rafael."

They walked into the room. Rafael was jumping up and down with a plastic bucket and a toy shovel. The boy was thin and tan with straight dark hair. "*Vamonos, vamonos,*" he said to Veronica.

Veronica slipped on her flip-flops. "English," she replied.

The boy frowned. "Can we go now? Please."

Veronica turned to James and Brittany. "This *must* be Brittany." She smiled with full lips and a round face. "I'm Veronica. I've heard so much about you."

Veronica hugged Brittany before she could respond. After a moment, they separated.

Brittany looked at Rafael, then to James. "This is your son?"

James grinned. "He's four."

"Do you want to make a sand castle with me?" Rafael asked Brittany.

"Sure," she replied.

"Yes!" The boy raised his shovel straight over his head in celebration of his new friend.

"Why don't we let Daddy catch up with Brittany first," Veronica said. "There'll be plenty of time to play."

The boy scowled. "But you said we could go now."

Veronica smiled again at James and Brittany. "I'll take him to the beach. He needs to burn up some of that energy. It was really nice to meet you."

"It was nice to meet you too, Veronica."

"Are you ready?" she asked.

"I've been ready the whole time," Rafael replied, his brow furrowed.

The door clicked as the boy and his mother headed for the beach. James and Brittany walked out on the balcony. They leaned on the railing, watching the ocean. Cesar, his boys, and Rene were still bodysurfing.

"Yolanda's boys." James chuckled. "They're not boys anymore."

"That's my fiancé out there."

"Dr. Rene Gautier. I looked him up."

"I love him dearly."

He turned to Brittany. "I'm happy for you. Rene, the wedding, your job, everything." He smiled. "You did it."

"How do you know about my job?"

"The wedding announcement said you guys met at Woodbridge General."

"I forgot that we put that on there. We posted wedding announcements on all these little local websites, hoping that we could attract you but not the authorities."

"I don't think they care much about me anymore. Besides, James Fisher doesn't exist. I'm Jaime Espinosa, born in Mexico. You can buy just about anything here, even a new identity."

"Can you come back to the States?"

"With my son, it's not a risk I can take."

She nodded.

"So where to after the wedding? Do you have a honeymoon planned?"

"We'll be here for a week, and then we'll go to a small village in southern Chad."

"Chad? Like the country in Africa?"

"Rene grew up there. We're heading up a relief mission for his village. They've had major problems with the water. It's making people sick, and the women have to walk too far to get it." She deadpanned, "Some of them have been attacked on the way."

He winced. "Do you have everything you need?"

"I hope so. We're bringing medical supplies, water filters, food. We'll be building a clinic, and installing a well and rainwater-harvesting tanks. We have a team of people, mostly friends of Rene."

They watched Veronica and Rafael amble onto the beach hand in hand.

"How did you two meet?" she asked.

"She was my Spanish teacher."

Brittany grinned. "I guess that makes sense. She seems nice."

"I'm very lucky."

"How did you know what was gonna happen with the money?"

He smirked. "Math and history."

"Did you see what happened with Apple, buying up all that silver? Silver prices doubled overnight."

He nodded. "They're afraid they won't have the silver they need for their electronics."

"I did what you said with the money. It's worth more than I could ever spend. You should have it."

He shook his head. "You keep it. I can see you're doing good things with it. Do you remember when I insisted on digging up something?"

"You had a stash of gold and silver?"

He laughed.

She gazed out to the ocean. "I can't believe we're here ... after everything."

He turned to her. "I'm proud of you."

She glanced at James for a moment, then her eyes settled on the beach, on Rene. "None of this would have ever happened ..." She wiped the corners of her eyes with her sleeve. "Without you I'd be ..."

James watched his wife and son. "So would I."

Dear Reader,

I am thrilled that you took precious time out of your life to read my book. Thank you! I hope you found it entertaining, engaging, and thought-provoking. If so, please consider writing a positive review on Amazon and/or Goodreads. Five-star reviews have a huge impact on future sales. The review doesn't need to be long and detailed, if you're more of a reader than a writer. As an author and a small businessman, competing against the big publishers, every reader, every review, and every referral is greatly appreciated.

If you're interested in receiving my new book releases for free, go to the following link: http://www.PhilWBooks.com. You're probably thinking, what's the catch? There is no catch.

If you want to contact me, don't be bashful. I can be found at Phil@PhilWBooks.com. I do my best to respond to all e-mails.

Sincerely,
Phil M. Williams

Made in the USA
Las Vegas, NV
27 December 2023

83540661R00146